BOOK 6 OF COURAGE ON THE OREGON TRAIL SERIES

I0582189

FIERCE DREAMS

A.T. BUTLER

FIERCE DREAMS

An Oregon Trail Western Adventure

A.T. BUTLER

CHAPTER ONE

"Thank you so much for holding the baby," Mrs. Rayburn said as she sat.

"Of course, ma'am. I'm happy to help."

Pretty, eighteen-year-old, Nora Cole sat quietly in the Rayburn sitting room on a crisp October afternoon. Outside the maple leaves were turning a brilliant orange, and the church's plans for a bonfire that weekend in celebration of the harvest had all the children collecting twigs and sticks. While their mothers caught up with the family gossip, Nora held the Rayburn baby on her lap, cooing into his ear. What a handsome boy, with his round cheeks and fine light brown wisps of hair. Little Jory was only a few weeks old, and his mother seemed grateful for visitors and any help the neighbors could offer.

"Aren't you just the sweetest thing?" Nora murmured to the pink-cheeked child who grasped her finger in his tight little paw. "I could just eat you up."

Though she hadn't finished the quilt squares she had

meant to sew that day, Nora was not about to miss a chance to visit the Rayburn house. Instead, she would finish her sewing by candlelight later that evening, even if it ruined her eyesight. Nora and her mother had come to bring Mrs. Rayburn some of the last summer tomatoes they had finished canning.

When she sensed a lull in the conversation, Nora looked up from the child. The mothers were cozy, leaning toward each other from either end of the settee on the other side of the sitting room. The Coles hadn't seen any of the other members of the family since they arrived twenty minutes earlier.

"Is Jimmy around?" she asked, trying to arrange her face in an expression of innocent inquiry.

"No, dear," Mrs. Rayburn said, smiling at her. "He's helping Mr. Turret bring in their harvest this week. I fancy we won't see him till long after dark." She turned back to Mrs. Cole, lowering her voice conspiratorially, but Nora had already stopped paying attention.

Nora frowned—when she had seen her best friend Betty Turret the night before, she hadn't told her that Jimmy Rayburn would be helping her father with the harvest. Betty usually always told Nora everything; she had a gift for conversation and loved sharing details. Every fall Mr. Turret hired several of the local boys, and Nora had never paid much attention to who in previous years. But Betty knew how Nora felt about Jimmy, about how interested she was in every aspect of that young man's life. If she had known Jimmy would be spending the entire day at her family's farm, wouldn't Betty have told her?

Nora looked down at baby Jory babbling in her lap

while the women discussed the details of the new schoolteacher that had started just a few weeks earlier. Though she had not attended school for two years now, Nora's younger sister Amy would still be under the new teacher for a bit longer, as would most of the Rayburn children.

But then, that would be the last of the Coles. Just Nora and Amy. It was lonely at times, with just the two of them, but that was another reason why Nora was so looking forward to getting married and starting a family of her own.

Jory Rayburn, on the other hand, would get to grow up with a bevy of siblings. She looked down at the little boy in her lap and took a whiff of the top of his head. That lucky child had six older brothers and sisters, the oldest of which was just about Nora's own age. Every time she was with the Rayburns Nora felt that enveloping feeling of familial love that surrounded them all. The chance to marry into that family was one of the things Nora loved most about Jimmy.

She had known Jimmy Rayburn as long as she could remember; making mud pies with him was one of her oldest memories. She had loved him almost as long. As she sat with the baby, Nora kept glancing at the door, even though she had no reason to expect him. The habit was too deeply engrained in her. Every Sunday at church, all through the years they were in school together, even when she was making social calls, Nora was constantly on alert for his presence. His smile that lit up a room. His attentiveness that made her feel like she was the only person in his mind.

But he would not be walking in that door any time

soon. Nora would have been better off staying at home to finish her patchwork quilt than to sit here if Jimmy wasn't home.

She sighed, louder than she intended to. Her mother looked up at her sharply.

"Are you feeling all right, Nora?"

"Yes, of course, I was just thinking ... You know, Mother, I still have so much to do on my quilt. I wonder if we should be getting back."

"Oh, Nora, dear," Mrs. Rayburn said, "that reminds me. There's a basket of scrap fabric there by the stove. You're welcome to take anything you find for your patchwork. I know Jimmy told me you like a variety when you quilt, don't you?"

"I do. Thank you."

Flattered that Jimmy had remembered such a detail, Nora stood, still with the baby in her arms and crossed to the wide woven basket. She was in the middle of her third patchwork quilt. The first she had given to a cousin for her wedding; the second donated to the church fundraiser the previous summer. But this one she intended to keep for herself. Many an autumn afternoon she had spent stitching together the small pieces of fabric, piling up the squares that would soon be the top of the quilt.

And all of those sewing hours she had spent daydreaming about her future—her husband, her home, her children. The bed that would one day be home to this quilt and the love that would surround them.

The top layer of the basket was a threadbare—even burnt—kitchen towel that had seen better days. Below that was a small boy's trousers, too worn in the knees to be patched any more. Nora kept digging with one hand, holding the baby in her other arm while the mothers continued chatting away. She wasn't looking for anything in particular; she could be content to wait until all the right pieces of fabric came across her path.

Then she felt a soft linen and pulled it out of the stack to look at in the light. It was a dark, almost brick, red, worn and soft and well-loved. Like the trousers, however, it was beyond patching in the elbows and in spots near the collar. No wonder it had been discarded to the scrap pile.

But when Nora held it up, her breath caught. She recognized this shirt. It had been Jimmy's, though she hadn't seen him wear it in months. The last time she had seen it had been at the school's harvest festival the previous year, in fact.

"This is perfect," she said softly.

"Oh, good, I'm glad you found something," Mrs. Rayburn said with a glance. "I'm sure it will take me months to go through that whole stack."

"Thank you!" Nora tucked the shirt under her arm.

Her words were almost drowned out by the kitchen door banging open and a young man's voice calling through the house.

"Mother, do we have any string? Like the kind you use for packages?"

Nora's heart hammered. She would recognize that voice anywhere. Silently, she prayed Jimmy would come into the sitting room looking for his mother and see her there. She willed him to look at her, to see her holding the baby. To see her as the very image of domesticity.

"Mother?"

And then he was in the doorway. Tall and broad-shouldered, with his honey-blond hair just long enough to brush the top of his collar.

"Nora. Mrs. Cole. Nice to see you." He nodded politely at the women, before turning his attention to his mother. "Do we? Sorry, it's just that Betty's pa is waiting on me."

"Yes, check on the top shelf of the pantry. I believe I tucked the last of it away in there."

"Great!" he said over his shoulder, before darting out again.

Nora felt herself deflate. She clenched her jaw, willing her disappointed tears to remain at bay.

"Come along," her mother said, standing. "We'd better get back to make supper. Goodness knows your sister won't be any help."

Nora kissed Jory's chubby cheek before handing him to his mother. "Tell the rest of your family we said hello."

"Of course, dear."

"Jory is just darling," she added, afraid she may have embarrassed herself by paying too much attention to Jimmy.

As Nora and her mother walked home in the autumn afternoon, Mrs. Cole talked on and on about what chores and laying in for the winter they still needed to finish before the first snow fell. By the middle of November, though occasionally earlier, their neighborhood just outside of Detroit, Michigan, would be covered with a fine layer of snow which almost never left until spring.

Nora tried to listen, but she couldn't stop thinking

about her conversation with Betty the night before. The other girl had come over after supper, ostensibly to borrow an apron pattern, but all members of both families knew that was just an excuse for the two girls to see each other at the end of an otherwise work-filled day.

Sitting out on the steps of the Coles' front porch, Betty and Nora had daydreamed together about the harvest festival the church would be hosting in another couple weeks.

"My new muff should be ready by then, I hope," Betty had said. "I'm to go to town with Pa next week to collect it. Wait till you see it, Nora. It's just the loveliest shade of green, lined with the softest rabbits' fur."

With veritable stars in her eyes, Nora sighed happily. "I can just imagine. It's going to look so lovely, Betty. You must be so excited."

Betty leaned back against the rail and sighed happily. After a quiet moment, she added softly, "That's what I love about you, Nora Cole. There isn't a jealous bone in your body."

"Of course not. Why would I be jealous? I want you to have everything your heart desires."

"You really mean that?" Betty asked urgently. "Even if it's something you want yourself?"

Nora had shrugged, unconcerned at the time and not thinking anything of such a question. Her friend's muff sounded lovely, but she didn't need one herself. "I don't see why not."

Now, though, the next day in light of the fact that Betty had perhaps not told her everything the night before, Nora wondered where such a question had come from. She didn't think Betty had ever had reason to doubt her sincerity before.

"Nora," her mother said. "Nora, did you hear me?"

The girl shook herself out of her musings to focus on the moment at hand.

"No, Mother, sorry, I was…"

"Daydreaming about some boy, I have no doubt," Mrs. Cole said with a smile. "That can wait for the moment, my love. I was asking you if you thought your sister might be ready soon to start with cooking lessons in earnest."

"Amy? Cook? On the stove, with all that fire and danger and the potential to poison us?"

Her mother laughed. "You know, maybe if we put it to her as if it is a science experiment, she would be more likely to show some interest."

"Oh, goodness, as long as she doesn't want to experiment on how best to cook cockroaches or earthworms. Can you even imagine? She'll come in from the barn, start mixing up the gravy and half a dozen spiders will fall out of her hair into the pan."

Mrs. Cole laughed again. "Oh, my poor girl. Well, I suppose she's only thirteen. Plenty of girls her age aren't ready to keep house. There's still time for Amy to find her way."

"I'm not sure." Nora tried to keep her tone light, but this was a problem she had spent many hours worrying about. "Not if she doesn't set aside some of the creatures or curiosities she's always so fascinated with. Can you imagine her being able to find a husband willing to put up with such ramblings? It might be best to just try to teach her to stay quiet."

"Now, don't be cruel. Your sister is ... unique. There's no denying that. But I wouldn't want her to be anyone other than herself. And I pray every day that her future partner loves the same things about her. You'll see. But, as I said there's no reason to worry too much now."

"I suppose the first thing she needs if she's going to be able to find a husband at all is those cooking lessons. Maybe we can start her with something impossible to ruin."

"Did you have something in mind?"

"Do you think she could bake a potato?"

Mrs. Cole burst into a peal of laughter.

CHAPTER TWO

The next evening at supper, the Cole family sat down together to eat. Nora and Amy set the table, laying out the dishes and making sure that all four place settings had the right silverware. It had been a full day of finishing up the summer canning before starting Amy on her cooking lessons, meager though they were. The younger of the two Cole girls had been chattering away, informing their father of the strenuous, curious, and only somewhat satisfying afternoon she had spent in the kitchen.

"And therefore," she concluded, after blowing a piece of her brown hair out of her face, "it is my belief that whenever possible we should be eating our food raw." With that, she took her seat at the foot of the table.

"Sounds like everyone had a good day," her father responded absently.

"Father," Nora said as she took her own seat. "Did you hear what Amy just said? She was in charge of baking all the potatoes for supper. Today was her very first cooking lesson."

"Amy made this?" Charlie poked experimentally at the potato, before looking at his wife hopefully. "What about the roast chicken? Or the beans?"

"No, just the potatoes. We decided to start small." Laura Cole cut open her own potato, and tried to inspect the white baked flesh within without anyone noticing. Even from where Nora sat on the other side of the table she could see with not a small amount of relief that the vegetable had been cooked all the way through. It should have been difficult to ruin a baked potato, after all.

"A potato can be a full meal," Amy protested. "If that is all I am ever called upon to cook, it could still be plenty."

"Yes, yes. Let's say grace," Mr. Cole said, heading off any further excuses or accusations.

The four Coles bowed their heads, Nora closing her eyes to listen and hold gratitude for such bounty in her heart. It had been a long afternoon with Amy in the kitchen, but now she could rest.

"And thank you, Lord, for the years we have made this our home, and for what is to come," her father concluded.

When Nora looked up, she noticed her parents exchange a look of eagerness, but neither said anything.

"What is to come?" Amy asked point blank.

"Amy," Nora said. "Some things are not our business."

"Oh, I don't know," their mother said. "This might be something that you all can ask about."

"Let's eat first," their father said.

"But—" Amy protested.

"Eat," Laura Cole said.

Nora's younger sister sat to her right, across from their father, and looked at both her parents in turn before sighing and turning her attention to her plate. Amy carefully cut into her own potato. All that afternoon, as her mother had roasted the chicken and boiled the green beans, Nora had been tasked with keeping her sister on task.

It had been as good as impossible.

Even just helping Amy get the stove to the heat they needed it was rife with detours and scrutiny. Amy had wondered out loud about the different burning properties of various types of wood, even suggesting they get a handful of hay from the barn to stick inside the stove just to see if that was more or less efficient than the methods their mother had used for decades. Nora nearly lost her patience a dozen times, and twice had narrowly saved Amy from burning herself. Just as often, though, she reminded Amy that future cooking lessons could involve experiments. This very first one needed to follow their mother's explicit recipe, and for pity's sake stop trying to make changes right now.

"I still think we should have tried injecting the butter into the potato before we cooked it. Imagine how much more efficient your preparation would be now, with the condiment already cooked inside." Amy looked around the table expectantly.

Nora shook her head in exasperation.

"Well, I'll tell you what," Mr. Cole said. "In the spring, when we are traveling west on the Oregon Trail and cooking over a campfire every day, maybe that would be a good chance for you to experiment with food."

"Charlie!" his wife said in surprise.

Nora froze. "How— What— I— Uh... Oregon?"

"Very inarticulate, sister," Amy said. "Just ask him to repeat himself."

"Father, what did you just say about Oregon? Are we going to Oregon?" Nora asked, desperately.

Her father looked at his wife for reassurance and chuckled. "Well." He took a deep breath. "I said we will be heading to Oregon in the spring. Your mother and I have been talking it over for a few months now, and have decided we would enjoy the fresh start, somewhere it might not snow quite so much. Somewhere you girls could have more opportunities. More room to spread out."

"But ... Oregon!" Nora collapsed back in her chair, her meal forgotten. "We don't know anyone in Oregon. What opportunity could you mean?"

"Of course not," her mother said. "But we'll meet plenty. They say the folks you travel west with become a kind of family. By the time we get to the coast, we'll have all the new friends we could need. We've thought through all of this, I promise you."

Nora shook her head, still in shock. "But ... I ..."

"What do you think, Amy?" Mr. Cole said, taking another bite.

"Well..." The younger girl sat quietly thinking for a few long moments, while the rest of the family waited. Amy was generally quite precise in her language, but that did mean allowing her the time to formulate her sentence first. "While I admit I had not thought about the possibility of leaving Michigan, and I am mildly disappointed to not be consulted, on balance, I do think that the opportunities that such a journey affords will be to my advantage."

Mrs. Cole smiled. "Thank you, dear. Well said."

"Nora, I know you're surprised," her father said, "but we're not leaving tomorrow. You'll have plenty of time to spend with your friends before we say good-bye, and I'm sure they would love to receive mail from you once we're settled."

"When do we leave?" Her voice cracked as she said it, but none of the family commented on the emotion that seemed to be overwhelming Nora. "How long do we have?"

"Not until after the holidays," Mrs. Cole said. "Probably early January, if all goes well, but we'll be sure to be here for the Wilkinson holiday party as usual. One last time."

"One last time," Nora repeated.

Amy fired off a number of specific questions about the journey, but Nora had stopped listening.

This was not what she'd had in mind for herself, for her future. Oregon might as well be a foreign country for all it related to her life. She didn't quite know what to think about this big change, but she wasn't sure she had any choice.

In all her dreams of her future, of a husband, a home and children, not once did she ever imagine herself living anywhere but here. This neighborhood, these friends, were all that she had wanted in life. But now that was all being taken away from her.

As her parents and sister discussed what Oregon

would be like and what they might expect while traveling—Amy was full of questions—Nora could only look for a way out.

———

"Well. It's official," Nora said, lying back on the counterpane. "I can't even believe it."

She and her best friend, Betty Turret, were sequestered in the latter's bedroom the next afternoon. The two girls spent as much time as possible at the Turret home, given that Amy Cole was perpetually filling their own home with stray animals and the beginnings of science experiments. It hadn't been a week earlier that Amy had smuggled an actual toad into bed with her and Nora had not found it until the following morning.

"What is?" Betty asked. She sat at her vanity and had almost finished braiding her heavy dark hair.

"Oregon. Father told us last night. They've decided for certain that by this time next year they want to be settling in the Oregon Territory. Twenty-five hundred miles away."

"No!" Betty turned to face her friend. "What? Oregon! You can't leave Michigan. What will I do without you?"

Nora sat up and shrugged. "I don't know what choice I have. I can't stay here on my own. I have nothing else."

"Maybe you can. You just turned eighteen!"

"Yes, but eighteen doesn't mean I can provide for myself. There's not much I can do. I suppose the only option I have is to get married."

She said it lightly, as though she wasn't serious, but

both girls knew that such a step really was Nora's only real chance to stay in Michigan. Her family would not leave her behind unless she was being cared for by someone.

"So," she continued, "unless I can find a husband in the next three months, I guess I'll be leaving in January with the rest of my family."

Betty rose from her seat at the vanity and sat beside her friend on the bed. Without saying anything, she took Nora's hand in her own and squeezed. Oregon might as well be the moon; the two girls knew that once the Cole family left Michigan, she would never see Betty again.

Nora looked at her friend. She was somewhat surprised to see that Betty looked at her with an expression Nora couldn't interpret. It was almost like pity, but she could think of no reason why her best friend would feel so sorry for her. True, she hadn't yet managed to attract Jimmy's courting, but she still had plenty of time. Or she thought she had, before her father announced their big move.

"I'll figure something out," she murmured. "I have to. I can't leave... you. You all. Everyone here that I've known my whole life."

Betty wrapped both arms around her and hugged her tightly. "I'm going to miss you so much," she whispered.

Nora felt a tear slide down her cheek.

CHAPTER THREE

Dinner that night and news of their coming journey had set off a tornado of activity. After the decision had been made to pick up their stakes and move to the Oregon Territory, there was no time to lose. The Cole family had to go through all of their belongings, decide what to keep and what to sell. What they would need to buy before leaving and what they could do without until they reached the west coast. What treasures they would protect and haul west no matter what it took. What cherished belongings they would have to put from their minds, gifting to someone here who could take care of it.

For close to ten months, Michigan to the west coast, the family of four would be living out of a wagon and every option would be limited. Decisions needed to be made now to make that time more manageable.

Though there was plenty of other work to do, Mrs. Cole insisted that Nora finish the quilt she was working on before the end of the year. Better to start fresh once they had left, she told her daughter. And so, Nora spent many hours over the next few weeks getting all the patchwork pieces lined up and arranged. While her hands sewed the tiny stitches, Nora's mind daydreamed about how she could better get Jimmy Rayburn's attention, how she could delicately hint to him what she hoped for.

Jimmy finally realizing that he was in love with Nora would solve all of her problems.

"That quilt of yours will be exactly what we need for the journey," Mrs. Cole had said, before listing off several other projects she wanted her daughters to take care of. "Those cold nights in the mountains just before we cross into the territory. And it will be better to take a completed blanket with us into the wilderness, than to give away a half-finished project, don't you think?"

Amy, though almost fourteen, was too flighty and distracted by her bottomless curiosity to take on the same responsibilities that their mother required of Nora. One of these days, they told themselves, Amy would settle down and be trusted to sew her own dress or bake a cake without forgetting to put in flavoring. Until that happened, however, it would be Nora's responsibility to look after her younger sister and help their mother with the housework as much as she could.

But, that was what she had been doing her whole life, Nora reasoned. A few added responsibilities now before they left their childhood home altogether was not much. Nora was happy to do her part.

While Nora helped Mrs. Cole get the family's home and belongings in order for the big move, Amy roamed the farm with their father. She could be easily distracted by the formation of geese overhead, flying south for the winter, but she could help repair a fence as well as any boy. If her father was there to give instruction and keep her on task, of course.

One evening, shortly into November, her father entered the kitchen in the early afternoon. He almost never came in from the fields this early in the day unless he was ill, and his family was immediately concerned.

"Is everything all right?" his wife asked.

Nora and Laura both had hands covered in flour, as they prepared half a dozen pie crusts to be filled with cherries. Among the other projects they had to manage before leaving Michigan, was using up or giving away all the canned goods that Laura had put in over the previous years. Making cherry pies for their closest neighbors would help ease the shock of their going, as well as make good use of the last year's crop of fruit.

"Everything is wonderful." He wrapped an arm around his wife's waist and pulled her tight. "Perfect, in fact. Working out exactly as we hoped."

"Charlie," she murmured as he kissed the soft spot on the side of her neck. "What has gotten into you?"

"I have good news," her father said. "I have found a buyer for the farm."

"Charles Cole!" Laura turned fully toward her husband and threw her arms around his neck as the two embraced. "Thank heavens. That was the one thing I was worried about getting taken care of before we left."

"Now we can plan properly. We'll be able to leave Michigan after the new year, and be in Independence in time to team up with a wagon company before they leave this spring."

"Wonderful," Laura said. "Is it anyone we know?"

"James Rayburn."

Nora felt her cheeks flush at the name, but kept her eyes lowered pinching the edges of the dough as she fit it into the pie tin.

"My understanding is he's buying it for his oldest boy," her father continued. "He knows our plans, and we can stay until the end of January if need be."

"Goodness! We should celebrate!"

"Let's open that cider you've been saving. No better time than now."

A jolt of surprise shot through Nora at that news. James Rayburn's oldest boy was Jimmy. *Her* Jimmy. Did that mean he would be living in this house? If Nora married him, would she be living in her childhood home? Would he propose before the Coles were supposed to leave for Oregon?

All of this coursed through her mind in the short time before her father spoke again.

"I guess he's marrying Betty Turret in the spring, after the cherries come in, so that will give him some time to pay his father back before the wedding."

Nora's stomach dropped.

"What?" She cleared her throat; she tried to sound unconcerned, and hide from her parents the utter betrayal and panic that threatened to overwhelm her. "Did you say, um, they were getting married?"

"Betty didn't tell you yet?" her mother asked, as she pulled out the cut glass goblets from the highest shelf. "Oh, goodness, I suppose we'll need to give these glasses away before we leave. They'd likely just get broken jostling around the back of a wagon."

"Mother, wait," Nora said. "Did you just say Betty? You knew about this?"

"Her mother said something to me weeks ago. I knew they weren't announcing it yet, but I thought she would have told her best friend. I'm so sorry, darling, but I'm sure she had her reasons."

When she finally turned to face her daughter, Nora felt the pressure and scrutiny in her mother's expression.

"Nora? Are you all right?"

Tears threatened to spill down her cheeks, but Nora couldn't bear the pity. How had everyone known but she? Were they all laughing at her, as she had panted after Jimmy even as he courted her own friend?

"I have to..." she began, as she hurried toward the kitchen door. "I should go offer my congratulations."

Nora shouted this over her shoulder as she plunged into the autumn evening. The sun was just about to set behind the low hill of the Vandenberg farm, and she shivered under the slight cold, but she didn't want to turn back to grab a shawl. Hastily, she tried to wipe the flour off her hands onto her apron, before taking it off and crumpling it into a ball in her hands.

She didn't want anyone to see her cry. She didn't want to have to talk to a single person until she had heard the news directly from her best friend.

Why hadn't Betty said anything to her?

How could she have kept this from her?

The Turret farm was a quick walk through the spruce wood that divided the two families' land. How nice for Betty that she'd be living right next to her family after she was married, Nora thought sullenly. How long had she been planning this conquest?

A glance through the window as Nora approached the farmhouse told her that the Turrets were just sitting down for supper. She climbed the steps to the porch and rapped briskly on the front door. After a quick shuffling inside, the door swung open.

Warm light from the kerosene lamp fell on Nora's face.

"Why, Nora!" Betty exclaimed, frowning. "What are you doing here? Are you sick?"

"Is everything all right, Nora?" Mrs. Turret called from the doorway into the kitchen.

"Yes, ma'am. Thank you." Nora gave Mrs. Turret a small smile. "I just needed to check one thing with Betty, if that's okay? Just a quick question about, um, Jimmy."

"Take her up to your room, Betty," her mother said quietly. "Supper can wait yet."

Betty cleared her throat, offered Nora what she was sure was a false smile and led her up the stairs. "Come along."

Nora felt as though she were outside her own body, as though she were watching herself climb the stairs behind a stranger. The sounds of the other Turret children floated up the stairs after them, and Nora faintly heard Betty shoo her little sister out of their shared bedroom before she closed the door.

Silence fell over the room.

Still shaking, Nora crossed and sat on the edge of her friend's bed but kept her eyes cast down. She couldn't look at Betty. She didn't even know where to start.

"Nora?"

She looked up. Betty still stood by her bedroom door with a concerned look on her face.

"Nora, you *must* have known... I didn't realize you didn't. I... I'm sorry. Jimmy has been telling me that I needed to make sure you heard it from me, but..."

"Jimmy said that?" Nora's voice cracked. "Why? Why would he be so concerned about my feelings?"

Betty swallowed. "Nora..."

In a flash, Nora could picture all of it. Her best friend and the love of her life, happily gossiping about her behind her back, falling in love, forgetting Nora existed at all except as the punchline of all their jokes. It spoke well of Jimmy if he at least knew enough to urge Betty to speak to her, but the fact that he would do so because he knew of Nora's hidden love for him cut deep.

"You told him," she whispered. "You told him about me. How... Betty..."

In her embarrassment and anguish, Nora could not do much more than shake her head. She didn't know what to do next, how to react to such a hurt.

"I'm sorry. I didn't want to hurt you, not ever, but... Jimmy and I have known each other just as long as you, and over the last year we've... Well, you remember that night almost a year ago, at the annual Wilkinson holiday party? You left early because Amy got sick, and then he—"

"That long?" Nora cut in. "Since last Christmas? How could you have kept it from me?"

"I'm sorry," Betty said again. "I didn't want to, but you were always so... I didn't think the little flirtation would go anywhere, and I didn't want to hurt you. But then once it became clear that... I didn't know how to tell you. And so much time had passed. I'm sorry."

Nora looked up at Betty. She had been friends with her for so long; it was easy to recognize the expression of real regret on her face. But Nora was too hurt, too betrayed and lost to do anything more than register the emotion.

She looked back down at her hands.

"Well. We're talking about moving the wedding up till Christmas. Before you leave. I hope you will be there," Betty concluded softly. "I love you, Nora. I didn't want it to be this way. I didn't want you to find out like this."

"I have to get home," she said, standing. "I have to start packing."

CHAPTER FOUR

Five months later, Nora stood on the boardwalk outside the general store and held a small basket full of straw-cushioned eggs looped over one arm. She looked around the bustling frontier town, wide-eyed and welcoming to everything she saw. Independence was unlike anything she had seen, even over the three months it had taken the Cole family to travel from Michigan to this far side of Missouri. Everywhere she looked was a rugged mountain man, a terrifying Indian, or even a dark-skinned servant walking a pace behind their master. White, settler families choked the streets, desperate to acquire the last supply they need for their summer on the Oregon Trail.

Each person had a magical story or mysterious past. And Nora wanted to drink it all in. She was determined to arrive in Oregon ready for the next chapter in her life.

After her fight with Betty back in November, Nora had not spoken to her best friend for several weeks. Instead, she threw herself into the Coles' preparations to leave for Oregon. There was so much to do, both to be ready to travel and to get the house ready to be sold. Though every day was painful, thinking about Jimmy and Betty living in that house after their wedding, thinking of her friend living the life that Nora herself had wanted, she was not insensible. If it was not meant to be, it was not meant to be, or so she reminded herself.

It was time for the next step.

By the time Betty's wedding came around at Christmas time, Nora had thawed enough to attend. She had gone to the Turrets' early in the afternoon to help the bride with her attire. Though at times it felt like an act, Nora managed to be enthusiastic and supportive at the wedding supper after. She could do this for her friend. She could set aside her own pain. It was the last time that she and Betty would be together as friends. Nora mourned the loss of the friendship of her youth, but as soon as the wedding was over she turned her attention to her future.

She couldn't stay in Michigan after this heartache, and so looked forward to all the new people and new opportunities that would cross her path over the two thousand miles until Oregon.

Now, just a few more months later, the Coles had made it to Independence, Missouri. The gateway to the west. Though a small part of Nora felt as though she might send her old friend one last letter before they set off into the wilderness and the trail, in her heart she knew there was no point. Betty Turret had been her best friend all through her childhood, but Betty Rayburn now would have a whole new life apart from Nora.

Independence would be her fresh start. The Oregon

Territory would be her life now. She would find the love of her life here on the frontier, rather than in the stagnant community of her previous home.

And so, as she and her younger sister Amy walked through the frontier town, Nora kept her eyes open. Anything could happen out here on the edge of civilization. Any one of the young men they walked past while procuring supplies could be a friend. Mr. Cole had secured the family a spot in the Sullivan-Mills wagon company, but they had yet to meet many of the nearly fifty families that would be traveling west with them. Nora could easily imagine herself nursing some young man's injury or being sought after by the mothers of the company to look after the children while making their way west. She pictured her hair adorned with prairie wildflowers and the healthy glow of her cheeks after being outdoors. The romanticism of such imaginings buoyed her up through the drudge of the muddy streets of Independence.

"Come on," she told her sister, pulling her away from the crowd of boys watching the blacksmith. "We need to get back to camp with these eggs. And, besides, a smithy is no place for a young lady."

"Why do I have to be a young lady?" Amy asked, though she followed her sister uncomplainingly. "Father liked it when I helped him on the farm."

Nora guided Amy between two pairs of women their mother's age, each one of them intent on their own list of errands that needed to be completed that day.

"Because if you don't act like a lady, no one will ever want to marry you."

"That's okay."

"And then you'll have to live with Father and Mother until you die."

Amy was silent for a moment, considering. "Oh."

Nora laughed. "It wouldn't be all that bad, but you'll never be able to talk Mother into letting you bring your rodents into the house."

"Rats are very smart!"

"Yes, you've said. Many many times. And yet that still has not convinced Mother, has it?"

"But if I get married," Amy continued, "I'll have my own house and can bring as many of the rats as I want."

"I suppose," Nora responded with a groan. "Just maybe let's get you asked to dance first or something first. One step at a time."

"I don't know how to dance."

"Well, then, we'll work on that too."

They continued their walk through the streets of Independence, to the small campsite that had been cobbled together a few blocks away. Families were coming to Independence from all over the country, and the hotels and boarding houses had long ago filled up. Instead, the Coles, like many others, lived out of their wagon for a few weeks more. What was that little bit of inconvenience tacked on to the beginning of another six months before they even reached Oregon?

As the Cole sisters returned to their camp, Nora was awed by the sight of so many new wagons. Whole families of emigrants that had showed up just in the few hours they had been gone. A big family with several grown sons. A small family with a young boy and girl. An older couple who seemed too fragile to make the journey any farther. And everyone in between.

"How many could you get?" Mrs. Cole asked, when she saw the girls approaching.

Amy went straight for the back of the wagon, climbing in and all but ignoring their mother.

"Only half a dozen. The more folks coming into town, the fewer Mrs. Strauss has available, I imagine." Nora handed her mother the basket with the fresh eggs packed gently with clean hay. "But she was happy to trade for the dried cherries we had. I don't see why we can't take a chicken with us in the wagon, though. Then we could have eggs all the time."

"Ask your father, but I for one do not want to have to worry about keeping a hen alive on top of everything else that needs my attention. Did you see anything else interesting in town?"

"Mother, do you think that I could be a blacksmith?" Amy asked. She had climbed back out of the wagon and now sat cross-legged under the shade of the rear wheel, drawing shapes in the dirt.

"Oh, I..." She looked to Nora for guidance, who just shrugged. "Well, it seems like the kind of vocation that you would need to be much stronger for, in addition to all the other considerations."

"Yes, but that seems like an easy problem to solve."

Nora walked away, leaving the two to their hypothetical discussion. It didn't matter how much Amy was able to talk their mother into supporting her potential future career as a blacksmith. The truth was Amy would find something completely different to interest her in the next month, if not sooner.

The Coles' wagon and campsite was in the middle of a broad, mostly dirt, open area near the edge of Independence. The family had arrived several weeks earlier and in that time more and more families had come to camp nearby. Each family made their preparations to continue on to Oregon or California. Each family full of hope for their future, despite the limitations of their present.

As she walked through the wide route between two rows of wagons, Nora felt that same infectious optimism, almost like waves coming toward her. Each of these families that she passed had given up a life farther east in the hope that what was ahead of them would be worth the sacrifice. Nora herself'd had to give up her dream of marrying Jimmy Rayburn, but she had faith. She believed. Whatever God had in store for her would be better than what she'd had in Michigan.

Movement near the edge of the campsite caught her eye. Nora turned to see a young man, probably about her own age lifting a young boy up over his head to reach the high branch of a tree. He was tall and lanky, though plenty strong, his shoulders barely straining in the effort to lift the child. He laughed and tossed his head back, which made his hat fall into the dirt. There was another little boy hovering nearby and watching intently who ran to pick up the hat. Nora was intrigued and drifted closer to see what they were doing.

As he held the little boy as high as he could reach, the young man guided him toward one of the branches.

When she got close enough, the little boy still on the ground noticed her.

"What are you doing?" Nora asked.

"We're on an adventure!" the boy on the ground

exclaimed. "Jasper says it's an expi... Expo... What is it?" He looked up, with a scrunched-up face.

"Expedition. We're searching for bird's eggs," he explained to Nora, as he set his charge back down in the dirt. "I think I saw some newly hatched babies in this tree just a couple days ago, and Will wanted to see."

"Jasper says we might get to see them try to fly," the other little boy chimed in.

"Why don't you two run along home?" the young man who must be Jasper said to the boys, claiming his hat and guiding them gently away. "We'll finish our expedition tomorrow, maybe. Ask your mother."

The boys frowned at Nora, with something akin to envy in their expressions, before running back to their own wagon. The young man turned back to Nora, offering her his full attention.

"Jasper Stephens. Formerly of Indianapolis," he said, tipping his hat and grinning at her. His smile favored his right side, and Nora thought she had never seen any smile so cute. "And I'm going to Oregon."

Nora laughed, charmed by the frankness the young man offered. His wavy dark hair curled down around his ears in a way that reminded her of Jimmy Rayburn, but she pushed that other man out of her mind. Jasper's warm smile and twinkling eyes gave her such a sense of being noticed that she had never gotten from Jimmy.

"You know, I suspect many of the families around here are also going to Oregon," she replied, gesturing generally to the campsite full of wagons.

"You don't say. Well, that is a coincidence. Are you traveling on your own, missus...?"

"It's miss. Nora Cole. Thank you." She could feel

herself blushing, acutely aware of the implication intended in his fishing for her name. "I'm going west with my family. Parents and a younger sister."

"Better and better; I'm doing the same. Only my sister is older."

"I ... Well... That's lovely. Goodness!" Nora was at a complete loss for words. She couldn't remember the last time a young man as charming as this had flirted with her. Had talked to her at all, in fact.

But Jasper seemed well able to maintain his side of the conversation at least, and didn't draw any attention to her awkwardness. She was so grateful for this kindness that she almost missed what he said next.

"...leaving in two days, with the Sullivan-Mills wagon company. It's a shame you and I didn't meet sooner."

"Sullivan-Mills!" she exclaimed, latching on to the name. "Yes, me too! That is, my family has joined that wagon company as well. We're leaving in two days as well. I'll be there with you. Or, I suppose, with everyone..."

"What a treat," Jasper said in a low, confidential tone. "I imagine we'll be seeing a lot of each other, then."

Nora blushed. Her heart pounded and she almost felt as though she could not catch her breath. She took a half step closer to him.

"Nora!" Amy called. "Nora, can you help me with this? Please?"

Nora tore her eyes from Jasper reluctantly. Even from this distance she could see that Amy was struggling under the weight of their father's tools, as she tried to pull the box out of the wagon.

"Is that your sister? Can I help?" Jasper asked, concerned. He took half a step toward the Coles' wagon.

"No, no, thank you," Nora interjected, mortified that Jasper's first impression of her family was this. "She's fine. She just... Well, she got it into her head she wants to be a blacksmith, and Mother told her she needed to be stronger, and so I assume this is the result." She sighed. "I'm sorry. I should go make sure she doesn't get crushed under that."

Jasper laughed heartily. "And if you find *you* need help, just call for me."

"I— Um, I will." Nora stumbled as she took a couple steps back. "Thank you. It was lovely to meet you, Mr. Stephens."

He tipped his hat again and watched her return to her wagon.

CHAPTER FIVE

Before they had even left Independence for the Oregon Territory, Jasper Stephens was lodged in Nora's mind. She wouldn't have it any other way. The attention and consideration she had hoped to inspire in Jimmy Rayburn was now coming her way in the figure of the tall, handsome man from Indiana.

Or would be, Nora knew, once they had more time to spend together. It was so clear just from the few moments they spent together that she and Jasper could have a future. Both helping others, both cheerful about the adventure ahead. She just hoped he saw the same potential she did.

The following two days were a whirlwind of activity, of last-minute errands and packing the wagon for the hundredth time. Checking and double checking. And yet, amidst all this busyness, Nora still kept one eye open for the handsome Jasper Stephens. With as spread out as this campsite was, his family's wagon was just out of direct line of sight from her own. Over those two full-to-bursting days, she would invent reasons why she needed to go collect more water, or check something on the other side of the wagons next to them. The Waters family, with their two wagons and six grown men, seemed to take up so much space, and Nora just wanted a glimpse of Jasper.

Her parents were too consumed with their final preparations to worry about Nora's errands, but Amy was as full of questions as ever.

"What are you looking for?" the younger girl asked when she tagged after Nora.

"Nothing." Nora peered this way and that. She paused when they turned a corner around another wagon, and she saw a different tall, thin man before she realized it wasn't Jasper.

"Well, hurry up, then," Amy insisted, hurrying ahead to the spring where they had been collecting water for the last few weeks. "I want to get back and help Father check the mules' shoes."

As her sister ran on ahead, Nora allowed herself to be distracted by the wide array of emigrants that were clustered in this campsite on the edge of Independence. Though the various wagon companies leaving from Independence were all on different schedules, every emigrant was eager to get moving west. If they left too late in the season, there was not only the danger of not getting over the mountains before the snow fell in the fall, but also the increased likelihood that all the teams and animals that had gone before them will have eaten all the grass. Nora's family would be leaving the next day, but so would many of the families she passed as she walked through the maze of wagons.

She reached the creek to find that Amy had already filled their bucket and was waiting impatiently for her before returning. There were only so many excuses Nora could make without arousing her sister's suspicions and finally, after walking around the long way, the girls returned to their wagon.

"Mother, look what I found!" Amy reached into the pocket of her apron and withdrew an enormous beetle.

Nora gasped. "Where did you get that?

"It was near the base of the shrubs when I was getting water," she responded. "I'm going to study it while we are traveling west."

"No, Amy," their mother cut in, "you cannot bring the beetle with you."

"Mother—"

"Amy. I assure you, we will find plenty of insects and creatures for you to study on the prairie between here and Oregon. There is no need to house one in the pocket of your apron."

"It's dead!" Amy insisted, holding out her palm to better display the two-inch-long bug.

Nora smiled to herself as she heard her mother lose patience with her sister. There was always something with that girl. Nora did her best to help her, but Amy didn't seem to want to fit into any society. It was late in the afternoon, and the pressure of needing to get everything done before the morning was putting everyone on edge.

Mrs. Cole had started supper, including baking a whirligig with the last of their fresh eggs and some of the dried cherries they had brought from Michigan. After months on the road from their previous home and then weeks in Independence, it was finally time to leave town, finally time to tie up all the loose ends and hit the road. The following morning, the Coles would cast their lot with the Sullivan-Mills wagon company and spend the day traveling northwest toward their first campsite.

"How early are we leaving in the morning, dear?" Mrs. Cole called to her husband. He and Amy were checking the hooves of the three mules that would be hauling their wagon westward.

"Early. Or, rather, early enough. I imagine getting that many wagons and families all coordinated could take all morning. We'll just have to see. Mills assured me they'd be going right past this campsite, and we would just need to fall into the caravan where we found a spot."

Nora felt a thrill run through her. It was all starting. Tomorrow was the day. The rest of her life, the love and adventure and everything that went through it would be hers. She went to bed that night hardly able to sleep for the excitement.

It seemed as though the big day would never come and when the morning finally arrived, Nora and the rest of the Coles were awake and ready with plenty of time to spare. Their journey from Michigan had already established the rhythm of days spent traveling. Charlie Cole was past master at guiding their team of mules into the harnesses, with Amy on hand if needed. Laura Cole could whip up a filling, healthy breakfast in what seemed like the blink of an eye. Amy could follow directions, but most times was left to her own devices.

Nora filled in the gaps here and there, as required. At times she was in charge of gathering water and fuel, at other times reorganizing the rear of the wagon to make room so they could reach a trunk in the far corner. She thrived on feeling useful and ever since they had left Michigan that had been a daily staple, steadying herself with the assurance that she was needed.

About mid-morning, Nora had gone through a range of anxious emotions while waiting. Time seemed to stand still. She was rebraiding Amy's hair after her sister had crawled under a bush chasing after a lizard when they heard their father call out.

"There they are! It's time to go, ladies!"

Nora looked up excitedly. The clean white canvas of a wagon top passed on the road, onward north, with an older man at the helm. Hurrying to finish Amy's braid, Nora kept her eyes on the caravan, wagon after wagon passing their campsite.

Charlie next called to his team of mules, goading them into movement. They were slow at first but once the wheels of the wagon got moving the animals hauled it forward with ease. Mr. Cole guided the team out into the road, behind another of the stark white, brand-new wagons that was heading out of town behind Captain Mills. From where the Cole family was in the rear of the caravan, Nora could not even begin to guess how many other families and wagons would be joining the trek westward. There seemed to be dozens.

For the first time in two days, thoughts of Jasper's adorable, crooked smile were far from her mind. Instead, the sight of so many people, so many animals, wagons, and all the folks' earthly belongings heading out of town arrested her attention. Where they were going there would be no outhouses, no general stores. Goodness, there would not even be any buildings with roofs, aside from the handful of Army forts peppered at long intervals.

And Nora was striding bravely into the heart of it.

The long, spring afternoon on the trail passed quickly for Nora. The dirt trail, with deep grooves worn down by hundreds, if not thousands, of wagon wheels curved away from the town into the prairie. Her father had told Nora it would take most of the day for them to reach the site of the first camp; there they would stay for an extra day to allow any stragglers to catch up. That meant miles of walking in April sun, parallel to the caravan, in the tall grass of the prairie.

The rainy period of late March had given way to the veritable carpet of wildflowers that stretched as far as she could see. Nora overheard snatches of her sister's conversation, asking about the different kinds of poisonous plants that they might encounter on their journey, but she shut it out as best she could. She preferred to walk alone, at least this first day, and drink in the breathtaking scenery where she found herself.

There was no stopping for food at midday, but Nora was perfectly satisfied with her fistful of jerky and canteen to nourish her. Just the adventure of their first day on the trail gave her plenty of energy.

When the wagon train finally turned off the trail to the sprawling campsite at the end of the day, Nora looked everywhere for a familiar person. In spite of all the families she had met in Independence, there were new faces everywhere.

"So many people!" she exclaimed. "Were there even this many families in Independence?"

"There was, though likely more spread out through

the neighborhood," her mother said. "Here it's far easier to get a sense of how many are heading west with all those stark-white wagon tops drawing the eye. Each of those wagons is home to at least a couple people, sometimes four or more."

At that moment, out of the wagon that had parked next to the Coles, three children popped out of the back of the wagon. The little girl waved to Nora when she noticed her looking; Nora waved in return.

Supper that first night was a tired affair; to Nora, food seemed uninteresting compared to all the new people and sights around them.

After they ate, she couldn't sit still any longer. "I'm going to go walk around," she told her mother, as she stood.

"Don't be long, please, dear. We have a long day tomorrow, and I'm going to need your help."

Nora wrapped her crocheted shawl around her shoulders and set off into the night. With so many wagons, so many campfires, even this long after dark there was plenty of light for her to see by as she strolled between the camps. Everywhere she looked was a harried mother washing dishes from supper, or a frowning father brushing down the family's one precious horse. Children of all ages laughed and played, pleased to be on their adventure at last.

Somewhere in the distance, Nora even heard the delicate lilt of a fiddle, playing into the night.

She wandered around the wagons for nearly an hour, watching, listening, and dreaming about it all, before heading back to her own wagon and bed.

Nora felt the community around her like a warm

embrace. The Waters family with their half-dozen young people, all excited to spread out throughout the Oregon Territory. The Valentine family, who had a daughter Nora's own age. The Stephens family, Jasper's irresistible charm and his sister's sad widowhood.

Who cared that Jimmy Rayburn hadn't seen her value? It was no matter that Nora had had to leave behind her best friend, and the entire community in Michigan that she had known since she was born.

Now she had a new chance to build a life exactly what she wanted, to expand just like the country full of pioneers and adventurers were expanding across the continent.

Hers were the same fierce dreams of love and home that so many women before her had dreamed.

CHAPTER SIX

The campsite where the Sullivan-Mills wagon company had stopped was expansive, offering space to several wagon companies to organize before heading west. As such a busy site, the privy and water supply were busy from dawn till dusk. The following morning, Mrs. Cole sent her daughters to collect more water that they could use throughout the day. Since they had a full day to spend in this campsite, they would wash the quilts and linens that had been well-used since they had left Michigan.

"Why didn't we do this before we left Independence? There are too many people here," Amy said, as she and Nora collected all of the family's empty buckets.

"Because there were a thousand other things to do that had to be done before we left. This is one chore that could wait."

"Until now," she replied sullenly.

"Until now," Nora agreed. "Grab that other bucket,

please. There's bound to be a crowd at the river this morning. Let's get moving."

She wasn't wrong about the crowd. The girls had to wait their turn to even reach the water's edge, and then squeeze their way between other women to leave again. After the girls had each collected two buckets of water, Amy asked her sister to wait while she examined something interesting she had found just off the trail.

As Nora waited, she daydreamed about meeting Jasper Stephens here, somewhere, today. Surely, he would be somewhere in this broad expanse of wagons. If they were in the same wagon company, he should be here for another full day. Maybe he was even looking for her too.

"Excuse me."

"Oh!" Nora started when she heard someone speak to her. She noticed a woman, a mother with dark hair pulled off her face, trying to get by. She turned back her sister. "Amy, move. Get out of the way. Let this woman through."

Amy seemed surprised to be pulled out of the way. It was as though her feet had not yet caught up to her brain, when Nora tugged on her arm. She had been too focused on watching the activities of a spider weaving its web between two branches to notice anything else.

"It's fine," the woman said. She smiled at the Coles as she snuck around them. "Not to worry. We'll likely all find ourselves in the middle of somebody's path between here and Oregon. Are you two with the Sullivan-Mills camp by any chance?"

"We are!" Amy said, finally looking away from the web. "We heard there was a doctor with that company.

Do you know about that? Do you think he does dissections?"

The woman spluttered awkwardly. "I'm sorry?"

Nora blushed. She could forget the strangeness of some of Amy's speeches most of the time. Hearing her say such things in front of a stranger brought them back to mind in a hurry. "Never mind her. *I'm* sorry. Nora Cole. And this is Amy, my sister."

"My name is Mrs. McKinnon. And to answer your question, I think if the doctor ever did dissections, it's unlikely that he will do any of that on the trail."

"Oh." Amy seemed disappointed. "That's probably true. Amputations, though, maybe, right?"

"Amy," Nora scolded under her breath.

"Um. Yes, maybe. You know, I have a daughter about your age," Mrs. McKinnon said to Amy, trying to smooth over her sister's embarrassment. "Her name is Claire. She helps me a lot with my younger children, and the chores and such, but maybe the two of you, or three of you, might like to play together some time."

"We'd love that," Nora said brightly, before Amy could answer. "But of course we have chores of our own to get to."

"Of course."

"It was lovely to meet you." Nora smiled, handed one of their buckets to her sister and nudged her back up the trail away from the water.

"What?" Amy asked, before they were very far away. "We were talking!"

"Amy," Nora said with exasperation. "Maybe... I don't know. Maybe just get to know a person a little bit more before you start talking about amputations."

"You don't know!" she protested. "Maybe such discussions interest her. She has children. I bet she has thought about them losing limbs before."

"Oh, Amy," was all Nora managed to say before they arrived back at camp. She loved her sister, she really did, but she had never realized how much of her life was spent explaining and excusing Amy to other people until they had left Michigan and all the families they had known their entire life.

After three more trips to the water—the last one without Amy—the Cole women had all they needed for their day of laundry. The repetitive scrubbing and wringing out of water gave Nora all the time she could wish for to daydream about Jasper and their life together in Oregon. She kept these thoughts to herself, of course, but she didn't think there was any harm in a little wishful planning.

As there was so much laundry to do, Nora found herself keeping close to camp for most of the day. But when her mother began preparations for supper, Nora heard someone playing fiddle elsewhere in the camp and couldn't stay put.

"I think I'll go see where that's coming from," she said, standing. "If that's all right."

Her mother pursed her lips. "Be careful. I don't like you going alone. Maybe Amy should go with you."

"No, thank you," her sister called from where she sat near the front wheel of the wagon.

Nora chuckled; she hadn't even realized Amy was listening.

"I'll make a friend there, maybe. I promise to be safe

as safe can be, stay near the light, and in the crowds, not venture off into the wilds of Missouri. No wolf will get me."

"I hope you do make friends," Laura said, ignoring Nora's teasing tone. "Don't pretend that leaving Michigan was so easy on you, Nora Cole. I know the truth."

She didn't respond, but simply hugged her mother around the waist, grabbed her shawl and set off through the camp.

The sun was just setting. The light of dozens of campfires illuminated the whole camp, as Nora wove between the wagons. She wasn't the only one drawn by the sound of music, either. Four or five different individuals, all around her own age and older, seemed to be streaming toward the sound of the fiddle too. As more of the emigrants finished their supper or their chores, they made their way to the source of the music that had wafted over the whole camp.

With no competing music or loud sounds out there on the prairie, it wasn't difficult to find the wagon where the fiddler resided. When Nora reached it, she was far from the first to have arrived. Three couples had already begun a lively waltz. Nora was reminded of the Wilkinson holiday party, one of their final weeks in Michigan. That too had been both boisterous and spare, with limited musicians. There as here, so much joy could be made out of so little. The emigrants who had chosen the hardships of the Oregon Trail were not about to turn their noses up at a dance just because it had only one fiddle.

Just outside the circle of light from the campfire, stood a young man of about Nora's age with a shock of jet-black hair. He seemed utterly focused on the worn, beat-up instrument in his hands. Though he occasionally glanced up at the couples dancing in the clearing on the other side of the campfire, he said nothing. He stood alone as he played, with seemingly no thought outside of the boisterous music he was producing.

Two other young men, both with the same jet-black hair of the musician, lounged at the back of the wagon. They laughed and passed a flask between them while the fiddle played on.

"Supper's ready, Martin!" one of them called.

An older man with a long gray beard stood over a big pot that sat on the smoldering coals of a campfire. He dished out some of whatever delicious smelling stew he had been making for supper and called again to the fiddler.

"Martin, if you don't come eat now your brothers will have all of it!"

Martin shook his head, grinned, and kept playing.

"Would you like to dance?"

Nora was surprised to find a well-looking young man standing in front of her offering his hand. Though not much taller than Nora, he was barrel-chested and seemed pleasingly steady. Safe.

"Oh, I..." She stammered.

"Arthur Davis," he said. "Oldest son of the Rupert Davises, and will be traveling west with the Sullivan-Mills wagon company. And now we're acquainted, you don't have to tell your mother you danced with a stranger." He winked at her. "I promise not to step on your feet."

Nora laughed and dipped a funny little courtesy as she introduced herself. "Nora Cole and ..." She felt a surge of expansive hope. Maybe creating this new life outside of Michigan could be easier than she thought. "Yes, well, then... thank you."

She took his hand and before she knew it, he had whisked her into the crowd of dancing couples.

They whirled around the small clearing, too quickly for there to be any conversation between them, but Nora didn't care.

After the first two songs, another young man cut in and, though he said his name, Nora didn't catch it over the music and her own laughter.

But it didn't much matter.

All that mattered was how she felt in this moment. It seemed such a small thing, but being able to find this joy again, this magic of dancing and meeting new people, just confirmed for her that heading west was the best choice for her. The next six months would fly by if every day was like this.

While dancing, she looked everywhere for Jasper Stephens, but he never made an appearance. Nora could think of plenty of reasons why that might be—anyone traveling to Oregon must have an unending list of chores and tasks to take care of every day. And only a small number of folks even peeked their heads out to come listen to the music. Maybe he came and left without even seeing her. She wouldn't take it personally. It wasn't possible he was avoiding her, was it?

Yes, Nora told herself as she walked back to her own camp alone, the fact that she had not seen Jasper at all that night meant nothing at all. There could be a new opportunity every day to speak to him, to run into him by chance, or to even share a dance with him.

It would all work out.

CHAPTER SEVEN

The sun peeked over the horizon, dawn breaking on the first morning the Sullivan-Mills wagon company would be heading west. Nora Cole rose with the sun. She was so excited to start, so ready to be on her way to her new life that she could barely sleep. In the quiet dawn, she went to the water to wash her face and collect a bucketful for her family's breakfast before many other people had gotten out of bed.

By the time she returned to her own camp, however, the bustling of other families was all around her. The camp was moving. In no time, everyone in the Sullivan-Mills wagon company had eaten breakfast, packed up the last of their things and harnessed the dozens of teams of oxen and mules for the long day ahead.

The appointed time the company was supposed to leave came and went, but Nora was too excited to be bothered. Every tiny change thrilled her. Every sight of a wagon, that promise of adventure, put a smile on her face. She had total faith that every step of this journey would get her closer to her true destiny in Oregon; she could be patient with tiny hiccups.

Finally, somewhere off on the far edge of the collection of wagons, Captain Mills set off, leading the caravan, guiding the emigrants west. One by one wagons fell into line behind the Mills family's wagon, until finally it was the Coles' turn. Leaving camp, the Coles pulled their wagon into the long caravan of vehicles just behind the Sheldon family. Though Nora had not yet had a chance to meet them, her mother had spent a while the day before speaking to Mrs. Sheldon, and learned all about the half a dozen dairy cows her family was driving west. The oldest of the four Sheldon children, along with their dog, was tasked with herding the animals west, matching the pace of the wagons.

The wagon that fell in line behind the Coles was home to the Gilroys, a man, his wife and her grown nephew so recently arrived from Ireland that at times Nora had difficulty understanding their accent. They had a big plan for their settling in the Oregon Territory. Mr. Gilroy—Sean—was a blacksmith, and as soon as Amy learned that she pestered the poor man with questions for more than an hour until Nora dragged her away.

The company of fifty wagons would be their community until they reached the Willamette Valley. These two families would be the Coles' neighbors throughout the entire five or six months that it took for the wagon company to reach Oregon. Every morning they would fall into the caravan with them, and every evening they would camp beside each other. Nora had never had trouble making friends, and though the Sheldons did not have any children her own age Nora was still very much looking forward to making the family a part of her life. The Gilroys' nephew Caleb was a bit older than Nora and seemed kind enough but had been too busy with chores to offer much conversation.

But there was time. There was so much time ahead of her to build this new life. These families—this wagon company as a whole—would be the foundation on which her future in Oregon was built. Many would likely band together to form a new town, once they reached the territory and claimed land. Others might form another company to travel north to Puget Sound or south to California. They would get through all of it together.

And so, when the wagon company first set off on that trail, Nora was ecstatic, soaking in every detail and treasuring the start of her future.

The wagons rolled westward. The morning wore on, with the April sun warming her shoulders. Thank goodness for the sturdy, bright bonnet that shielded her face and reflected the light. Because they had been late starting, the wagon company was not stopping for a midday meal, so Amy and Nora shared a handful of dried cherries with their new friend Claire McKinnon as the three girls walked along the trail near the Coles' wagon.

Nora had been walking in the grass, parallel to the trail, with her sister and Claire. The latter, a lovely dark-haired girl just between the Cole girls in age, had approached them earlier that morning while the wagons still waited in camp. Whatever Mrs. McKinnon had told her daughter about the Coles had evidently piqued her interest; once the wagons had begun their slow roll westward, she had again sought out the sisters, shyly introducing herself and grinning at their welcome.

"Nora has never had a beau," Amy said, apropos of nothing. Claire had been telling them about the swimming hole in their town in Pennsylvania where they were from.

"Oh?" Claire walked between the two sisters, and she turned to Nora at this shift in conversation. "That doesn't seem possible. Really?"

"The boy she liked married someone else," Amy offered.

Nora sighed.

Claire focused on her even more intently. "Is that true?" she prompted, sounding both excited and sympathetic. "Tell me everything."

"Amy, what are you doing?" Nora asked. "Why would you even bring that up?"

"I think it's very interesting. Some people read novels about stories like that. You should be proud to have such unique experiences."

Nora groaned. "Tonight, you and I are going to have a chat about what information is private and what is for sharing."

Claire laughed, but before she could ask any more questions, all their attentions were pulled by the fact that the wagon train had slowed to a stop. This far back in the caravan, they couldn't see far enough ahead to be able to identify the problem, though it seemed as if the wagons were being diverted off the trail.

"Why would we have to move?" Amy asked. "It seems inefficient to detour like that, doesn't it?"

"Something is blocking the trail," Nora responded. "Maybe a bison carcass or fallen tree?"

"What do you think happened?" Claire asked in a whisper.

"Do you think someone died?" Amy asked darkly.

"Amy Cole," she scolded. "Bite your tongue."

"I'm going to go find my mother," Claire said. "She might need my help. I'll come find you girls maybe tonight."

When the Coles were alone, they made their way closer to their own wagon, walking beside their father as the wagons inched their way forward more slowly. There was always something comforting about their father's presence; if the delay was hazardous in any way, Nora knew he would make sure they stayed safe.

The caravan of wagons snaked off the well-worn wheel ruts into the tall prairie grass. The air was especially fragrant as the bright blossoms of wildflowers were crushed under the heavy vehicles and ox hooves.

When they drew close enough, Nora realized what obstacle in the middle of the trail was. She gasped.

"How... What could be so strong to do that?"

One of the wagons that had been ahead of them in the caravan was tipped completely on its side, upended with much of the supplies spilled across the trail. One of the wooden ribs that had held up the white canvas top had snapped, the wagon cover now crushed in the dirt beneath the wagon.

"The oxen," Charlie murmured. "Get them going the wrong direction or spook them somehow and they are plenty strong to do that."

But as they inched forward, the sight only got worse.

Just past the wagon, a woman sobbed, as she held two small children close to her. The little boy had thrown his arms around her waist and was burying his face in her side. Nora's heart stopped and her hands grew clammy. What had happened? This poor woman. This poor family.

Then she noticed movement, down near the ground, by the wagon wheel.

An older man Nora guessed to be the doctor knelt in the dirt, next to the body of a man, his shirt rust red with the spread of blood. A broken wheel leaned nearby. Even at this distance, even with her limited knowledge, Nora knew there was nothing to be done for the man.

She looked again at the wailing woman.

The Coles wagon was now around the obstacle and returning to the trail, following the Sheldons. The caravan wasn't stopping, though many of the members had stepped up to help. Men and older boys were coordinating to lead the oxen away, to lift the heavy things out of the wagon making way for eventual repairs. But it wasn't clear that anyone was stepping in to help the woman or children.

Nora felt tears sting her eyes.

That poor family.

"I'm going to see if there's anything I can do to help," she declared, looking back over her shoulder at them.

Her mother paused in her walking to peer into Nora's face. Gently she laid a hand to her oldest daughter's cheek. "My sweet girl. I love your heart. But are you sure that is a responsibility you want? I worry about you taking on too much of other people's burdens and not caring for yourself enough."

"I won't, Mother. Or I'll try not to. But I can't just sit here while I know that this woman or her children could use a friendly face. She can't handle this all on her own."

Laura nodded. "All right. Be careful. I know it's useless to try to stop you."

Nora squeezed her mother's arm and ran back to where the doctor was consulting with the woman. The oxen had been unyoked from the wagon, and four men were consulting quietly near where the body was still pinned under the wagon.

Nora approached the scene carefully, slowly, not wanting to startle the woman who was likely quite fragile with the shock.

The wagons continued to slowly roll by, and Nora thought she might have glimpsed Jasper Stephens, but she had more pressing things to think about.

Taking another step toward the poor family, Nora reached out one hand, as though she was soothing a horse.

"Ma'am?" she ventured tentatively.

One of the men who had been helping noticed Nora and gestured her forward. The grateful expression on his face told Nora she was right to do what she could for this new widow.

He leaned in to whisper. "See if you can get her to lead the children away. We don't want them to see the body once the wagon's been moved."

Nora nodded and turned again to the woman.

"Ma'am?"

At this second attempt, the woman turned toward Nora though her expression was blank.

"Ma'am, my name is Nora Cole." She stepped closer and gently placed a hand on the woman's arm. "I imagine you're likely in shock right now. I want to see what we can do about that. Are these your children?"

She nodded, before looking down at the small heads cuddled close to her bosom.

"What are their names?"

The woman didn't answer for a moment, as though she had to reach deep into the reaches of her mind to recall any fact beyond that she had just lost her husband.

"Um... This is... um, Betty and, um... Johnny." She took a deep breath that seemed to calm her somewhat.

Nora felt a jolt, missing her best friend. The name Betty might always do that for her.

"And what's your name?" Nora prompted the mother gently.

The woman blinked several times, shook her head as though to clear cobwebs from her mind, and then stood up a little straighter before answering.

"Alma Buchanan."

"Well, Mrs. Buchanan, I'm here now. You don't have to worry about any of this alone. Let's start with getting the children maybe a little ways away while the men take care of your wagon."

The widow looked back at where her husband had expired in the dirt under their wagon. The doctor, or someone, had covered the body with a quilt. She turned back and offered Nora a weak smile, but nodded and allowed herself to be led away.

CHAPTER EIGHT

Nora could not stand by and watch; she couldn't just continue on with the rest of the company. The sight of a man crushed beneath the wheel of a wagon was heartbreaking, but such a tragedy spurred Nora into action. Where someone else might feel stuck, unsure of what to do, Nora found innumerable ways to help.

After leading the new widow away from the scene of the accident, she spent the rest of the afternoon with Mrs. Buchanan, and her children Betty and Johnny. While the men took care of the practicalities of moving a broken wagon, Nora looked after the surviving family. Food. Water. Shelter from the sun. Campfire once the wagons stopped in camp for the night. There was plenty to do. There would always be plenty to do. Nora wasn't the only woman to put aside their own concerns to help a neighbor in need, but she was the only one that didn't have children or siblings that she needed to return to.

As such, she was on hand to answer questions that men brought to her about the Buchanans' wagon, and keep the children occupied while their mother made necessary decisions. The widow slowly began to emerge from her shock as Nora helped create a secure, safe place for her to mourn. Without having to worry about building a campfire to keep her children warm, Mrs. Buchanan was better able to attend to the emotional safety of the children. Nora watched as she gathered the little ones to her, speaking quietly to them, managing to keep calm.

Nora tried not to eavesdrop; learning your father had died would be a traumatic conversation, even if you hadn't witnessed it in the middle of the wild frontier. When she heard Mrs. Buchanan first say, "your father," Nora walked a few more steps away, keeping her back to them. She tried to give the family privacy while still keeping a listening ear out in case she was needed. But there was plenty to do elsewhere as well, and Nora set to work sorting out the family's bedding from the mess of supplies.

The Buchanans' wagon had just been delivered back to them, albeit with absolute chaos within. Sean Gilroy, his nephew Caleb, and one of the Jameson men had fixed the broken wheel with some wooden scraps they had on hand, while two of the Waters brothers had tended to the animals. Working together, all the young men were able to ensure the task was completed as quickly as possible and the family did not get left too far behind.

They were a community now, and a community helped each other.

Nora was grateful, admiring how these near-strangers had all banded together, without question or hesitation, to help a family in need. Each one of those men had their own chores and responsibilities to their own families, but when they saw that the Buchanans needed them more, they stepped up.

All these thoughts percolated in Nora's mind as she went about righting the wagon's interior. She started by pulling out the Buchanans' corn husk mattresses that had been smashed against the side of the wagon when it had tipped over. Looking around for anything she might use to stuff the pallets again, Nora realized this campsite was well picked over from the trains that had come through already that week. Maybe over the next few days she could enlist the children to help pick prairie grass to dry and fill. Tonight, any cushion they slept on would have to just be blankets.

It was while engaged in solving this problem for the Buchanans that Nora got the chance to meet the captains for the first time. When the wagon company had left Independence, Captain Mills was at the head of the line. Mr. Cole pointed him out from where they watched for their turn to enter the caravan. A tall man with a bushy brown mustache, George Mills exuded the strength and confidence anyone would want in a leader.

And so, when Nora saw Captain Mills and another tall man approaching the Buchanans' makeshift camp, both with hats in hand, she knew to stop what she was doing.

When the men reached the glow of the fire Nora had built, Mrs. Buchanan noticed them immediately and pulled herself away from her quiet conversation with the children. Nora set aside the pile of quilts she was going through. The coffee was almost done, so she picked through the tumbled over crates in the back of the wagon for the coffee mugs.

"Oh! Captains... goodness," Mrs. Buchanan said wearily, getting to her feet. "How kind of you to come by."

"Please, Mrs. Buchanan. Have a seat again," the man who must be Captain Sullivan said. "Don't mind us. We don't want to take up any more of your time than we have to."

"Thank you," she murmured before sitting.

She leaned down to the children and whispered some instructions to them, before they too got up and disappeared into the interior of the wagon. Nora tried smiling at the children encouragingly, but they didn't even look at her as they passed.

"As you know," Captain Mills began, "we don't have much time to dally before continuing west. I've asked Pastor Montgomery to lead a burial service for your husband tomorrow morning, but after that we need to leave. I'm so sorry, Mrs. Buchanan. I wish we could offer you a proper mourning time, but that's just not possible."

"And as you know, there is far more than just mourning that needs to be taken care of," Captain Sullivan added.

Though he spoke gently, Nora could hear the steel in his tone as she busied herself pouring the coffee. The captains would not be distracted from their objective: getting the entire company west as quickly and as safely as they could.

"I'm sure I can help," Nora interjected, as she

brought Mrs. Buchanan a cup of hot coffee. "Everyone can help. You don't have to do this on your own."

"What do you mean?" Mrs. Buchanan asked.

"Well..." Nora thought quickly. "We need to leave tomorrow, right? Maybe there's a family with extra room that can take in one or both of the children. Or if you decide to turn around and go back to Independence, surely one of the older boys can help make that trip and come back to meet the company."

"Miss Cole is right," Captain Mills said gently. "Decisions must be made. I'm happy to advise you however best I can, of course, but the rest of the wagon company will need to be leaving in the morning."

"I understand, Captain, and Nora, dear, I appreciate the suggestions but I've already made up my mind." Mrs. Buchanan sat up a little straighter. "I'll be traveling west with the rest of you all, but in my own wagon, with my own things. I already lost my husband; I won't be having the rest of my family separated any sooner than Providence decrees."

"Very well," Captain Mills said, placing his hat back on his head to prepare his departure. "You know, I trust, that it won't be easy. But it is certainly not impossible. With that decided, though, the rest of the details can be sorted out. You'll need help driving the wagon, no doubt, but with so many families in this company there's surely to be a way that can be managed."

"Well, off the top of my head," Captain Sullivan added, "I know the Waters and Davis families both have an abundance of young men who might be available. Maybe the Jamesons too. I'll ask around and see what's what."

"I'm happy to pay, of course," Mrs. Buchanan added. "I don't expect any charity, and I want young men who are willing to be hired on for the rest of the journey, who I can depend on day in and day out. If you could find me a couple likely boys like that, Captain, I'd be mighty grateful."

Nora thought about the kind of young man who would be so unselfish and industrious to take that on. As the conversation went on around her, she allowed herself a tiny daydream, imagining such a man driving the Buchanans' wagon and noticing Nora's own altruism at the same time. They could bond over a shared desire to lift up those around them. Love matches have been made with less, she told herself.

She was pulled out of her dreaming as the captains said their good-byes, promising to bring her a few names the next day before they left camp. Nora finished pulling together a small supper out of the food that was easiest to find in the wagon. As the whole vehicle had been overturned, the organized stacks and thoughtful arrangements were a mess. Nora did what she could to pull it all into some semblance of sense, and cleared the path so the children could find a place to sleep for the night, but there was still much to be done.

"You should get back to your own family, dear," Mrs. Buchanan said more than an hour later, after she had put the children to bed. The sun had set long ago. "I can manage now."

"But, I'm happy to—"

"No," she cut her off kindly, while Nora stifled a yawn. "Please. You've done so much, and I'm so appreciative, but I... I need some time to be alone. Please. Please understand."

Nora thought back to her own shock and experience of losing Jimmy. Though she knew quite well that the circumstances were not the same, she also knew that being alone and not having to be social was what helped her finally gather her thoughts and get through it.

"Have a good night, Mrs. Buchanan," she responded, bowing her head deferentially to the new widow. "I'm so sorry about today."

Her voice cracked, and though she wanted to make big promises about fixing things or coming back the next day to help, Nora didn't trust herself to talk.

Mrs. Buchanan inclined her head in return, but didn't say anything. Nora walked back to her family's camp, but when she looked back over her shoulder she saw the widow sitting by herself, staring blankly at the remnants of the campfire.

For the next several days, Nora checked on Mrs. Buchanan many times, but each time she seemed to be doing better and needing less help. Nora was not more than an extra set of hands to help move a trunk inside the wagon or to entertain the children while their mother lugged buckets of water. Ralph Davis and Billy Whitson were hired to drive the wagon all the way to Oregon. Other women had checked in with Mrs. Buchanan, and now that things were more settled, Nora was less necessary.

And without some assistance to offer, Nora felt herself a bit lost.

CHAPTER NINE

The wagon company pushed on westward; the emigrants fell into a rhythm of survival and struggle. After the death of a member of the company, many of the emigrants seemed far more subdued than they had been when everyone first set off from Independence. Although each man and woman knew that losing people was possible—if not likely—during the five to six months they would be traveling west, no one had expected it to happen so soon after setting off.

The shock of such a violent death had cast a pall over the company.

Nora dealt with the struggle the same way she always had: by putting others' needs ahead of her own. She could easily forget about her own troubles when helping someone else handle theirs. But there was only so much that needed doing. After three days of making herself available every moment she could, Mrs. Buchanan gently suggested Nora return to her own camp.

But not twenty minutes after Mrs. Buchanan had

sent her away, Nora was sitting with two of the girls her own age, Abby Mills and Katie Valentine, helping them rip up an old dress into long strips of ragged fabric.

She had been walking back to her own campsite; it was still before supper, so she decided to walk the long way around the camp and take her time. It had been days since she had even seen Jasper Stephens amidst all the chaos of leaving Independence and dealing with the death of one of their own, though she wasn't looking for him specifically. Truthfully, Nora was just looking for somewhere she might be needed.

The sun would be fully set in the next half an hour, and the golden light cast over the camp made even the outdoor living seem homey. Smells of coffee and bacon wafted after her as she passed campfires. Nora was not ready to go home yet.

Captain Mills and his family had made their camp on one of the edges of the group of wagons, the better for the men to keep an eye on the cattle they were driving across the continent. As Nora approached, she noticed Abby and Katie sitting near the fire with their laps full of something and were diligently working away.

"Hello?" she called to them.

Katie looked up and waved Nora over to where the two girls sat near the Mills family's campfire.

"You look like you could use a break," Katie said.

"Mama told us how much you've been doing for Mrs. Buchanan," Abby added. "Sit with us. We're going through these fabric scraps."

Nora sat nearest to Abby, also facing the campfire. Mrs. Mills had started something cooking already; Nora took a big whiff, settling in. Butter and wild onions, maybe, but delicious whatever it was.

"I almost have enough to make a braided rug," Abby said happily. She gnawed on the hem of the dress sleeve to start the rip. "Mama wanted me to save the pieces to make a patchwork quilt, but I like this idea better."

"We're just making this all into strips?" Nora clarified as she reached for the cloth Katie handed her. It seemed to be an old tablecloth; Nora made a mental note to steer clear of the food stains. "You don't need anything more specific or a certain number or ...?"

Abby shook her head and dove into describing how she would be making the braided rug full of whatever fabric she could find. Though Nora had never made one herself, she understood exactly what the other girl was looking for. As she listened to Abby's plans, her fingers sought out the hem of the tablecloth, deftly picking out the thread.

Katie was distracted, though. She seemed to be looking past Nora, over her shoulder toward something outside of their little circle. When she spotted a shy smile on Katie's lips, Nora peeked over her shoulder at what the girl was looking at.

There, about thirty feet away, Abby's older brother Daniel stood in the midst of the Mills's cattle talking to a few other young men. She recognized Benjamin Findley, who she thought was Daniel's best friend, as well as Caleb Kelly, the Gilroys' nephew. With a stab of surprise, Nora realized that the fourth man was Jasper Stephens.

Nora abruptly turned back to the tablecloth draped over her lap.

"I thought maybe if I make enough of these," Abby

was saying, "I could sell some when we got to Oregon. I don't know though. Mama seems to think that most women would want to make their own. But they don't take up much room. Worth trying, maybe."

Nora nodded, murmuring something encouraging, before looking back over her shoulder.

Jasper was watching her.

She thought—though the distance made her doubt— that he was looking right at her.

Or maybe he was looking at Katie.

Nora looked back toward the other girl, who was now looking down at the strips of fabric in her lap.

"Daniel!" Abby called out.

Nora took one last look over her shoulder to see that Abby's interruption had broken up the men's discussion. Daniel Mills headed toward his family's camp, while the other three men dispersed. Jasper seemed deep in conversation with Caleb and didn't look over at the girls again.

"Daniel, when are you going to give up that shirt?" Abby was saying. "It's riddled with holes, and I can use it."

Nora half-listened to the siblings' banter while she kept her eyes on her work. Jasper had seen her; he must have. Wasn't he looking at her? But he didn't come talk to her. She hated to admit how much that bothered her, so instead she busied herself with helping Abby.

Later that night, once she was back with her own family, in her own wagon, her own bed, though, thoughts about what Jasper might think about her—or not think about her—whirled around her mind, keeping her from sleep.

Thoughts of Jasper were not the only things keeping Nora awake.

Before the wagon company could emerge from under the dark cloud of Jeb Buchanan's death, they crossed into Indian Territory. Nora had known it was coming; one of the subjects about which Amy had asked innumerable questions had in fact been the native tribes of the plains. Thinking it would help prepare her, their father had let his youngest daughter read the guidebook they had for the journey. It wasn't enough for Amy; she still felt her knowledge woefully meager and worried about what might happen. Repeatedly and vocally worried, often within earshot of her sister. As such, Nora seemed to have adopted some of the stress and uncertainty that her sister betrayed when they found themselves under danger of attack at any moment.

"Well, not *any* moment," Amy clarified, the first morning after the captains had instituted a stricter security policy. "It's possible we will see or hear them coming, I would guess. Then maybe we'll have at least a few moments of warning."

"Maybe," Mrs. Cole said. "But remember, dear, this is their home. This land is where these tribes have lived their entire lives and they know every hill and river far better than we do."

"This isn't helping my fear," Nora murmured.

"We'll be just fine. The captains know the best way to cross this land, and the best way to protect us as they do. Your father will have to take guard duty every few nights, but everything will be fine."

"I hope so," Nora murmured.

CHAPTER TEN

For days, Nora had been hearing about the wagon company's preparations to cross the Kansas River. The Sullivan-Mills wagon company was on the trail not long after dawn every day, traveling west as many miles as they could push the animals, striving to get over the tall mountain ranges before the snow fell. But after days and days of flat, easy prairie, they finally reached the first real obstacle that the land had to throw at them.

The Kansas River was slow moving, several hundred feet wide at the crossing, stretching north and south into the distance. It was not fordable, though some men would caulk up the gaps in their wagon and float it across like a raft. There was only one ferry in this stretch of river, which created quite the bottleneck in getting families to the west bank.

Amy had read their Oregon Trail guidebook innumerable times (and reminded her family of that repeatedly). Into every conversation she peppered facts and tidbits about the journey, and now the Kansas crossing.

Reminding her sister of the danger and what was at stake. Constantly explaining to Nora how they would get all fifty families, their animals, and enormous wagons across the river in just two days.

"There's the ferry," she exclaimed, pointing when the trail crested a low hill. "Those men will get us all on the platform and then use those long sticks—can you see them?—to push the ferry over to the other bank. It's so interesting. Who thought of this? I wonder how thick those sticks are. They look like they could break, don't they? Not nearly sturdy enough to push a platform with all these thousands of pounds."

"This is in no way reassuring, Amy," Nora said. "Why don't we talk about something else?"

"I wonder what would happen if the platform were to tip. You know? If a wagon and team and everything were to fall into the river. I'm not sure how deep it is. I bet all the supplies would be lost."

"Goodness," Nora murmured, her heart beating faster just imagining what Amy described.

But she didn't take her eyes off the ferry. The wagon company arrived on the banks of the Kansas River in the afternoon and made camp. Each family would need to wait their turn, so they may be there a while. Only two wagons could cross at a time, after which the platform would need to be brought back to the eastern bank and loaded up with another two wagons again. The process of getting the entire company to the west side of the river would take all of two days.

The Cole family was in the second half of the company and had plenty of time to wait. On the first day, Laura kept the girls busy with repacking the wagon, but by the second day, Nora had run out of ways to distract her sister. Amy suggested that they go down to the water to watch. Their father had tried to explain to Amy the concepts of leverage and momentum, going over exactly how the wagons would be transported, and Amy wanted to see it all for herself.

"It'll be like school," she insisted, when asking her mother if they could go. "Like a physics lesson."

The girls crossed through the camp to the water's edge, careful to stay out of the way of the men focused on getting the wagons and animals across. When they passed the ferry, Nora spotted Katie Valentine holding the hands of two of her younger sisters and guiding them onto the platform. She waved, but didn't stop, didn't want to distract them from what they needed to be safe. The banks of the river were high above the water line on either side of the ferry platform, and Nora found a spot nearby for them to watch. She sat in the grass, her knees pulled up and her arms resting on them as Amy chattered away.

"This says that the ferry company was founded by three brothers," Amy began, before launching into a recitation of how the guidebook described the business of getting hundreds of enormous wagons from one side of the Kansas River to the other.

Nora was only half listening to her sister, as her eyes scanned the faces of the families loading up their wagons and tentatively crossing. From here it looked as though everything were running smoothly and safely, but there was no guarantee it would stay that way.

Amy lapsed into quiet, intent on devouring the next chapter of the book.

After an hour of watching the platform go back and forth, Nora realized that the Sullivan family was crossing with their two wagons. The Coles' chance to cross would be not long after this.

"Come on," Nora said, as she stood. "It will probably be our turn soon. Let's go see if Mother and Father need any help."

Amy didn't respond, other than to get to her feet, still reading. She seemed utterly consumed by the book.

"Amy, just... don't trip, I guess," Nora said.

She pulled lightly on her sister's arm to lead her back to their wagon. With her nose still in the book, Amy followed and the two girls walked along the bit of trail back toward where all the wagons had made camp for two days. Her mind was occupied thinking through what she would need to do to help keep the animals calm, and keep the wagon steady when it was finally their turn to cross the river.

Jasper Stephens crossed the trail only fifteen feet or so ahead of her.

Nora stopped in her tracks, unable to decide if she should call his name or pretend she didn't see him.

Amy, unfortunately, still had her eyes in the book and hadn't noticed that her sister was no longer walking. She walked directly into Nora's back, knocking her sister into the dirt.

"Amy!" Nora cried out as she fell to her knees.

"What?" Amy said, finally looking up.

Fortunately, Nora was able to catch herself before she ended up sprawled across the trail. Frustrated at her sister, Nora took a deep breath, quelling her temper before she rose again. Though she wasn't badly hurt, she had been jostled severely. Her right knee felt like it might have twisted unnaturally; the pads of her palms were bruised and roughly scraped by the pebbles when she had caught her fall.

"Let's take a look at those injuries."

Nora looked up to see Jasper Stephens standing over her and reaching out a hand.

"I'm sorry I wasn't close by enough to catch you," he said with a grin. "But I can at least get you home safely. Do you need to be carried?"

"Jasper!" she said, getting to her feet. "Mr. Stephens, I mean. Hello." She cleared her throat and could feel herself blushing. "I'm fine."

"Are you?" His tone sounded more serious, as he looked closely at the bruises on her palm. "This should heal quickly, but we should clean the cuts."

"I..." Nora cleared her throat again, stalling as she wavered over what to say. "How embarrassing to be caught like this. I'm sorry. But, um, thank you. I'll do that. Clean the cut, I mean. I... um. I haven't seen you in a long time."

"Ah, but I've seen you," he teased, gracefully passing over her stammering. "I think your wagon is maybe five or six ahead of us every day, and I spot you and another girl walking out in the grass often. Is this your sister? The one who was going to be a blacksmith?" He looked down to Amy who was just standing dumbly by her sister, watching the exchange.

"Yes, this is Amy. Amy, who knocked me over because she was too busy reading," Nora said pointedly.

"I'm sorry." She turned to Jasper. "How did you know I'm going to be a blacksmith?"

"Mr. Gilroy. He seemed a bit impressed by all your questions."

Amy beamed, while Nora took a deep breath and turned back to Jasper. "We were just going back to our wagon. I think it will be our turn to cross soon, and I want to see what I can do to help."

"Yes, I heard you like to help. Word of what you did for Mrs. Buchanan reached me, too. That was really kind of you, how much time you gave to that family."

"Oh." Nora laughed embarrassed. "It's nothing. Really. I... I like to help. I'd do it for any of the women in the company. Any of the *people* in the company," she amended.

"Nora, come on," Amy said, tugging at her sleeve. "Father will need us. And I want to see the ferry close up."

"That may be true," Jasper said, still focused on Nora, "but not everyone would. I think it's admirable. I was really impressed when I heard."

"Thank you."

"Nora," Amy prodded.

Jasper grinned. "Seems like you should get a move on. But maybe I'll catch you on the other side of the river. And you can tell me all about your exciting river crossing."

"Hopefully not very exciting. But, yes. Thank you. Yes. I would love that," Nora said breathlessly, as Amy pulled on her arm, dragging her away. "Come find me."

He waved until Amy had pulled her around one of the other wagons and out of his sight.

"That was very rude," Nora scolded. "Mr. Stephens was just trying to help after you knocked me down."

"I didn't mean to knock you down," Amy protested. "And besides, he didn't do anything to help. Just told you to wash the cuts. Which you already knew to do. He just wanted to flirt with you. That's not important."

Nora laughed. "Well, at least you noticed that, even if you didn't notice anything else."

They had reached their wagon, with not much time to spare. Nora hurried to clean the dirt from her palms before they had to get everything packed up in the wagon.

"All right, Father," she called out as he started to yoke up the mules. "What can I do to help?"

CHAPTER ELEVEN

After two days waiting on the banks of the Kansas River, it was finally the Coles' turn to cross. Nora's father slowly led their team of mules onto the wooden platform. Two wagons could fit on the platform at once, and the Cole family was loaded onto the wide wooden ferry with the Gilroys. All of both families' animals crowded onto the platform. Heavy wedges of wood were placed behind the wagon wheels to keep them from moving too much. The men tried to keep their teams as calm as possible, but with the very boards under their feet tilting, the animals were rightfully petrified.

Nevertheless, the Coles and the Gilroys made it across the Kansas River with nothing dramatic happening. The animals, the wagons, and all the men and women made their way off the ferry and headed toward the campground that was already well established.

Nora, however, stayed on the bank of the river to watch the next few crossings. She stood alone on the high bank, admiring the view of the lazy, dangerous river, while all around her the families that had crossed safely made camp for another night. There were only maybe twenty or so wagons left to cross. The Stephens family—Jasper—were not far behind them, and she should be able to see when it was his turn.

Several families were ferried over. Dozens of scared animals soothed and led across to the opposite bank. And still Nora watched, until she recognized the tall figure of Jasper. He and his father had control of their team of oxen, guiding it onto the platform alongside the other wagon.

The ferrymen pushed off from the far bank.

Nora held her breath.

Now that she was safely across, she was more scared for Jasper's crossing than she had been for herself or her own family. It seemed to inch its way across, each ferryman pulling the weight of the platform and all its cargo as steadily as he could. Little by little, the platform made its way toward the western bank.

But then, as Nora watched, the platform seemed to tip. From this distance it was difficult to say precisely what was happening, but she could see the men seem to hurry around more desperately than they had before.

She stumbled forward, skidding down the bank until the toes of her boots rested in the small lapping waves of the river.

As she watched, it seemed as though the team of oxen on the ferry were panicking, that maybe— No! Nora could not believe what she saw. Was the wagon rolling toward Jasper?

A strangled cry got caught in her throat. It was so

difficult to see what was happening from this distance, and there was nothing she could do.

Somehow, seemingly in an instant, the ferry seemed to right itself. Balance was restored. The ferrymen again were pushing the platform toward the opposite bank. Everything could change in a breath, and it seemed it could change back as well.

Nora tried to take calming breaths as the ferry with the Stephenses reached her bank safely, and in one piece, with no one stampeded or crushed under a wagon wheel.

Without a thought, without hesitation, Nora ran to the dock. She ran straight to Jasper, almost throwing herself into his arms. He looked pale under his cavalier smile; her heart thudded.

"Jasper," she said breathlessly. "Are you all right? Were you hurt?"

"We keep meeting like this," he teased, as he slowly guided his team off the unstable platform onto the solid ground of the riverbank.

"What happened?"

"Just a little problem with the balance, which spooked the team. We're fine. We're all fine." He was speaking in a soothing voice to his team, now leading them farther away from the water, and not looking at Nora at all.

"I'm so glad. I was so worried."

"Were you?"

At that, Jasper finally looked at her—*really* looked at her—and smiled. She could not help but smile back, willing him to understand her concern, to take her offer of help seriously.

"I hate to worry you, Miss Cole," he said in a low

voice as he shifted his weight to be towering over her, "but I must say it's quite flattering to have such claim on the thoughts and attention of a lady like you."

"Oh, I... uh..." She blushed. Would she never be able to put together an entire sentence in front of this man? That smile of his absolutely turned her world upside down.

He chuckled gently and stepped closer.

Nora tried to steady her nerves by taking a deep breath, but in doing so his scent—leather, coffee, a hint of campfire—washed over her, further unsteadying her.

"How will you spend the rest of your evening?" he asked casually. "Does Abby need more help with whatever you and Katie were doing with her the other day?"

"Oh! You noticed. I—"

"Nora!"

Nora whirled around, looking for the source. That was Amy calling her somewhere in the distance; she would recognize her sister's voice anywhere. She couldn't see Amy from where she was at the edge of the water, though. She couldn't see Amy anywhere.

"Amy?" she called back.

"Is she okay?" Jasper asked.

"I... I don't know. I suppose..."

"Go find her. Look after her," he assured her. "I'll be fine."

"Nora!"

"I'm sorry," she said fervently, looking over her shoulder again to where Amy still called for her. "I'm so sorry, but I need to make sure she's all right."

"Go on, then," he said with a smile. "We'll talk later."

Nora swallowed hard, bobbed her head in thanks and

turned to seek out her sister, praying that she wasn't too hurt.

"Nora!" Amy yelled again. She sounded more scared, more vulnerable than her sister had ever heard her.

What had happened that could make Amy cry out like that? Though she still couldn't see her through the maze of white-topped wagons, Nora ran to where she thought her sister must be. Alone and hurt somewhere.

"I'm coming, Amy!"

Nora darted around the outermost wagon, to the stand of trees on the edge of the campsite. As she quickly approached, she spotted her younger sister at the foot of one of the bigger trees, sitting against the trunk in the shade. Her book was again open, but over-turned on her knee, as though she had only just stopped reading when she heard her sister coming.

Nora raced to her side, looking her all over desper-ately. "What is it? What's wrong?" she asked breathlessly. "What can I do?"

Amy looked down at her arm, on the side closest to Nora. "My wrist! I think I broke my wrist."

"How?" Nora asked as she carefully, delicately ran her fingers down her sister's arm, looking for where the injury would be. "Oh, Amy, if you've broken your arm..."

She didn't want to finish that thought. The possi-bility that her sister could be so physically limited out here in the wilderness for months to come was too scary.

"I, um, fell. I was trying to climb the tree and fell out and I landed on this arm and it hurts so bad."

Nora leaned closer, looking for a scrape or bruise or bump or anything on her sister's wrist that could explain the pain she described. "But, you know better. Why were you climbing the tree?"

"I don't know. Um..."

Nora squinted at her sister. Amy never was at a loss of words.

"I guess maybe to see farther?" she suggested. "I didn't have anyone to talk to, since you were just staring at the water. What else was I supposed to do?"

"Amy, what on earth are you on about? There are dozens of people literally within sight of this spot. I was not the only person you could have called. You could have found Claire. Or Faith or Abby. Even Mr. Gilroy. You've never been shy. None of this makes sense. What's the real reason you were climbing?"

Amy only shrugged and looked away.

Nora peered at her sister more carefully. There was no injury to Amy's arm that she could identify, not even a scrape. And there was only one real reason that she refused to meet her eyes.

Nora sat back with a start, her mouth hanging open. "Why are you lying to me? You're fine. You're not hurt. Why would you lie to me about that?"

"I wasn't lying..." she equivocated. "I was just... embellishing."

"Embellishing what? Amy, stop talking nonsense and tell me what is going on. Start at the beginning. Why did you yell for me?"

Amy looked away again, but this time it was as though she was looking for some distraction, for someone else to save her from the conversation.

"Amy Cole," Nora said sternly. She settled against the

trunk of the tree next to her sister, happy to wait her out.

"I just ... I wanted you to come be with me. Claire's busy. I didn't want to be alone, and you would only come if you thought I needed you."

"I was busy. I was talking to someone else. It's very rude to have interrupted me at all, but to do so with a lie? Worrying me and making me have to be so abrupt with the person I was talking to? That's just..." Nora shook her head. "What were you thinking?"

"If I hadn't, you would have stayed there with that boy all afternoon."

"Come, now, that's not true—"

"It is true. You hadn't paid attention to me the whole time we were watching the crossing, and then we ran into that boy and all your attention was on him, and it's not fair."

"Not fair? Amy Cole, what on earth does fair have to do with it? I'm with you all the time. *All* the time. Morning, noon, night, and then we sleep next to each other in that tiny, crowded wagon. How can you possibly think it right to *deceive* me in order to spend even more time with me? Are you out of your mind? Are you so clearly untethered from what is considered reasonable in polite society as to make up a story to get someone to do what you want?"

Amy seemed to shrink back at Nora's vitriol, but she didn't stop.

"This is something you're going to have to deal with sooner or later. I am going to meet a man and fall in love and get married and leave you one day, and you're going to have to deal with that when it happens. Maybe it's better if you start getting used to not having me around now, if it is going to be so difficult for you to deal with."

"No, wait, don't say that..."

Nora felt tears welling up. She didn't think Amy had ever lied to her before, and to do it for such a selfish reason shocked her. "I'm really hurt," she said in a whisper. "I really... I just can't believe you would do this."

Amy looked down at her hands and mumbled, "He's just a boy."

Instead of replying hotly, Nora forced herself to slow down and think. To consider what Amy saw of it. Regardless of who Nora had been talking to, what her sister had done was wrong. There was no question about that.

"He's not just a boy."

Amy snorted derisively.

"Or, okay, you're right. But, Amy..." The pleading in Nora's voice was clear. "I like him. I like Jasper, or I guess Mr. Stephens, a lot. This could be... It could be really special. And I want you to be happy for me."

"You don't know that."

"No, of course not. I don't know that, because I haven't gotten hardly any occasion to speak to him. And this one chance I had, especially after he could have just been terribly hurt, you interrupted."

"He was hurt?" Amy looked contrite for the first time in the conversation.

"No. At least, I don't think so. I hope not." Nora sighed. "He was on the ferry and... It doesn't matter. That's not the point."

Nora rested her face in her hands. This whole journey west was supposed to be a new chance for her to find the love she was destined for. The wide-open spaces of the prairie were going to bring her the passion and romance that she had expected with Jimmy Rayburn. Nora had never suspected that her sister would be so selfish as to try to keep that from her.

"I don't know what to do," she said, mostly to herself.

"Just... talk to him again," Amy said, matter-of-factly. "It's not hard. Do you want me to go with you?"

"Oh, Amy," Nora groaned. She didn't know if she wanted to laugh or cry. "I'm still mad at you."

"I know." Amy shrugged. "But I'm your sister. You'll forgive me eventually."

"Maybe not," Nora said, teasing and weary. "Not if Jasper Stephens never speaks to me again. Do you really not see how handsome he is?"

Amy opened her mouth to respond, but stopped at a new sound. A cry, unmistakably genuine. The girls turned toward the wailing, heart-broken and crazed. It seemed nearby.

"Did you hear that?"

Amy nodded, looking stunned.

"From the river?"

The pain and agony in the cry they had heard put Nora on edge, and she whispered this last question. Whatever was happening at the river would be unsettling, dangerous, and risky.

The sisters put aside their disagreement and crept toward the water's edge where a crowd was beginning to form. It was difficult to see around the dozen or so people who were drawing close to the water's edge, but the heart-broken cries continued unabated.

At a break in the line of people, Nora spotted a woman with dark hair trudging out of the water, her skirts wet to the waist and the weight of the drenched fabric slowing her steps. In her arms she held something large clutched to her. When she turned slightly, Nora realized who it was.

And who she was carrying.

"Mrs. McKinnon," Nora said in a whisper. "I think... Amy, is that her little boy? What is Claire's brother's name?"

Amy gasped. The two sisters looked at each other in shock.

The Oregon Trail had claimed another victim.

CHAPTER TWELVE

For a second time in mere weeks, death had touched the wagon company. The girls later learned that small, five-year-old, Alexander McKinnon had wandered away to play by himself and apparently gotten caught up in the current at the edge of the Kansas River. Nora couldn't imagine how heartbroken and anxious all the mothers in the company must be. Knowing that death and injury were a risk every moment of every day would be exhausting.

And Nora didn't know how to help that. This was one thing she couldn't fix for them.

After the Sullivan-Mills wagon company left the Kansas River the next day, and with it the tiny grave of Alexander McKinnon, Nora felt lost. She made a couple attempts to be of service to Mrs. McKinnon the way she had with Mrs. Buchanan, but was rebuffed at every turn. She insisted she was all her family needed, keeping her oldest daughter close to home and turning inward.

Nora was helpless to do anything about it.

The fact that Nora was distracted by thoughts of Jasper didn't help either.

Her annoyance with Amy was unabated, but her sister either didn't notice or pretended not to. And it certainly didn't help that her sister had yet to apologize for her deceit and manipulation.

"We should check again to see if Claire wants to come walk with us," Amy called to Nora that first afternoon after leaving the river. "Maybe her mother has changed her mind. It would be nice for her, don't you think?"

Nora had been walking parallel to the trail, but farther out into the prairie grass than her sister. Amy was trying so hard to get back to the easy back and forth the sisters had, but Nora was wary. She had tried to deceive her once; would she do it again? So, instead of fighting any more, Nora just tried to avoid her sister. Every time Amy seemed to be drawing closer, Nora moved farther away, though she didn't say anything to draw attention to her choice. Finally, after three attempts to reach her sister, Amy just yelled after her.

"Do you want to come with me to ask?" she continued. "Come on, Nora. It will be a nice thing to do for her. Don't you want to?"

Before Nora could even think how to respond, a crack of thunder sounded in the distance. Both girls looked toward the horizon, at the heavy gray cloud that seemed to be speeding toward them. With the flat land, Nora could see for miles, and the misty blur in the distance told her they were about to experience their first prairie storm.

"Did you see that lightning?" Amy asked.

But Nora had already dashed past her on the way to their wagon.

Thunder clapped again; the storm was moving even faster than she had expected.

Nora reached the back of the Cole family wagon, hurrying to keep up; the men weren't about to stop their westward progress just because of a storm. They would just trudge through the rain as long as they could. Timing herself with the rotation of the wheels, Nora picked up her skirt and stepped onto the rear lip and up into the wagon. Somewhere in here were the oilskin wraps Mrs. Cole had purchased to protect them from weather.

The wagon jostled and rocked on the uneven trail. Nora held one of the beams above her head to keep her balance while she looked.

"The trunk there, behind the cot."

Nora turned to see her mother walking behind the wagon, while still trying to lean under the canopy to offer instruction.

"Hurry now," Mrs. Cole said. She looked up, peering into the sky above.

The heavy gray clouds had reached the wagon company, blotting out both the blue of the sky and much of the light. Nora had to let her eyes adjust to the near-dark of the wagon interior, as she made her way to the trunk her mother had indicated.

"Did you find it?" Amy asked. She had also appeared in the opening to the wagon. "Hurry. The rain is starting."

"Give me a minute," Nora snapped.

"Nora," her mother said gently.

She took a deep breath and turned again to the task at hand. The trunk her mother had pointed out was under a sack of rice. Moving the heavy bag to the floor, Nora was able to access the quilts, heavy coats, scarves and, finally at the bottom, the oilskin wraps that should protect them from rain. They were big, and heavier than she expected, but Nora managed to tug them out from the bottom of the trunk and turn back to her mother.

She held out two of them as Laura leaned into the wagon.

"I'll take it to your father," she said, reaching for the oilskins. "You girls stay in here if you want to. Out of the mud."

Nora handed over two of the wraps, and her mother disappeared from view as she hurried to take some measure of protection to her husband. At the same time, Amy climbed awkwardly into the wagon, her skirt already showing some damp patches where the rain had found her.

Nora backed up into the gloom of the wagon, trying to move out of her sister's way, trying to avoid dealing with her at all.

"Why didn't you answer when I suggested we go see Claire?" Amy asked, as she sat on the small cot to the side of the wagon.

Outside the rain had begun in earnest. In the distance, Nora could hear a few of the men shouting, instructions it sounded like. She didn't envy them the difficulty of keeping the animals and wagons moving through the torrent.

Nora looked into her sister's face. Amy seemed utterly guileless and innocently wondering why she had behaved the way she did. For as smart as Amy was, she certainly had some glaring blind spots.

"I don't know what to say, Amy," she said, tiredly. "I don't know how to explain to you that what you did really bothers me. Still. I don't know why you don't see that."

Amy looked up at her blankly, as though expecting more of an explanation. "But I was sorry."

"Were you? Because you didn't actually apologize. You made excuses. I know that in your mind your version of events is always the right one, but you really need to start considering other people's feelings."

Nora felt tears of frustration well up and was grateful for the dimness of the wagon. Any display of emotion Amy would just use to further disregard whatever her sister was saying.

"I'm sorry," Amy said in surprise. "I didn't know you would be so upset. I just wanted—"

"I know. You just wanted what you wanted and didn't think about other people."

Amy, at least, had the grace to not argue with her sister, and for that Nora was grateful. Trying to convince her sister of her own flaws was more than Nora felt she could manage right now.

"I trusted you," she said finally. "You've never lied to me like that before, Amy. I trusted you and now I don't know what to think."

"I'm sorry," she said again.

"Are you? I don't know if I believe that."

The sisters looked at each other in the gloomy light. The wagon rocked from side to side, like a rowboat on a lake. As the rain poured down, Nora thought it fitting that the weather so perfectly matched her mood. She was frustrated and tired and a bit hopeless. The pattering on the canvas over their heads grew louder, more insistent, just as Nora's thoughts of everything they still had to get through before her happily ever after in Oregon.

She looked at Amy, wondering if her sister would continue to demand her attention, to soak up everything Nora could provide. Her big dreams of a new life in the western territory would never come to fruition if Amy couldn't find her own independence.

"I'm going to walk," she said, before grabbing one of the remaining oilskins and climbing out of the wagon.

As she threw one leg over the back of the wagon to exit, Nora looked up at the sky, fat raindrops sneaking under the hood of her bonnet and wetting her face so she couldn't know where the tears started.

When they had lived in Michigan, rain and inclement weather had naturally dictated their days. Snow meant that the family would stay indoors as much as possible. A day of blue sky and sun forced them out-of-doors to tend to the farm from dawn till dusk. Here on the Oregon Trail, however, there was no such luxury as adjusting plans to fit the weather. As the days wore on, the dirt turned to mud, churning up with every ox hoof or wagon wheel that struggled to continue westward.

For more than two full days the emigrants lived under the blanket of the storm. Even small breaks in the rain weren't enough to build a campfire, to make fresh biscuits. To ever feel like they would be dry again. The mud caked up to their ankles, sucking each footstep down into the mire. Nora clenched her jaw and kept on, step after step determined to get through this. She knew that a storm was far from the worse the Oregon Trail would throw at them, but she couldn't help hoping it would be.

Finally, just when it seemed as though they would never see the sun again, a hint of warmth shone on her shoulders. Nora looked up and sighed in relief to see a peek of blue sky through the clouds.

That evening, the wagon company made camp on the banks of a narrow river, and the captains sent word that they would be staying here for a full day. Many of the men needed to make repairs to their wagons, caulking up the cracks where leaks threatened their stores. The women needed to fully air out their clothing and bedding, after days of musty stagnant air.

Nora looked forward to the break, to not being on her feet all day. Maybe it would be time enough to give Amy another chance. Or maybe, instead, it could be time enough to spend with Jasper Stephens.

CHAPTER THIRTEEN

Nora stripped out of her wet dress, rubbing her neck where the fabric had chafed. Her underthings were a little damp here and there, but with the patchwork quilt wrapped around her shoulders, Nora was finally able to dry out after two days of thunderstorm. She sat on her cot, listening to her mother build their campfire just outside the wagon so she could get started on supper. Closing her eyes to the brick-red linen patches that reminded her of Jimmy Rayburn, Nora let the dry warmth of the quilt thaw her limbs before she dressed again.

The Sullivan-Mills wagon company was gratefully making camp for the night. Hurriedly, fathers built fires and stationed their children as close as possible to warm. Mothers took the soaked-through clothes to drape over the limited shrubs that were scattered around the campsite. They would have a full day in this campsite on the shores of a river so each and every member of the company could have a chance to catch their breath and take care of what needed to be done.

Living out of a wagon for six months as they trekked west was difficult enough as it was, but to do so while also managing inclement weather, limited food supply, and the risk of Indian attack was pushing each person further than they had ever been pushed. The gift of an extra day, a little more time to breathe and to rest, was greatly welcomed. Nora went to bed early that night, snuggling down into the blankets without worrying about the day ahead.

When Nora woke that next morning, she all but bounded out of bed. The sunshine and warmth and newness of the day called to her. Somehow the knowledge that she would not need to walk ten miles alongside the trail gave her more energy than it would have taken to walk those miles. She had a wealth of options ahead of her and could not wait to get started.

As she combed her hair and pinned it up again, her eyes lit on her sister's still sleeping form. Nora had spent most of the time since the company had left the Kansas River avoiding Amy. Her disappointment in her sister's behavior just made it too hard to make idle conversation.

But things couldn't continue that way forever, Nora reminded herself as she dug out a clean apron to tie over her dress. Amy was her sister; they would be sisters forever. She would need to speak to her again soon.

Not this second, though.

With a quiet sigh, Nora tucked that thought away to deal with later. Now it was time for her to get started on her day. She climbed out of the Cole family's wagon, careful not to wake Amy, and stepped into the early morning quiet.

Many of the other travelers were still in bed, lying in for the first time in weeks. But not Nora. There was something about mornings that always made her feel as though anything were possible, that people would say yes more often, or that luck would turn on her side. This early in the morning both of her parents were already up and starting on their chores; it occurred to Nora that maybe she had gotten her love of mornings from them.

"Good morning, gorgeous," Mrs. Cole said, leaning forward to kiss her daughter. "Is your sister still sleeping?"

Nora nodded, as she crossed to where the empty buckets sat along the side of their wagon. "She didn't even stir when I got up."

"Ah, well. She's growing. Might as well let her sleep since we have the day."

"I'll go collect some water, and when I come back you can tell me everything we need to do?" Nora suggested, as she took a few steps away.

"You're an angel," her mother replied, before turning her attention again to slicing off a few slices from the salted bacon she had pulled out of the wagon for break-fast. "Have some dried cherries before you go."

Nora took a handful of the fruit from the small bag near her mother's feet, put a few in her mouth and set off toward the river.

The previous evening when they made camp, the Sullivan-Mills wagon company had pulled all of the wagons into a circle as usual. Ever since they had crossed into Indian territory, this had been the ritual. A tight, chained circle of wagons served as their best protection against any attacks from the outside. The animals would be safe within the center, and the wagons themselves would be chained together to keep the circle secure. The arrangement was a constant reminder of the danger that the emigrants were in as they crossed the wilds of North America.

In the morning, however, in the light of day, to Nora it felt almost like the cozy, meandering streets of a beloved neighborhood. She strolled across the open land in the center of the circle, swinging an empty bucket in each hand. As she walked, she passed by families that she knew well, some she knew only in passing, and others she had yet to speak to. The women who recognized her waved hello. Some of the children stared and grinned as she passed.

This was her home, albeit a temporary one. And these families would be her friends and neighbors potentially for the rest of her life.

She had to cut through part of the circle of wagons, then climb over some of the chains to get to the river they had camped nearby. The captains had wasted no time in determining where they could gather water from, where they could bathe, where the privy would be, farther away from their water source. It was all very efficient and very safe, and Nora hummed to herself as she made her way to the water.

"Miss Cole!"

With a broad, welcoming smile, Nora spun toward the voice, then froze when she saw who it was.

Jasper Stephens was stepping over the chains that

locked two wagons together, and then striding across the grass toward her.

"It's early," he said as he approached. "Barely dawn. But you're already up and doing chores I see."

Nora looked down at the buckets in her hand, as though she needed to be reminded what she was doing.

"Yes." She laughed self-consciously, though she knew there was nothing she should be embarrassed about. Merely being spoken to by this man was enough to make her flush. "I just love mornings. And I love getting things done as early as possible."

"And then maybe you can rest the rest of the day?" He winked at her.

"Oh, ha! No, no not really. I don't know that I'll ever be the type of person to do that. There's always so much to do. If not for my family, then surely someone else needs help, don't you find?"

He looked down at her admiringly. "I suppose you're right. Although I tend to take so long doing my own chores that I rarely get to anyone else's. It's really kind of you to do it."

Nora blushed under his praise. "It's nothing."

She looked down at her feet and mentally berated herself for not knowing what to say. There was something about Jasper's charm that overwhelmed her, that made her speechless, that drove all coherent thoughts from her mind. He would never admire her if she stayed mum like this. He would never even seek out another conversation with her if she couldn't be more captivating.

"That reminds me," he continued. "My mother and sister have some big thing planned. This afternoon, I think, for all the ladies. You might have heard about it, but you should come. I won't be there, of course, but maybe you can..." He trailed off and shrugged. "Help them out?"

"Maybe I can," she repeated. "I didn't hear anything about it though, do you know... Well, where should I go, if I have a chance to later?"

"The river. Early afternoon. You can... you know. Get to know my family a little better."

She blinked at him in surprise and felt her grin growing wider.

"Your family?" she repeated. "That is, I would love to. That would be lovely. Your sister seemed just..."

"Lovely?" he completed, after she had cut herself off.

"I'm sorry. I'm flustered. I just ... I didn't expect to run into anyone this early in the morning. My mind must be elsewhere." She realized she still held a fist full of dried cherries. "Would you like some? Cherries? Sorry. I'm... I guess I'm a mess."

"There's no reason to apologize." He stepped closer to her, smiling warmly, and accepting the gift she held out. "Thanks for these. Why don't I walk with you? It'll give you time to get used to the idea of talking to another person."

"I would love that," she said with an awkward laugh.

"Let me help."

He took one of the buckets from her, but not both. She wouldn't know what to do with herself without something to do with her hands. They turned as one and walked down the narrow trail that led from the wagons to the water.

"What will you do today?" she asked, realizing

suddenly that she knew very little about this man who so consumed her thoughts. His good looks and his magnetism were undeniable, but she knew she couldn't —or shouldn't—make any judgment off of only that.

"I'll be with Mr. Gilroy and Caleb most of the day, I think. There are some men who need Gilroy's help with their hardware, the axles and tire irons and things. He needed an extra hand if we're going to get it all done before we leave camp tomorrow."

"Oh, do you know much about blacksmithing?"

"Not really. I'm learning though. Actually." He looked around, as though worried they were being overheard. "I haven't told anyone this. I haven't even spoken to Gilroy about it."

Nora felt a thrill at being brought into his confidences.

They paused at the top of the trail; the river was only a dozen feet away.

"Do you think I would make a good blacksmith?"

She blinked in surprise, her mind immediately going to a memory of Amy insisting that she was going to be a blacksmith. "Really? A blacksmith. How long have you been thinking about it?"

"Not long. It's just, I got talking to Gilroy, and heard about what he was planning on the other end. I lent a hand earlier, back when Mr. Alden needed a couple of his tools repaired. Caleb doesn't really like it, so I think Gilroy could probably use an apprentice. I haven't mentioned it to him yet. Just something I've been thinking about. Could be a good career. You know? Provide for me and a family for years." He looked at her earnestly, uncertainty plain on his face. "What do you think?"

"I love it. Truly. If you think it's work you would enjoy—"

"I would," he said. "I really would. I mean, I do already, the little bit I've seen. I've never felt like this before. When we were in Indiana, I was just doing whatever my pa needed, but with this... I don't know..."

He looked uncomfortable all of a sudden, as though he regretted his moment of vulnerability.

"I'm sorry." He grinned, deflecting from the apparent emotion. "I'm distracting you. You were on your way to get water."

"No, it's fine. I'm glad you found me. I'm glad you told me this."

He nodded, and looked as though he might say more, but just grinned widely again. "Don't forget what I said, though. This afternoon at the river. My mother and sister should not be hard to miss."

He handed back her bucket, tipped his hat to her and turned to go back to the circle of wagons.

Nora watched him walk away, grateful that she'd had this moment with him. Thrilled that he had trusted her enough to share this desire with her. All she wanted was more time with Jasper Stephens.

After so many weeks of daydreaming about the boy, the reality seemed to be even better.

It wasn't until after they said good-bye that Nora realized she still didn't know what it was he had invited her to that afternoon. But she would go. His family needed help, Jasper had said. Who better to aid them than Nora?

CHAPTER FOURTEEN

Though Jasper hadn't given Nora details about what his mother and sister would be doing at the water that afternoon, the rumor made its way around camp throughout the course of the morning. This community of emigrants, though numerous, was intimate and connected. Everyone knew at least a little something about everyone else. And the little Nora heard—hot water, relaxation, being of service to the other women—intrigued her. Nevertheless, the idea of presenting herself to these virtual strangers, these women who she hoped might one day be her family, petrified her.

"Are you all right, dear?" her mother asked, after the third time that Nora had paced out to the middle of the circle of wagons and back again.

She nodded. "Just, um, thinking. Do you think you'll go down to the water this afternoon?"

"To bathe?" Mrs. Cole shook her head. "It sounds lovely, but I simply don't feel as though I have the time to spare. You should go, though."

"Don't you need me to stay here and help you with... with whatever is keeping you here?"

"No, dear. I'm fitting your sister in a new dress, so there's no need for another pair of hands here. You would just end up watching most of the time. You should go, though. Have fun."

Nora nodded, but in spite of this blessing still didn't feel ready.

But feeling ready wasn't always the reason things got done. About halfway through the afternoon, Nora finally found the courage go down to the water where she knew Jasper's mother and sister were. Or, rather, she made herself walk toward the water whether she felt ready for it or not.

Before she could stop herself, Nora gathered her towel and checked on her sister. Amy was occupied, sitting under the rear wagon wheels, and peering at something in the dirt. Nora could get away without worrying about her sister following. With a quick wave to her mother, Nora made her way to the wide, calm river. It was to a spot slightly downstream from where she had gathered her water earlier in the day, to where she had seen a steady stream of women and girls heading throughout the early part of the afternoon. They would need help, she reminded herself. With this many women seeking out the comfort of hot water to wash their hair, surely Mrs. Stephens and Mrs. Tenney would be grateful for her assistance.

Nora swallowed hard, and made her way down the narrow trail to the water. She followed the other women at a distance until she could easily pinpoint the destination from the chattering and laughter coming from the bathers.

Pushing her way between the shrubs, Nora felt a moment of panic. She had only very briefly spoken to Jasper's sister, the widow Mrs. Tenney, and not at all to Jasper's mother. Not even once. What had they heard about her? Had Jasper said anything? Did they know about her strange sister?

Nora froze halfway down the trail, partially hidden amongst the low branches that had caught on her skirt. What was she thinking? How could she present herself to these women as someone that they should bother with?

Another woman passed by her on the trail, smiling kindly before moving on in the same direction Nora had begun.

She could do this. Everyone was a friend. There was nothing for her to worry so much about. Nora shook off the doubt, and reminded herself why she was there. If nothing else, she could help. That's what she had to offer. Even if no words were exchanged. Even if she left that evening with Mrs. Stephens not knowing her name, Nora could at least give her time and make someone else's afternoon a little easier.

There was nothing wrong with that, Nora knew. She could be okay with that.

She stood at the top of a little decline to the water, watching as Jasper's sister greeted one of the little girls who had darted up out of the water to ask for something. When the little girl ran away again, the other two women were left alone. There seemed to be a lull in the afternoon's action, and when she spotted them, Nora realized she was the only person nearby.

Just when she was about to turn around and go back, however, Mrs. Stephens called out to her.

"You okay, there, honey? Can we help you?"

"Mrs. Stephens," Nora answered gratefully, admiringly. "This is just wonderful. I thought maybe— That is, Jasper told me that, um... I thought I would check to see if I could help you, maybe? If you need it? It's just wonderful what you're doing and I..."

She trailed off looking around again. Internally she vacillated between being embarrassed by her forwardness and being proud of herself for the generosity. These women had given up their own afternoon to do this; hopefully they would admire her for doing the same.

"I think we have everything under control, dear," Mrs. Stephens answered with a smile. "But it's nice of you to offer."

Nora stepped toward them impulsively. "I just—" She could feel herself blush and stopped herself, shaking her head before taking a deep breath. Looking back up at the older woman, she added. "I've heard a lot about you both, and I wanted to... to help, too. If you need me. And even if not, I didn't want to miss all this. It seems just..." She gestured to the women in the river. "It's just wonderful."

"Thank you," Mrs. Stephens responded.

The young widow, Mrs. Tenney, looked behind Nora up the trail. "Your sister didn't come?"

"Amy is... No, I would have had to really work to talk her into it and I thought it better to just come by myself instead. I'm sure she is perfectly happy inspecting the ant colony she found just outside our wagon wheel."

The two other women exchanged a look. Nora held her breath, hoping to be let into this little circle of the women who knew and loved Jasper best.

"Well," Mrs. Stephens finally said, "if you really don't have anywhere you need to be, I'm sure we can find some way to put you to work." She gestured at the expanse of grass, just outside their circle of dirt where the fire was smoldering. "Why don't you set down your towel and take that bucket to get us more water? We can always have some ready."

"Yes, of course. I would love that. Thank you. Thank you, Mrs. Stephens."

Nora hurried to drop her towel in the grass and catch up the empty bucket that sat nearby. More gratitude and admiration bubbled to her lips, but she held her tongue. The edge of the river was nearby, and Nora busied herself collecting all the water the women could ask for. When someone new arrived, Nora hung back, following Mrs. Tenney's lead and jumping to help whenever someone looked her way.

Mrs. Tenney—Rebecca—was only a couple years older than Nora herself, and she was thrilled to be included. As the afternoon wore on, more and more of the women from the wagon company approached them, hesitant at first, just as Nora had been, but soon eager and grateful for the gift they were being offered.

Nora found herself answering questions, telling stories about her years growing up in Michigan. She had always found it easier to make friends when she was being of service. Katie and Abby came later in the afternoon. All of the Larson women. Two of the Hudsons, the oldest remarking loudly that she had other things she should be doing that day.

It was a full day, social in a way that Nora had missed from her home back near Detroit.

Finally, as most of the women had made their way back to their own campsites and the river was empty, Mrs. Stephens turned to Nora.

"You should go on home, dear. It's been just lovely having your help."

"If you're sure..."

"Absolutely. We heard about what you did for Mrs. Buchanan that first day, and I imagine you're the type of young woman who will just keep going until you're told to stop."

Nora laughed self-consciously. "That's probably true."

"Go on home, then. Tell your mama she should be proud of you."

Nora ducked her head in a shy good-bye before collecting her towel again—unused—and heading back up the narrow trail toward the circle of wagons. The company's day off was nearly over and she didn't get any chance to rest, but somehow what she had done was even more of what she needed.

As she crossed through the center of the circle toward her own wagon, she noticed Jasper at his own camp. He was too far away to speak to, too far out of her way to detour without being too obvious in her pursuit of him. But he must have been looking for her. As she watched him patching the crack in a wide wooden tub, Jasper looked up, caught her eye, and nodded to her with a smile. Nora wondered what he would ask his sister about her later that evening. She wondered what Mrs. Tenney might say. She prayed she had made a good impression, but there was always the possibility that she was fooling herself.

It was with these daydreams flitting through her mind that Nora finally arrived back at her own campsite.

"Where have you been?" Amy asked, with no hint of real curiosity. "Mother made me stand in the sun for hours. I needed you to read to me while I held my arms out."

"Mother fitted you for a new dress, you spoiled monkey," Nora teased. She was too pleased with how her day had gone to have any animosity still for her sister.

"It's not my fault I'm still growing," Amy whined.

"You know you're going to have to continue to get new clothes periodically, even after you've grown, right?"

"Ugh."

Nora laughed and kissed the top of her sister's head as she passed. She should have remembered: it was easy to forgive Amy. She was so guileless; it was impossible to stay mad at her.

"When's supper, Mother?" she called into the wagon. "Do you need help?"

Mrs. Cole emerged from beneath the canopy with her arms full of empty pans she would use for cooking.

"I would love some."

CHAPTER FIFTEEN

"Another couple buckets, please, girls," Laura said the next morning before they left camp. "This tub still has room in it, and we need to carry as much water as we can."

Spending the afternoon bathing and relaxing was exactly what the women of the Sullivan-Mills wagon company needed. It was a gift; when was the last time any one of them had had such a fulfilling few hours? There was time to rest and time to catch up. Even the women who did not wash their hair enjoyed the luxury of time. Many of the families spent their day doing laundry and baking extra biscuits. It would be days yet before they had such a chance again.

When the emigrants left camp that next morning, it was to begin a long stretch of the Oregon Trail that was devoid of any fresh water options. Each family would be in charge of hauling their own water supply. Before leaving that river, the Coles filled every canteen, jug, pan, tub, bowl, and bucket with as much fresh water as

could be carried. They needed to carry across the
Oregon Trail all the water that they would need for both
the family and the animals. The water would be rationed
and protected as well as possible, even as the wagon
rolled over rocks and ruts in the trail, jostling every
container they had.

"Why'd the men choose a trail route that doesn't
have water?" Amy asked. "Imagine being one of the first
pioneers to cross this, and not realize you're going to run
out of fresh water before you find more."

"They must have been very brave."

"Oh. I was going to say foolish."

That sent Nora and Katie into peals of laughter. The
Cole sisters walked alongside the wagon trail with two of
the Valentine girls later that day. The break of a full day
off had put a spring back in Nora's step, after the stress
of the Kansas River and her fight with her sister. The
attention of Jasper Stephens and the chance to spend
time with his family had kindled a spark of hope in her
that frightened her. It all seemed too good to be true.

Now, on this sunny afternoon as they walked, Amy
had been lecturing her, Katie, and her younger sister
Enid about all the ways Oregon would be different from
Michigan, everything she had learned from the guidebook that she had now read cover-to-cover five times.
Everything would be better, she was insisting. The
weather and the rivers and the soil. About how she
would be able to learn more about insects because there
would be less snow, and about how they might even get a
chance to see the ocean for the first time.

Nora was only half listening. All of Amy's supposi-
tions were interesting enough, but Nora's mind was on

the previous day. How Jasper had looked confiding to her his goals. How Mrs. Stephens had looked when she thanked Nora for her help. How Jasper had seemingly gone out of his way to direct her to his family.

She knew she should be guarding her heart, protecting herself from falling too quickly for a man who didn't think anything about her. A repeat of what had happened with Jimmy Rayburn could break her heart beyond healing.

But still... she thought about that smile of Jasper's, that quiet intimacy.

"Nora's never going to see the ocean," Amy said, pulling her sister's focus back. "She's going to want to stay close to home with a husband and babies and all that boring stuff."

Nora looked at her sister in surprise. "Why do you say that?"

"Because I saw you the other day. Talking to that boy. You're always talking to boys. It won't be any different in Oregon."

"No, I'm not," Nora scoffed. "That's absurd."

"What are we?" Katie asked, bumping lightly into Amy with her shoulder. "What if she wants to go see the ocean with us?"

"Exactly," Nora added gratefully. "We're here walking with two girls right now. Or what about Claire? Or when I helped Mrs. Buchanan? Or Betty back home?"

"Okay, not always. But you're always thinking about boys. Remember how often you'd beg Mother for an errand to take to the Rayburns? You were obsessed. You were in *looovvvee.*"

Katie and Enid giggled. Nora blushed and opened

her mouth to defend herself, but found that Amy was too close to the truth for her to deny it. She *had* thought she was in love. And she had done all manner of embarrassing things to show it.

"I was not," she muttered. "I was just ... smitten. It was a crush. That's all. Don't pretend you've never had a crush, Miss I'm-going-to-be-a-blacksmith."

"Wanting to be a blacksmith is much more about learning to use those tools and fire than it does any boy. Mr. Gilroy is much too old for me."

"What about Caleb?" Katie demanded. "He's our age."

"And Katie thinks he's handsome," Enid added.

"Besides, I don't even know if I want to be a blacksmith anymore," Amy concluded dismissing the subject. "It doesn't matter." She grinned and looked over at her sister. "I'm right about you, though. Don't deny it. You would be married already if Jimmy had asked you."

Nora smiled self-consciously and shook her head. Blushing, remembering how special she had felt with Jasper even calling her name, Nora looked up ahead, toward the horizon and specifically avoided looking at her sister. "You enjoy being right far too much."

"That's not 'no.'"

Nora and the other girls laughed; it turned into a sigh. "Well, that's all over now anyway. Jimmy Rayburn is hundreds of miles behind us and I'll never see him again. Plus, he's married. That's why we're all going to Oregon, though, isn't it? New life? Fresh start?"

"Katie had a boy back home too," Enid said.

"Not really," Katie protested. "It's not the same thing. It's not like Felix announced his engagement to someone else. He just … left. He showed me a little interest, but then he and his older brother went to Boston a few years ago and we haven't heard from them since."

All four girls were silent for a few moments, walking across the hard earth.

"See?" Amy finally said. "This is why I think I should become a blacksmith. Then I can take care of myself—of both of us—and we don't have to wait for any man to decide to marry us."

"I love you," Nora said with a laugh, hugging her sister around the shoulders as they walked. "You have a good heart even if you are a pain in my neck sometimes."

"Do you think you'll get married soon?" Katie asked.

"Me?" Nora clarified. "I don't… Who would I marry? I mean, yes, I would like to but…" She blushed. "It's not as though I'm being courted by anyone. And no—" she said, cutting Amy off before she began. "Not even Jasper Stephens. We've spoken a handful of times. That's all."

"Maybe once everyone is settled it will actually turn into courting. When we're not sleeping on the prairie and eating over a campfire. Things will be different when we get to Oregon," Katie said, wistfully.

"That's what I keep saying!" Amy insisted.

Nora squeezed her sister's hand as the girls walked on. There were still miles to go before they could rest for the day.

By the time the Sullivan-Mills wagon company finally made camp at sunset that night, talk of courting and marriage had been dashed from Nora's mind. Any future happiness was pushed aside by the immediate need of water.

"I'm thirsty," Amy said, putting words to everyone's thoughts.

Walking miles in the hot sun took a lot of stamina. Nora thought they had become acclimated to a full day with reduced resources, but her body cried out for water. Each person in the wagon company drank as little water as they could get away with, just enough to get by so the water could last as long as they needed.

By the time they stopped to make camp that night, Nora felt as though her mouth was full of sand. The more she thought about how long she needed to make her canteen of water last, the thirstier she got. That evening, when they stopped for camp, Amy helped their father with the animals, while Nora helped their mother with supper. She eyed the full bucket of water longingly, but kept her discipline.

Carefully measuring out enough for one cup of coffee for each of them, Nora said to her sister, "You can have this cup of water now, or I can make it coffee for you. Which do you prefer?"

"Now please," Amy answered, reaching for the cup.

"Have you seen Claire recently?" Nora asked, returning the dipper to the bucket.

Amy shook her head. "Not since her brother died."

Nora was struck by the truth of that statement. "Not since her brother died," she repeated under her breath. "That poor family. We should probably go see if there's anything we can do, don't you think?"

"Should we?"

Nora smiled with gentle exasperation. "Amy, just because you like being left alone doesn't mean everybody does. Let's just go offer to help or something. We won't know until we check. After supper, okay?"

But after supper, when they made their way to the McKinnon camp, they were turned away by Claire's mother.

"No, girls," Mrs. McKinnon said impatiently. "Not tonight. There's nothing. No one can help us. You should go on home to your own poor mother, and not be traipsing about like this."

The stunned expression on Amy's face mirrored how Nora felt. The two girls backed off, into the darkness in the middle of the circle of wagons and made their way back to their own camp.

"That was weird," Amy finally said in a low tone.

Nora was grateful she had waited until they were out of earshot of the McKinnons.

"She must be very stressed. I can't imagine how scary it must be to know there's a river crossing coming up when you lost your son at the last one."

"Well, yes, but still... You would think she'd be grateful for someone else to wash her dishes or something, right?"

Nora chuckled in spite of herself. "Some people just feel better when they have control over everything they can. Accepting help doesn't actually help them."

"I still think it's strange."

"We'll just have to be on the lookout for other things we can do, I suppose. Claire probably knows to come see us when she can."

"Maybe after the Platte."

Amy began filling her sister in on all the details about the Platte River she had learned in her many readings of the guidebook. It was rumored to be a mile wide and a foot deep, and so muddy as to not even seem like water.

"We will have to follow along it for a couple days before we cross, though. Since it's so wide."

"Well, I'll just be grateful if it's an easier ordeal than the last," Nora said, as they arrived back at their wagon.

CHAPTER SIXTEEN

After days of walking through the hard, parched land without even a spring to quench their thirst, the wagon company finally reached the low hill that looked over the Platte River Valley. Nora paused, as the wagons rolled on next to her. Amy had been right; from this distance she practically could not even see the other side of the river, it was so wide. The sun reflected off the water, creating a broad expanse of bright landscape, highlighting the barrier they would need to cross.

But that would not be for a few days yet. The wagon caravan made its way down the low hill and turned slightly north. They followed the river past the worst of it, until they absolutely had to cross it.

Finally, where the Platte River was narrowest, the company would take a few hours for all the wagons and teams to ford across. There was no ferry, no need to float a wagon across to the other side. The Platte was wider even than the Kansas, but it was so shallow as to be barely ankle-deep in places. With focus and care, it should be an easy traversing.

Several wagons could cross at once, so the wait until it was the Coles' turn was short. Nora's father would lead their mules, while the women would walk across, picking their way across the muddy water. Checking one final time that neither of her parents needed her help, Nora started through the river on her own. The water was shallow enough that she had no fear in fording it. She lifted her skirts, though the hem still dipped into the water every couple steps as the river bottom was uneven. With focused, deliberate steps, Nora made it easily to the other side.

Amy was only a few steps behind her, and soon they were out of the water.

"There can't be any fish in water this shallow, can there?" she asked as she stumbled up the bank behind her sister.

"I have no idea. Let's get out of these wet boots and stockings though. We don't want to get blisters."

Moving slightly upstream, out of the way of the other crossing wagons, Amy plopped down on the grass and tugged at her boots.

"Do you think everyone will get across okay?"

"I hope so," Nora murmured.

When she had peeled off her stockings, Nora stood in the grass, wiggling her toes to help her feet dry before she went any farther. While the sun baked the water off her feet, she watched the rest of the wagons cross the Platte. There were still about a dozen families waiting to cross the river, including that of Jasper Stephens.

He was still on the opposite side of the water,

focused on getting his team and wagon across the shallow river. Leaning into one of his oxen, Nora could see him petting the animal's neck and seemed to be whispering into its ear.

Well, at least this would be safer than the Kansas ferry, she thought.

"Nora! Amy!" their mother called, as their wagon climbed the bank. "Come help me, would you?"

She nodded, and turned reluctantly away from the river, away from Jasper.

Once the Sullivan-Mills wagon company had crossed the Platte River, though, they still couldn't rest. There were still several more miles to cross before they could stop for the night. Though each person in the company was exhausted from the travails of the day, there was nevertheless a thrum of anticipation throughout the campsite. It was as though each person had been holding their breath, on guard against the chance that they might lose another member of their company to the dangers of the west.

Nora walked gingerly across the dirt and grass until she could climb into her own wagon to get the dry stockings she had set out on her cot. The boots were still wet, but she could manage the last of the journey that day. They would be fully dry by the morning.

Partway through the following morning, Claire McKinnon sought out the Cole girls and the three walked together throughout much of the day. That evening, after the company had made camp for the night and the Coles sat around their fire eating supper, her mother asked Nora if she was planning on going to the dance that evening.

"While you were out walking with Claire this afternoon, Sadie Waters came by the wagon and told us about it."

"Seems like folks are looking forward to letting their hair down," her father added. "She seemed very excited."

The moment she heard the word dance, Nora imagined herself in Jasper's arms, whirling around the dance floor, his eyes only on her as they talked late into the night.

"Yes," she told her parents.

"No, thank you," Amy added, to no one's surprise.

And so, immediately after supper, Nora put on a clean dress, braided her hair afresh, and set off through the circle of wagons. She stopped by the McKinnons' wagon on her way, but Claire's mother wasn't about to let her out of her sight. All of her other friends were out of the way, so she approached music and revelry by herself.

Even from a distance, Nora could see that a crowd had gathered. Hannah Sullivan whirled by in the arms of the son Captain Mills's right-hand man. Three of the tall Waters brothers surrounded Miss Atkins, the schoolteacher. She was at least ten years older than all of them, but they each teased and flirted while trying to monopolize her attention. Ernie Schmidt and Florence Pierce had all but sequestered themselves near the end of the Jamesons' wagon where it was darkest and quietest. Nora wondered if they were already engaged; there had been rumors.

As she looked around the crowd, Nora realized she knew most of the folks of the wagon company by sight, though not all. As she hovered around the periphery, she looked for a friendly face, wishing again that Claire could have joined her. Maybe Katie was here. There was a small group standing near her; several looked over at her as she approached.

"Nora Cole," greeted the young man closest to her.

In the flickering firelight, she recognized Billy Whitson, the fifteen-year-old who Mrs. Buchanan had hired to help drive her wagon across to Oregon after her husband had died.

"Billy, good evening." She looked around appreciatively. "Just about everyone is here, it seems like, doesn't it?"

"Just about," he agreed. "That New York society girl that Hannah is friends with couldn't be bothered, it looks like, but lots of other folks."

Before she had a chance to respond, Nora's gaze found what she had subconsciously been looking for. There he was. Nora felt like her whole body was lifting up, floating on the mere promise of spending an evening with Jasper. He was approaching the group of revelers with his sister on his arm, escorting the widow, though some would frown on her being there at all. Nora opened her mouth to call out to them, but realized they were too far away. She would have to yell at the top of her lungs in order to be heard over the music and chattering.

She watched as he and his sister whispered to each other, and then he darted across the open dance space toward a group of young men even farther away from Nora. He greeted them, smiling, shaking hands, and then accepting a flask from one of them.

Nora felt buoyant just watching Jasper from the opposite side of the crowd.

"Did you want to dance?" Billy asked.

She turned to him in surprise, having completely forgotten that she had been speaking to him.

"Oh, um. Not yet. Thank you. I just want to watch and listen for a bit longer."

He took the rejection well, and turned instead to another in the small knot of people he had been speaking to before Nora arrived. She half turned to listen to their conversation, though she was distracted by all the movement and socializing around her.

At a quick glance, Nora estimated that there was close to three dozen dancers gathered, drawn by the high spirits of Martin Jameson's fiddle and warm rhythm of Davis Waters's guitar. By this time in the evening most of who would be attending were there.

She smiled to herself, as she listened. Billy and his friends standing next to her were discussing the fort that the company would reach in a few weeks, and how long it had been since they had slept in their own bed. All around her, young folks were letting loose, relaxed, and happy after so many days of hard travel.

This was precisely where she wanted to be—in the middle of all of it.

Just as Nora was about to turn back and ask Billy how the Buchanans were doing, her attention was seized by movement. On the edge of the dance floor a few feet away, someone had collapsed.

Without thinking, Nora hurried to help.

Mary Norton sat in the dirt, both hands around her

ankle, while her dance partner, Clark Whitson, squatted nearby. Nora kneeled next to him.

"I'm sorry, I'm sorry," he pleaded. "I'm so sorry, Mary, don't be mad. I knew I never shoulda tried to dance. I'm so stupid. I'm sorry."

"Clark, hush," Mary said. "I'm not mad. But I don't think I'll be dancing more with you tonight."

"I'm not sure you should be dancing with anyone at all tonight," Nora said. "Here, let me see."

Using gentle probing, Nora was able to determine that the injury wasn't too severe. Nothing was broken.

"It's just a strain," she said. "You should probably see Dr. Martell if the swelling isn't down by tomorrow. And ride in your wagon tomorrow, instead of walk, but if you're careful this should heal just fine in a day or two. How did it happen, anyway?"

Clark began apologizing again, but between the two of them managed to describe how he had been too ambitious in his dance leading, trying to twirl her in time to the music but instead only managing to tangle them up.

The crowd that had gathered when Mary first fell had now dispersed, but Nora still felt as though there were eyes on them. As she stood and helped Mary to her feet, Nora looked around.

Had Jasper Stephens been watching? Where had he gone?

She immediately turned back to Mary, to help her off the dance floor and give a couple final instructions, but she would have sworn that Jasper had looked right at her.

And after all, how could he miss her? No one could

have missed Mary falling to the ground, and Nora had been by her side almost immediately.

Not that she was doing it for the credit or the attention, of course, but Nora had expected Jasper to be by her side any moment.

Mary and Clark hobbled off through the night to the Norton family's wagon, and Nora turned back toward the dance, confused and a little hurt.

CHAPTER SEVENTEEN

Nora turned back toward the music, after seeing that Mary would be all right hobbling home on her hurt ankle. She had only been there a few minutes, but she was ready to dance, if only Jasper would ask her. The crowd of dancers and on-lookers thrummed. The air was full of the sounds of Martin's fiddle, girls' giggles, and the heavy steps of dancing. Nora watched it all, trying to find where Jasper had gotten to.

She froze, once she understood what she was looking at.

There, on the other side of the dancers, Jasper Stephens bent low over some other girl's hand. A dozen dancers whirled between them, but Nora could not mistake what she was watching. Her feet seemed rooted to the ground, as Hattie Larson demurred only briefly before accepting Jasper's hands. As the music started up again—a lively waltz—he whisked her off in his arms into the circle of dancers, her forest-green calico dress sweeping out in a wave.

The couple's movement propelled Nora into action. She turned on her heel and began the long walk back to her own wagon.

"Nora?" Billy called after her. "Are you all right?"

She blinked back tears as she strode away purposefully.

Trying to block the sound of the music from her ears, Nora was suddenly grateful that Claire had not accompanied her. She needed to be alone. Forty feet away from the gathering, in the center of the secure circle of wagons, Nora stopped and took a deep breath. It was still early in the evening, so early, in fact, that Nora couldn't bear to go back to her own campsite yet. Even if none of her family asked about the dance or who she had seen or why she was home so early, her sister would find some way to monopolize her attention. And Nora simply did not have the energy to deal with that.

Instead, she altered her route, crossing between the wagons of the Gladwell and Ulmer families and leaving the safety of the circle of wagons.

"Don't go too far now," a male voice called to her.

Nora looked up to see that Ralph Ulmer was sitting up on the seat of his wagon, with a rifle cradled in his arms.

"I'm on watch for another three hours yet, so just mind you stay within my sight, all right?"

"Yes, sir," she called back. "Thank you. I'm grateful."

And she was. She could be alone, she could have some space, but she could stay safe. It felt like such an immeasurable relief to be able to trust at least some of her own care to another person. As Nora walked slowly through the grass, careful to avoid any rodent nests or other holes in the dirt that she couldn't see, she thought about how much of her travel westward thus far had been about helping others around her and being helped in return.

She had thought that being a good person, offering assistance and herself, would be enough to attract the kind of man she wanted to build a family with. It *should* be, she thought. All she had ever wanted was to be admired for who she was naturally. Her parents had raised her with the belief that if she just worked hard and was compassionate to other people, everything in her life would fall into place. Her reward for selfless behavior would be everything she had ever wanted.

The evidence stared Nora in the face.

Either her parents and their entire worldview was wrong or ... maybe Jasper Stephens was not the man for her.

She had been convincing herself that he could be her future, after the connection they had made, after the conversations they'd had, after the way he had encouraged her, and the way she had thought he was confiding in her. If they could go through all that together and he could still flirt with another girl right in front of her, maybe she was wrong. Maybe she was wasting her time dreaming of the life they could build together.

He'd had so many opportunities to seek her out, not just this evening. And he hadn't done so much as look her direction that night. Nora didn't want to be chasing after Jasper the way she had Jimmy. She was done putting aside her self-respect while a man dismissed her.

And given that no other young man had showed her

such attention since they had left Independence, maybe she was destined to be alone.

Standing out in the darkness, far from the crowd and the warmth, Nora felt the hopelessness overwhelm her. The same fears and heartbreak that she had endured in Michigan before they left now swooped in again.

This journey was supposed to fix everything.

Uprooting her whole life was supposed to give her the fresh start that she so craved.

Nora had been so sure that she would meet the love of her life, if not on the trail, then at least in Oregon itself. Though they still had a long way to go before the journey's end, Nora wondered if there was any point in such dreams after all.

She stayed out on the prairie for a long time; it was long enough that by the time she returned, Ralph Ulmer called down that he had been ready to go out after her. By the time she finally returned to her own wagon, the rest of her family had gone to bed. Nora quietly settled herself in the cot next to her sister and closed her eyes.

Sleep was a long time coming.

CHAPTER EIGHTEEN

After a despondent night, the bright sun of the following morning went a long way to clear Nora's mood and frustration. The hurt lingered, but Nora tried to forget. Instead of thinking too much about what Jasper had meant to her and what he might be now thinking about her, Nora threw herself into work. There was plenty to do in support of her own family, but she sought out anyone else she could find as well. That deep drive in her to be of service would not be quenched, no matter what some fickle man might do. She wanted to believe that this was what her life was meant for; she couldn't let go of that faith.

The wagon company continued their relentless march westward. That day they would not cover as many miles, but they would have to overcome two big obstacles before they made camp for the night. The earlier they got started the better.

When the wagons unrolled out of the protective circle into the long line following the trail, Nora kept her eyes on the horizon. She wouldn't look back. She wouldn't think about her disappointment. She would keep on toward Oregon.

Amy, of course, insisted on walking with her. To her credit, however, Amy did not seem interested in asking about how the dance had been the night before. She was too excited to tell Nora about how she had finally gotten to talk to Dr. Martell.

"He came to our camp last night to thank you for helping Mary Norton, but since you weren't there, I got to ask him if he ever does dissections or amputations."

Nora smiled to herself, grateful for Amy's self-absorption in this instance.

"What did he say?"

As Amy plunged into a story that sounded to Nora as though the good doctor had the patience of a saint, Nora renewed her promise to herself to not give Jasper Stephens another thought. Her sister could use her attention as much as anyone.

By late morning, Nora had learned more about how amputations are done—along with half a dozen other medical procedures—than she could ever want to know.

"Mother and Father heard all of this conversation too? You all are just talking about tourniquets around the campfire?"

Amy shrugged. "Maybe. I'm not sure they were listening very carefully."

Nora was saved from responding when their father yelled to them from the trail where he was leading their team of mules.

"Girls!" their father called. "Look on up ahead."

Nora and Amy looked to where he pointed, up

toward the horizon, directly in the path of the wagons to the field they were about to cross. They closed the distance to the trail, walking alongside their father as the caravan approached the next obstacle.

"Wow," Amy said in a low voice. "What makes it look like that?"

After weeks of the flat, open prairie, the terrain the wagon company had to cross shifted dramatically. As far as they could see to either direction, a field of boulders, enormous rocks and stones blocked their path. The stony field extended over a small incline, but there was no way around it. The trail seemed to weave through this treacherous landscape, though Nora didn't see how that was possible. How could anyone get a wagon through that safely?

"I dunno," their father answered. "Could be thousands of years of land upheaval and moving about. Could've been some larger piece here broken down by the weather over time. There's professional men who spend all their time studying rocks and things; maybe they could tell you."

"But none of them are here," Amy finished, in frustration.

"Maybe once we get to Oregon you can write to one of the colleges back east," Mrs. Cole said, soothingly.

"But not now," Mr. Cole added. "Right now, we just gotta get to the other side. We can worry about how these rocks got like that when we're settled somewhere."

"Is there anything we can do to help?" Nora asked.

"Maybe just stay close. Be a second set of eyes for me. I should be able to keep pretty close to Sheldon's wagon, but you never know when things might shift or go awry."

And so, Nora spent her morning following as close as she dared to her father and their team. She wanted to be near enough to see the smallest change in the terrain, but far enough away that she couldn't get caught if the wagon became unstable.

She kept her focus on helping her father—or at least being available—and put everything else from her mind. He was counting on her. The wagons would only get through this impossible terrain with focus and deliberate action. She had to admit, though, some of Amy's more graphic descriptions of amputations popped into her head at times.

The way was slow. The ruts were deep. Nora did her best to move aside as many of the smaller rocks as she could, but it was like moving sand on a beach—she couldn't even pick out the spots she had just tried to clear.

Finally, they reached the opposite side of the field of stones and rocks that had so delayed the wagon company. Nora let out a long sigh of relief. There were still at least a dozen wagons picking their way through the terrain, but at least the Coles' wagon had made it through without incident. Not everyone was so lucky.

Nora turned to look back over the unearthly field of stones. Her eyes searched over the landscape, the rocky terrain they had only recently left, the chalky Platte River beyond that, and what she knew was miles and miles of arid country even farther east. They had already been through so much, and yet they were not yet halfway to Oregon.

And they were not yet out of danger.

When she turned back to face west, to face the next step, she was overwhelmed. Just past the worst of the boulders, the ground seemed to open up, driving the caravan toward a gorge. The next campsite was at the bottom of a ravine; each wagon needed to make its way carefully down the narrow trail cut into the rock face. By the time the Cole family had crossed the rocky terrain, the first of the wagons were already making their way down to the campsite and fresh water at the bottom.

Nora took a deep breath and went to her father's side, where he waited at the top of the gorge.

"We're chaining the wheels so they don't roll out of control," her father said, without looking up. He secured the chain through the rear right wheel, pulling it hard to ensure its stability, before finally straightening. "It's going to be steep, but we'll be fine. Go on, honey. You girls walk down ahead of me. Don't worry."

"If you're sure..."

Her father just nodded as he walked around to the other side of the wagon to secure more chain.

All around her, men and older boys were doing the same with their own wagons. The path down to the campsite wasn't long, but it was steep. It was treacherous. And the last thing the wagon company needed was for someone else to get injured, or die.

"Come on, Amy," Nora said, as she reached for her sister's hand.

Amy had been standing far too close to the edge of the ravine, looking over. Nora pulled her back.

"Did you see that hawk?" she asked in wonder. "I

think it had a mouse in its talons, but it flew too fast for me to see."

"I need you to pay better attention, please," she said, as Amy stumbled. It was as though her brain had not realized that her feet were moving, so intent was she on the sight of predator and prey. "We're walking down the campsite, and need to stay well clear of the wagons, just in case. Hurry, now."

The girls made their way to the top of the trail, joining a bevy of other women and children taking advantage of a break in the wagons to walk down to the bottom of the ravine. The descent was steep; Nora almost stumbled more than once.

It was over quickly, and the girls were safely at the bottom of the ravine.

"Let's go find the water," Nora said. "Father is right behind us and we'll make camp."

She glanced over her shoulder, watching her father slowly and carefully guiding his team down the steep trail. He seemed flustered, but Nora knew there was nothing she could do from here. She led Amy away toward the water, but before they had made it far, Nora heard a crack and looked back.

Her father and the Coles' wagon had reached the bottom of the trail when disaster struck. Charlie was peering at the rear left wheel and shaking his head. "Made it all the way through those rocks and now this," he muttered.

"What happened? What can I do?" Nora asked. She had hurried back to his side and was looking over the wagon anxiously.

"Nothing. Go on. It's fine. It'll hold till I can get it parked. I'll have to get a couple of the boys to help me."

He didn't have to look far. Within minutes, three men had congregated around Charlie, offering advice and help. They were able to get the wagon situated in the camp quickly, so the wheel could be repaired. One by one the wagons made it down the narrow path, into the ravine, and into the tight circle of camp to settle for the night.

Nora's father set to work to repair his wheel as quickly as he could. He needed to get the wagon lifted up off the axles first, and find a replacement piece of wood to make a new spoke. None of this could he do by himself, and as Nora hovered trying to find a way she could be of assistance, more men came by their wagon to offer themselves.

She stopped with a jolt when she saw Jasper Stephens crossing the grass toward her wagon. After such a tiring day, she had successfully put him out of her mind, even for just a few hours. And now he was presenting himself here, at her own camp.

She didn't know how she could avoid him.

As he got closer, Jasper caught Nora's eye. He grinned companionably and closed the distance between them as he joined the group of men lifting the wagon off the axles.

Nora turned her back on him, tears smarting her eyes. She thought she would be able to get over him eventually, but seeing him every day made it more difficult.

"Come on, Amy," she said, pulling her sister again. "We still haven't found the water at this camp."

She did not look back. She didn't want to know if Jasper was watching her.

Once all the families and all the wagons were safely at the bottom of the gorge, Captains Mills and Sullivan decided that they would stay at that campsite for a full day. There was plenty of fresh water and grass for the animals, and each person could use a longer break after the stress of their long trek without water, crossing the Platte, and then making their way through the hazards of the terrain since then.

Nora had avoided her family's campsite all afternoon, for as long as she thought Jasper might still be there. When she learned they would get a whole extra day, she finally settled in for the evening. Amy's non-stop chattering about catching frogs at the river helped give her the distraction she needed.

CHAPTER NINETEEN

When Nora woke the next morning, she had a moment of confusion. Her mind had gone immediately to the intimate smile on Jasper's face when he had come by the Coles' camp the previous afternoon. For a minute she felt a surge of desire to see him. But the memory of him dancing with Hattie Larson crept quickly in.

Nora sat up in her cot, exasperated with herself.

There were far better ways for her to spend her time than dithering over some boy.

Carefully so as not to wake her sister, she climbed out of bed and got dressed for her day. The Sullivan-Mills wagon company would be at this site at the bottom of the ravine until the following morning. They had plenty of water and grass for the animals. They had shade and time to rest. Pastor Montgomery was even planning a church service that evening.

This had all the promise of a beautiful day.

As long as she didn't let herself bother with what some boy thought of her.

But as she climbed out of the wagon and considered how to spend her time, Nora felt torn. The ease and relaxation were welcome, of course, but the last time she'd had such a stretch of free time had been the day that she had attempted to befriend and assist Jasper's family. That afternoon by the river had seemed so full of promise that had since been dashed. Though she had enjoyed being of service and couldn't quite count it wasted time, the whole situation just added to her disappointment.

Now that Jasper's feelings for her seemed to be clear, Nora didn't want the memory of that day cropping up at every turn. There were plenty of other families who could use her help. Nora told herself she would just make new memories.

With her feet planted in the dirt under the newly repaired wagon wheel, Nora stretched tall, toward the sky, and took a deep breath of pleasing prairie air. She let it out slowly as she relaxed her shoulders and looked around the camp.

"Good morning, love," her mother said as she noticed her. She was crouched near the campfire, feeding it from the collection of twigs in one hand. "Nora, I'm going to need your help today, please. I need to try to get those stains out of your father's trousers and finish Amy's dress. Could you bake a batch of biscuits for breakfast and then also some extra? Maybe a dozen or so that we can keep for the next couple of days?"

"Of course, Mother."

"Thank you. Oh, and keep an eye out for your sister. She said something about going down to the water to look for frogs again. Probably as soon as she gets up, if I know her at all."

Nora smiled in acquiescence but inwardly was irritated. Amy was always too flighty, too unreliable to be depended on. Of course she went off to her frog adventure while Nora was stuck behind baking and cleaning.

But there was nothing she could do about it this minute.

Nora tucked a loose strand of hair behind her ear, and climbed into the wagon to find the ingredients she would need for the biscuits.

Breakfast on the Oregon Trail was unexciting for most of the emigrants. The Coles still had plenty of bacon for at least one thick slice a person each morning, though rationing the meat was a whole project. It was salted to last, but it wouldn't keep forever. They needed the protein to carry them as far west as possible, but they couldn't afford to let any of it spoil.

Because the Coles had brought several pounds of dried cherries from their orchard in Michigan, they had a rather more interesting breakfast most mornings than their neighbors. Laura would usually make cornmeal pancakes, flavored with small bits of the tart fruit.

Compared to most of their other meals, this felt like a luxury.

Biscuits would be made in large batches and eaten cold throughout the days, to save time cooking when they didn't stop long. Beans would be eaten for supper, with rice or more cold biscuits. This was not the first time Nora had spent a whole morning in camp making the food that was meant to last them several days.

Amy woke when she heard her sister rummaging around the wagon for the flour and salt.

"When you get up, will you get us a couple buckets of water, please?" Nora said when she noticed Amy sitting up. "For coffee and cleaning. And then I think we have the rest of the day to do as we please."

Amy stretched from where she sat on the cot. "Do you know how many frogs are down by the water?"

"I can imagine. Once you get me those buckets I'm sure you can go back and find some. But I have things that need to get done first."

Leaving Amy to her dressing, Nora climbed awkwardly out of the wagon again with her arms full. She had a full day ahead of her, traveling or not, and she was looking forward to getting started.

After breakfast, Laura set to work scrubbing out the stains from her husband's trousers, Amy had left to go find her beloved frogs and Nora was wondering if one of those poor animals was bound for a dissection. She should have asked. Maybe she should go after her sister just to check. She was mixing up the dough for her several batches of biscuits when she noticed Jasper Stephens walking toward the Coles' camp.

Nora felt as though her heart had stopped. What was he doing coming here?

Her hands were a mess, covered in wet dough, with dried flour sprinkled up her sleeves.

From still a dozen feet away, Jasper caught her eye, smiled at her, and tipped his hat, but didn't stop. Instead, he kept walking, past the Coles toward the Gilroys' camp and called out.

"Gilroy!"

Nora turned away, cheeks burning.

Of course he wasn't coming to talk to her. She should have known that.

Mentally berating herself for being so foolish, Nora doubled her effort, hunching over the bowl and trying to ignore the fact that Jasper had stopped at just the next campsite over.

That was nothing to her, she thought. Absolutely nothing.

But despite her attempt to mind her own business, the camps were only maybe ten feet apart. Nora sat in the dirt by her own fire, carefully forming her dough for biscuits, and couldn't help but overhear the men's conversation.

"When were you going over to help Emerson with his horseshoe?" Jasper was asking. "Later today? I can be free whenever you need."

Nora peeked over her shoulder. Mr. Gilroy leaned on the back wheel of his wagon, with a cup of coffee in hand, as Jasper approached. The two men launched into a casual conversation about scheduling and space, going over what they would need to help Mr. Emerson shoe his horse again. Nora turned back to her baking, trying not to listen.

Trying not to care or notice where Jasper Stephens was at every minute of every day.

Instead, as she worked, she made a mental list of all the families in the company who she should check on. There was Mrs. Buchanan, who she hadn't spoken to in weeks. She had heard that Mrs. Waters was feeling poorly and that Mrs. Van Anda's baby was due in the next couple months.

She was needed, Nora reminded herself. Even if Jasper didn't want her.

"Nora?"

Jasper's voice interrupted her thoughts. She felt her face flush, and her heart start beating faster, but she couldn't turn around. She wouldn't. The wound from him ignoring her at the dance was still too fresh. Though it was rude to shun him so blatantly, Nora didn't trust herself to have a calm conversation with him.

"Nora?"

This time his voice sounded gentler, more timid, as though he wasn't sure what to expect from her.

"Are you... Um, are you busy?"

From across the campsite, Laura peeked up at her. She was too far away to hear whatever Jasper had to say, but she'd certainly hear if Nora chose to make a scene.

Instead, she tried to calm her expression and turned to meet him.

"I am busy, yes, Mr. Stephens. Was there something I could help you with?"

"I..." He looked past her to Mrs. Cole and then back to Nora. "I won't keep you. I just... Katie just told me about the church service tonight, and I was wondering if you would be there."

"Katie told you that? Katie Valentine?"

Nora fumed, stunned. It seemed two girls were not enough for this man to have wrapped around his fingers. First her, then Hattie and now Katie too? She took a deep breath but her heart still pounded.

"I just saw her, back at the Gilroys'." He thumbed over his shoulder.

"I haven't decided about tonight. And if you'll excuse

me, I have several batches of biscuits to bake before it gets too hot this afternoon. I can't be traipsing about on social visits."

She turned her back to him again, proud of herself for not losing her temper. Though she couldn't quite get his hurt expression out of her mind.

"Oh, yeah, all right. Well, then maybe I'll see you."

She heard him walk away.

All the air left her sails. Somehow, the joy of her day of rest had left along with Jasper.

Nevertheless, the day at the bottom of the ravine went by too quickly for Nora's taste. She finished her chores and manufactured new ones. She stayed close to her own wagon most of the day, though Amy tried to get her to come to the water with her. Nora allowed herself time to be hurt and grieve the loss of her dreams, knowing that on the Oregon Trail such time was a luxury.

The following morning, the wagon company pulled up stakes early to begin the slow ascent out of the canyon back to the flat prairie. For the first hours of morning, the depth of the canyon kept the wagon company in the shade, but by midday they were high enough that all was gone. The summer sun was hot and direct, and Nora felt her shoulders baking.

But they were moving. They were making progress. They were headed toward Oregon. After the wagon company left the campsite at the bottom of the ravine and continued west, days past with little to mark them. A horse would throw a shoe, or a mother gave her boys all haircuts, but otherwise day after day looked the same. Another seventy or so days like this and they would have their new home.

They were well into June now, and the spring flowers were beginning to fade. Day after day, Nora walked westward. Occasionally with Claire McKinnon, the Valentine girls, or the Buchanan children. Usually with Amy. But always westward, under the sun and heat and bright, monotonous sky.

Despite the death and hardships the wagon company had experienced so far, Nora was optimistic. Despite her hurt and confusion over Jasper, she still had plenty of time to redirect her affection to a man worthy of them. There were still more than a thousand miles to go, but each day they were getting smarter, safer, and steadier about the journey. Surely the worst was behind them.

CHAPTER TWENTY

On and on. West toward the horizon. Day after day. Through sun and rain and heat and bugs and more sun. Through injuries and deprivations. Through the beginning of rationing. Through children getting lost and lovers being found. The Oregon Trail seemed unending and unrelenting, and still the wagons pushed westward.

Nora could hardly remember what her life had looked like before reaching Missouri.

One morning that initially seemed like every other morning, Nora had woken, eaten, and gotten ready to leave early as usual but then nothing else had happened. The wagon company didn't move; everyone stayed in camp well after their designated departure.

"Why aren't we leaving, Father?" Amy asked.

"Could be lots of reasons. Do you want to go investigate?"

She nodded, and ran away toward the captains' wagons before anyone could stop her.

Nora tried to busy herself while Amy was gone, but worry crept in. Their father was right and there may be all manner of reasons, but out here in the wilderness, in the clutches of the Oregon Trail, those reasons were more likely than not to have adverse consequences.

When Amy had been gone long enough that Nora began to wonder if she should go after her, the girl appeared from around the side of the Montgomery and Sheldon wagons. She rejoined her family full up with news.

"Sick," Amy said as soon as she was near, her eyes lighting up. "I saw the doctor and I got him to tell me. Do you know that most wagon companies don't have doctors? Why do you think Dr. Martell decided to come west? Wouldn't he have had a practice back wherever he came from? Maybe I'll ask him why he left it."

"Amy," said their mother, heading off a long rambling wonder. "Who is sick? What did he say?"

"Oh, right. Jeremiah Sullivan." She grimaced. "Their youngest boy. Measles, the doctor says. Or he thinks, at least. Why doesn't he know for sure? That's his job."

"Measles!" Nora and her mother looked at each other in alarm. "Oh, no, that poor family."

Nora had a flash picturing her own sister feverish and weak in the dark interior of the wagon. Helpless to do anything but watch her and pray.

"No wonder we haven't left yet," Laura added.

"Mills and Sullivan will have to decide what to do. Might need to leave the Sullivans here," Charlie said.

"Would they do that?" Nora asked.

"They might. Those captains have a responsibility to

the entire company, not just one little boy. I'm sure we'll hear something soon. Can't delay too long."

Nora's mind whirled and she needed to do something to calm it. Striding out through the scrub brush outside of the camp, Nora found some semblance of solitude. Measles in their camp! She and Amy had both had the disease as children, and Nora had been old enough that she still remembered those hard days. The rash and the cough were bad enough, but the delirium from the fever had almost been more than her tiny five-year-old body could manage. It had been downright scary at times.

She closed her eyes and said a short prayer, not just for Jeremiah Sullivan, but for his whole family.

When she opened her eyes, Nora spotted Jasper around the outside curve of the circle of wagons waiting to leave. He glanced at each family as he passed, but seemed to be coming straight to her. His expression was somber, determined. She felt a flutter of nerves in anticipation of speaking to him, but the moment was too dire for her to be caught up in her earlier feelings.

"Nora," he said, in a low tone. "I was looking for you. What are you doing out here? Is everything all right?"

She nodded, fighting back tears. "It's terrible."

"What is it?" He closed the distance between them, and though he didn't touch her, he did put out his hand gently inviting her to take it.

"It's the youngest Sullivan boy," Nora said dully. "Another child sick."

Jasper gasped. "Jeremiah? Oh, that poor family."

"I guess the doctor suspects measles. That's why we haven't left yet."

"Measles? That's ... That's really dangerous. They're letting him stay with the company?"

"I don't know, Jasper," Nora said despairingly. "I suppose so. I don't have all the answers. All I know is one of the captains' sons is sick. Really sick. And I don't know what I can do to help. And I hate how useless that makes me feel."

Her voice cracked at this last, and she hung her head, shoulders drooping. The last thing she wanted to do was show vulnerability in front of this man who had so hurt her, but the reality of the situation was just too much for her to bear right now.

"Hey, hey," he said gently. "It's okay. It'll be all right. Captain Sullivan is smart. He'll make the best decision for everyone, not just his family."

"I know, but ... That poor boy's mother. And sisters. What they must be going through."

He looked back to his own wagon. "I need to get back to my folks. Tell them what the holdup is. Will you be all right?"

"Yes. Thank you. Just... Maybe keep the news to yourself and your family? We don't want to panic anyone. I'm sure the captains will make sure everyone knows when they're ready. The only reason we know is because Amy asked the doctor directly."

"That's smart." He nodded, while reaching again for her hand.

As a reflex, without fully realizing what she was doing, she slipped her small hand into his big worn one, grateful for the comfort.

He squeezed her hand gently and leaned close. "Take care of yourself."

"You too."

As he walked briskly back to his family, Nora watched the tall, lanky form of Jasper Stephens disappear again around the curve of wagons. He seemed so sure, so sturdy, and reliable.

Somehow in that brief encounter, Nora could forget her hurt and doubt of the previous days though it was still there a bit. The feeling of being discarded that Jasper's behavior had woken in her was too deep of a wound. She wanted to ask him if he had seen more of Katie. If he was going to dance with Hattie the next time Martin got out his fiddle. But she also wanted to hear all about the start of his apprenticeship, if he had talked to Mr. Gilroy about it, what his plans were. She wanted to hear all about his life.

But all of that seemed so trivial compared to measles in the camp.

The wagon company pulled out of camp soon after that. Nora spent most of the day trying to forget her fear and the other part of the day preparing herself for the possibility that she may be called upon to nurse other members of the company who might come down with measles. Each person had to do their part.

The Oregon Trail did not discriminate.

In spite of the dozens of prayers sent up by the members of the wagon company, by the time they made camp that evening, Jeremiah Sullivan had died. His small body, already weakened by the journey and the shortened rations, had been unable to take any more. The news was whispered from camp to camp, Daniel Mills visiting many of the families personally to share the news.

Another child.

Another death.

Another hastily marked grave site left behind as the rest of his family kept traveling west.

It was a miracle that no one else in the company had taken ill; that was not to be taken for granted. But neither could they afford to stay any longer than the bare minimum it took to bury little Jeremiah.

As the wagons left the next morning, leaving behind the small grave piled high with stones to ward off scavengers, Nora made a promise to herself. There was no telling what would happen next on the Oregon Trail, and in the event of the worst she didn't want to have anything left unsaid. She told herself if she got the chance she would be kind to Jasper again. They might never return to their earlier promise of intimacy, but at least her conscience would be clear.

———

"There it is!" Amy exclaimed. "Do you see it?"

Nora peered into the horizon where Amy was pointing. After days and days of the same terrain, they finally had something more than just flat land and birds of prey to look at. The two sisters were walking with Claire McKinnon, parallel to the wheel ruts that led the company toward their destination. Amy had spent the previous half an hour explaining to the others about how they should be seeing these enormous rocks any day— any minute, she insisted.

"I told you!" Amy all but shouted. "The guidebook said. That spot on the horizon; do you see it?"

"That's Courthouse Rock?" Claire asked, likewise squinting into the afternoon sun. "It doesn't look very big."

"You'll see," Amy insisted. "That one is more than four hundred feet above the valley. And then a few days after that we'll see Chimney Rock and Scott's Bluff and a bunch more. You won't even believe it. You've never seen anything like it."

"And we might not ever again," Nora added, joining in the excitement. "Just think, girls, of all the things we've seen on the trail so far that were never part of our days back east."

Any bright spot in their journey was welcome. Anything that could break the monotony was highly anticipated. Courthouse Rock marked the beginning of several weeks' worth of monumental landmarks indicating their way west to Oregon. The days of repetition of sky and plains were behind them. There were days of travel between the large granite sites, but they dominated the horizon and the emigrants' view throughout those days.

Monuments of this size were impossible to miss on the horizon, and offered a clear visual path through the terrain toward where the emigrants needed to go.

Only a few days later, the company camped in the shadow of Scott's Bluff. Amy, as ever, had been full of details, more than anyone could ever need, about which men had found the huge cliff, what had happened, and how it had been named. Like Courthouse Rock and Chimney Rock before it, each one of these landmarks had an unforgettable story. When Nora went to sleep that night, she dreamt about men falling from cliffs and big stones growing up out of their graves.

She woke the next morning eager to set up rules for her sister about which stories from the guidebook she absolutely was not interested in learning about.

CHAPTER TWENTY-ONE

After leaving Scott's Bluff behind, the Sullivan-Mills wagon company had a few days' stretch of trail to get through, and then they would finally be reaching the first real civilized structure since they had left Independence. Fort Laramie was up ahead, and the emigrants would finally get the chance to replenish their supplies and stand within four log walls, if only briefly.

Nora was thrilled. Any of the landmarks along the way helped remind her of the progress they were making, but the fort was an even bigger boon.

Only a few more days to go.

One afternoon, Nora and Amy were walking through the grass next to the trail and discussing the possibility of going to find Claire McKinnon.

"She's been helping with her younger siblings a bunch," Amy said. "I bet she'd be happy to see us, though. Happy for the break."

"I bet we can help her too."

"Oh." Amy looked thoughtful. "Yes, probably. That's true."

"Oh, Amy," Nora said with a laugh.

Before any other decision could be made, the wagon train slowed. The girls hurried to their wagon to see what the problem was. Daniel Mills, the tall son of the wagon company's captain, rode his horse down the length of the caravan, shouting for the men to get ready for a hunt.

"Buffalo's been sighted," he called to all within earshot. "We'll make camp here the rest of the day. Men, be at the far side of camp in ten minutes with your rifles."

"Buffalo!" Mrs. Cole said, her eyes lighting up. "Goodness, fresh meat would be so welcome. You'll go, won't you, Charlie?"

"Try and stop me," he said with a grin, as he led their team and wagon after the rest of the caravan.

The next ten minutes were a whirlwind. Most of the wives and daughters took over the men's usual tasks of making camp so they could go hunt as soon as possible. Nora found herself brushing down the Cole family's mules while Amy fetched the animals fresh water. Settling in for the afternoon took a good thirty minutes longer than usual, given that a quarter of the company's members had left, but soon they had the open stretch of afternoon ahead of them to wait for the promise of fresh meat.

"I just don't know what to do with all this time," Laura said. "I almost want to take a nap."

"You should," Nora agreed. "Who knows when we'll

get another chance. What are you going to do this afternoon, Amy?"

"I dunno." She shrugged and looked more dejected
than usual. "I need another book to read. The guidebook is practically falling apart."

"Maybe Miss Atkins has something you can borrow?"
Nora suggested.

"I hope so."

The Cole ladies settled in for their quiet afternoon.
Nora thought about washing her hair or maybe going to
visit Mrs. Buchanan.

Or maybe she would take a nap too.

Nora looked around at the quiet campsite. As usual,
the wagons had been pulled into a wide circle, with the
livestock all grazing in the center. Some of the families
had started a campfire going, or begun to pull things out
of the wagons, but not many. With most of the men gone,
and a good number of the women taking the chance to
rest, the campsite seemed calmer than usual. There were
plenty of laughing, running games being played by the
children, but the adults were primarily quiet and subdued.

She walked dreamily out closer to the center of the
circle, between several of the oxen grazing on the little
grass available. It was a beautiful day and the promise of
buffalo meat lifted her spirits just as much as the afternoon off had. Tucking her bonnet under one arm, Nora
unpinned her hair from its loose chignon and ran her
fingers through the curls.

Relaxation and rest. That's what she needed most,
she thought as she ran her gaze over the campsites
around her.

Nora's heart thumped. Though the Stephens's camp was a good fifty feet away, it was clear that of the few men that stayed behind, Jasper was one of them. His father might have gone hunting, but the young man stood, plain as day, talking to his mother and sister next to their wagon.

Before Nora could even decide what she thought about it, a low, far-off rumbling captured her attention. It almost sounded like thunder, but there was barely a cloud in the sky.

"What is that?" Nora murmured.

Amy stood up, facing north with a look of concentration.

"Is—"

"Hush." Amy cut her off, and took two steps toward the noise still focused.

"Amy," their mother said softly.

"Hooves," Amy said, finally turning back to her mother and sisters. "Those are horse hooves. Dozens of them. Coming toward us."

Nora was confused for only a short moment. Were the men hurrying back from their hunt? But before she could form a question, she saw the truth.

On the north side of the circle of wagons, a mass of men on horseback approached. Men with long black hair, with brown skin toned darker from the sun. Men carrying bows and arrows, hatchets, and rifles. The kind of men Nora wasn't sure she would ever see.

And they were invading the emigrants' camp.

"Indians!" Amy shouted. She turned toward the center of the circle of wagons, where most of the women and children were still settling in for a lazy afternoon. "Indians!"

"Amy Cole, you quit your screaming!" their mother shouted at her. "We have to hide."

"Where?" Nora asked, frantically under her breath as she looked around. "Oh, where can we go? There's nowhere to run."

The warriors had timed their attack specifically when nearly every single man had left to hunt buffalo, and Nora was certain that was no coincidence. They must have been watching the caravan, inching its way across the plains, seizing the opportunity as soon as it was presented.

"Into the wagon," Nora called out. "We need to hide!"

With one arm around her mother, Nora hustled her toward the opening in the canvas at the back of their wagon.

"Get your sister," Laura cried. "Amy!"

Nora looked over her shoulder to see her sister still standing in the same place, staring at the attackers as they spread throughout the campsite.

The Indians had pulled apart two of the wagons, creating an opening in the otherwise secure circle where they could pour in. Whoever had not chained together their wheels would deeply regret the oversight. More than a dozen warriors had already begun to fan out, each approaching a separate wagon with weapon raised.

"Amy!"

But her sister, as usual, was in her own little world and paid Nora no heed. As Nora watched, Amy actually took a step closer to the danger.

Thank heavens none of the Indians had come their way yet.

As Nora moved to collect her sister and bodily force her into the wagon. Her attention was caught by Jasper Stephens, clutching his rifle. He ducked under his own wagon for cover, his navy-blue shirt helping hide him in the shadow. As quickly as he could, he was taking aim against the attackers.

"Amy!" Nora said fervently, grasping her sister's forearm and yanking her toward her.

The cry of pain Amy let out alarmed Nora; she hadn't thought she had pulled too hard. For a split second she was confused and almost scolded Amy for acting up. But then she noticed the rip in Amy's sleeve, exposing a shallow cut that had begun to bleed into the fabric.

"Gah!" Amy cried again.

"What...?" Nora looked around, still confused, before she spotted the arrow on the dirt behind them. Somehow in that moment of jerking Amy toward her, she had pulled her sister almost into the path of that arrow. Nora blinked rapidly, trying to determine the original trajectory of that arrow. Had it been aimed at her? Had she pulled her sister into the line of fire instead?

"I'm sorry, Amy, I'm so sorry!"

"Nora!" their mother shouted from the cover of the wagon.

"Amy, are you all right? It just grazed you, didn't it?" Nora glanced over her shoulder toward the now several dozen Indian warriors who were spreading throughout the camp. "You have to *move*!"

With that, Nora had finally gotten her sister's attention and gotten her moving toward the wagon. Looking over her shoulder one last time before she climbed in, Nora's gaze fell on Jasper again. As he was under the wagon, behind the wheel, she couldn't see much, but the rifle no longer seemed to be pointed out toward the attackers.

There was no time to dwell on it.

Jasper would be fine. He had to be. He had his mother and sister to think about.

And so did she.

"Come on, Amy. You'll be fine. We have to hide, though. Come on."

She kept up a steady stream of chatter, trying to both calm Amy and distract her away from the attack that was raining down all around them. From the far side of the circle of wagons, she heard a blood-curdling scream. Nora turned to look, to try to help, before reminding herself that she had a responsibility already in front of her.

If only Amy wasn't so muddle-headed. If only she could be trusted to take care of herself better.

"Come on. Climb in," she said, as they arrived at the wagon. Their mother hung out over the back, reaching for her girls. "Hurry!"

Nora looked over her shoulder again as she helped Amy climb in.

The camp was in in shambles. The attackers knew what they were doing, and were able to divide and conquer with devastating efficiency.

But she couldn't do anything to stop them now. All

Nora could do was hide and protect her family as best she could.

Nora all but vaulted herself into the wagon after her family.

"Shh," her mother warned, once she was inside. "Maybe if they don't know we're here they won't think to look."

"There are so many of them!" Amy said in wonder. "Where did they all come from? What tribe is it, do you think?"

"Amy, hush. Isn't Father's pistol around here somewhere?" Nora asked.

Her eyes hadn't yet adjusted to the dark, and she turned in place trying desperately to remember where she had seen the weapon. Oh, why hadn't they repacked the wagon recently? It was a chaos of half empty crates and stacks of unrelated items. Amy never put anything away after she had found it and now they would suffer for it.

A stern face, older than Nora, appeared in the gap between the canvas flaps. Dark eyes under heavy eyebrows scanned the interior of the wagon. The Cole women all held their breaths.

"Go away," Laura said in a shaking voice, almost too quietly for anyone to hear.

"We don't have anything you want," Nora added, though she knew it was unlikely that this man understood much English. Maybe if she could sound forbidding enough he would understand.

He looked directly at her with his steady gaze that didn't falter as he climbed into the wagon.

Nora swallowed a gasp and backed up a couple steps.

The warrior was only armed with a small hatchet, but that would be plenty to do them damage if he so desired.

With his broad, muscular shoulders, the Indian seemed to fill the cramped space, especially with three women cowering in the back. Nora watched him quietly, heart in her throat as he picked up this mirror, that heavy coat, before setting them down again uninterested. He pushed past Nora to the rear of the wagon, where more of the family's food was, and hefted a burlap bag of coffee beans.

Nora swallowed hard, her heart pounding.

After some almost casual consideration, poking into trunks and upending crates all around the Coles, the Indian had his arms full of sacks of coffee, sugar, and dried cherries. He moved to leave the wagon.

Finally, just before he climbed out with their food, he spotted something at the foot of Nora's bed that caught his attention. He reached for the folded quilt, with its memories of Michigan and patches of brick red.

"No!" she cried.

"Nora," her mother scolded. "Leave it alone."

But Nora couldn't. She wouldn't. She couldn't leave it alone. She had worked too hard to finish that quilt, poured too much time into it, to let it slip through her hands like this.

"You already have plenty," she cried at the man, still uncertain if he understood a word she said. "Take the rest, but leave this."

Grasping with both hands, Nora pulled the quilt toward her as hard as she could. The warrior resisted only a moment before letting go disdainfully, as though such a silly, feminine thing was beneath his notice.

With a snort that sounded suspiciously like a laugh, the Indian left them alone again. He carried with him much of their food, but at least he was gone.

At least he had left Nora's quilt.

"Goodness, child," her mother gasped.

She pulled Nora to her, almost pulling her off her feet.

"Don't you ever do something like that again, you hear me? At least not where I can see it. You about gave me a heart attack."

"I'm sorry," Nora murmured. But she was only just paying attention. Too much of her was focused on the sounds outside their wagon.

Behind her, Amy seemed to be breathing hard.

"I think..." She listened hard. "I think they're leaving."

Amy burst into tears.

CHAPTER TWENTY-TWO

Though the attackers had left, the chaos had only just begun. Each person was unsettled; each wagon was topsy-turvy. And there was still no telling when their men would be back.

As soon as the attack seemed to be over, Amy had burst into sobs with an intensity that Nora had never seen from her.

"Shh, shhh," their mother said, pulling her youngest daughter close. "Your nerves are overwrought. You're in shock. It will all be all right. Just hush now, dear."

With her mother's hands full, Nora took charge. She climbed out of their wagon and took stock of the situation. All around her women were crying, calling out for help, or trying to assess the damage to their stores. The Sheldon children, in the campsite next to hers, seemed to be in the same state of shock that Amy was, clinging to their mother and asking questions incessantly.

But they seemed physically safe enough.

Amy had been injured, but it was just a scratch fortunately.

But there was no doubt that some—if not many—other members of the company were likely injured. She had heard dozens of gunshots, and whether those were from the emigrants or the natives Nora had no idea. It was impossible to believe that none of them had hit their mark, though.

Yes, the first thing she needed to do was see about any other injured person and see how she could help.

Nora knew she would feel better about the entire attack if she could just help someone else. That was how she could steady herself.

Without a look back, Nora began to walk to the next campsite over to check on others.

"Nora!" Amy called out, and the desperation in her tone made Nora cringe. "Aren't you going to help me? I hurt my arm! They shot at me."

With a flash of guilt that Nora hurriedly stuffed down, she stopped and turned back to the wagon.

"I can't," she told her sister brusquely. "You'll be fine. Mother can help you just as well as I can. She'll wrap it for you. There are other people who need my help."

"But—"

Nora didn't stay long enough to hear Amy's objections. She had spoken the truth—there were plenty of other people who needed help. Her sister's cut wasn't even all that deep. Their mother could clean it and bandage it in the time it took Nora to explain it to Amy.

No, there were other places Nora needed to be now in this first chaotic aftermath of the attack.

Making her way quickly past the campsites, Nora

soon realized she was headed straight for the Stephens family's wagon. She had to know if Jasper was all right before she could concentrate on anyone else in the company.

Somehow, settling his safety in her mind could settle her nerves.

Whatever that meant about her feelings for him, she didn't have time to examine. She just made her way to his side.

When she got close enough to the Stephens family's wagon it was clear that this family had not escaped the attack unscathed. Jasper's mother and sisters had not yet emerged from their wagon, but Jasper had gingerly climbed out from underneath it. The sleeve of his navy shirt was soaked through with blood. The dark patch all over his upper arm tugged at her heart. The arrow shaft stuck from him at a wide angle; the arrowhead must still be embedded.

Nora's heart broke for him, and she ran to his side.

"Jasper," she gasped out. "Mr. Stephens, oh my goodness, are you all right? Of course you're not all right. Oh my goodness, what can I do?"

She touched his arm lightly. When he grimaced, she shrunk back.

"I'm sorry. I'm so sorry! Let me help. I'll be gentle," she said in a quiet voice.

He nodded and tried to offer her a smile, but that too turned into a wince.

Nora took a deep breath and focused. The first thing to do would be to get the arrowhead out of the muscle. She couldn't do it painlessly, but she had to try.

"Do you have a knife on you?" she asked.

"Miss Cole!" Mrs. Stephens exclaimed. "Goodness, child, you don't have to do that. Let me help you."

Before she had to do anything drastic, the rest of the Stephenses climbed out of the wagon to assess the damage to their campsite. Nora didn't notice them until she heard her own name.

"Ma," Jasper said. "What took you so long? We didn't know how long you'd be in there. This thing smarts like the dickens."

Relief washed over Nora. "Oh, thank you. I didn't want to hurt him, but ... Thank you."

Mrs. Stephens returned to the wagon to fetch her medical kit. Mrs. Tenney smirked at her brother, though Nora pretended not to see that.

"Nora, why don't you hold his hand?" his sister said. "So we can keep his arm steady. It's gonna hurt, and I don't want him to flinch. Jasper, you squeeze if you need to, but you hold your arm still."

Nora swallowed hard but tried to hide her nerves. She offered Jasper her hand. When he wrapped his fingers around hers he gave her a light squeeze.

She squeezed back.

"What kind of man do you think I am?" Jasper challenged, though without his heart in it.

"A man with an arrowhead deep in your arm. Come on, now. Don't fight me on this."

Between the three women, they managed to extract the arrowhead from his muscle and clean and bandage up the wound without too much more damage. The yelling they couldn't do anything about. Nora felt like her fingers were about broken with as hard as Jasper crushed her hand during the worst of the pain.

When they were almost done, Mrs. Stephens and Mrs. Tenney started laughing, teasing Jasper about the fuss he was putting up.

"How about I dig around in your arm with something sharp and see how you like it?"

That only made them laugh harder. Nora didn't think Jasper could even make a convincing threat of such violence, let alone carry it out.

The intimacy between the Stephenses, the way they interacted and how close they all seemed reminded Nora so much of the Rayburn family. Though, of course, there were fewer siblings, that closeness and love was there all the same.

"All right. Of course," Mrs. Tenney said, as she placed the clean folded fabric against the open wound. "We're done now. Just don't get shot again."

Nora watched as she secured the bandage. She felt at a loss, superfluous, and she almost made her excuses to leave the Stephenses' camp, when the other two women left instead. Mrs. Stephens and Mrs. Tenney left Nora and Jasper alone while they attended to their own inventory and what they had lost. Nora thought she saw Jasper's sister wink at him as she walked away, but she wasn't sure.

She was alone with Jasper.

She had rushed to his side in his moment of need and now she was alone with him.

Nora blushed, but kept her focus steadfastly on the bandage, checking the tightness with the tips of her fingers, as though his mother had not just done that very thing. The two sat in the dirt, leaning against the front wheel of the wagon, as alone and far away from listening ears as they could get in a crowded camp like this.

"Thank you for coming to check on me," Jasper finally said, lightly.

Nora looked up at him. It had been so long since they had been this close together, and she had forgotten how green his eyes were. Though his tone seemed almost glib, his expression was earnest. He really did seem grateful for her attention.

She smiled shyly. He grinned back and nudged her.

"Thank you," he said again.

Nora looked over her shoulder where his family had disappeared to. She wasn't sure how long she had until his mother returned, or until they would have a quiet moment like this. She couldn't be sure that the chance for such honesty would ever present herself. Reminding herself how much she had hidden her true feelings and hopes from Jimmy, Nora knew she had to speak frankly. Though the prospect was utterly terrifying, she forced herself to be brave.

"I almost didn't," she admitted. "I was so embarrassed about how rude I was the other day, and there are so many others that I could help." She gestured to the camp. "I wasn't sure you wanted to see me."

He frowned. "I did wonder why you seemed so ... so distant. I wasn't sure if I had done something wrong or not..."

He trailed off, giving her space to speak.

"I was..." Nora frowned, and resettled herself so she could look directly at him rather that sit shoulder to shoulder. "Mr. Stephens— Jasper, you ... You really hurt me. The other night, the dance after the Platte River. I mean, I know we haven't known each other very long, let alone made any kind of promises to each other, but I did think you would at least have acknowledged me somehow."

"What are you talking about?"

"And then to see you dance with Hattie was just—"

"Wait, Nora. The dance? I think maybe we have been misunderstanding each other. I didn't know you wanted to dance with me. I saw you helping Miss Norton, and that was so kind of you, but it made me think you were probably too... too busy. You seemed like the type of girl to be too serious and responsible to want to do something as frivolous as waltz. I asked Hattie to dance because I assumed you would turn me down."

Nora felt a wave of relief wash over her, tempered with disappointment. "Oh. All right. Yes, I suppose I can see how that might happen."

"I'm so sorry. It was wrong of me to assume."

Nora nodded, taking it all in.

"All right. I ... I'll have to think about this."

"Okay." He nodded. "If there's anything..." He ducked his head and looked away. "Gosh, Nora. I'm sorry. If there's anything I can do to make it up to you. This misunderstanding is just ..."

"I know," she said softly.

They sat in silence for a few moments, each lost in their own thoughts. Nora wanted nothing more than to believe him whole-heartedly. She could admit she was wrong. She could put it all behind her.

But, then, if she was wrong she might get hurt again.

Nora resolved to be cautious. Optimistic, but careful.

She placed a hand on Jasper's good arm, gave it a light squeeze, and got to her feet.

"I should get back to my own camp. My sister got hurt too, a little, and my mother will need help."

He nodded. "Of course. Thank you again. I can't thank you enough."

The men returned from the hunt not long after Nora made it back to her own camp, and they had the excitement and stress of telling her father all about the attack. Amy was upset that her sister had left, but Nora found time to return to Jasper later that night and then again the following morning just before the wagons left. Though others in the company had been injured just as badly, Nora's focus on Jasper Stephens was lost on none of the members of either family.

She just told herself he needed help, and that was one thing she was always happy to offer.

CHAPTER TWENTY-THREE

Captains Sullivan and Mills did not make the frightened emigrants stay any longer in that place, with all its memories of the attack, than they had to. Early the following morning, the wagons were on the Oregon Trail, headed west. The boon of the buffalo meat helped keep everyone's spirits up, though it wasn't enough to replace all the food and staples that the Indians had stolen.

Nora was grateful—and a bit guilty—that they hadn't lost more. They could manage. Some of the families in the company had lost so much, either stolen or destroyed, that they were distraught. Mothers were left uncertain that they would have enough sustenance to feed their children. The Coles, at least, had enough for now.

But they didn't have long to wait. After only a couple days hurrying westward, the wagons reached Fort Laramie. It was originally built as a trading post, the previous year the U.S. Army had purchased the fort, and stationed soldiers there to help the Americans heading west feel safe. The fort boasted fifteen-foot-tall walls all around the center square where emigrants could take refuge in the event of another attack. Two guards were posted at either corner, watching over both the Americans and the native women who had built huts just outside the walls of the fort. Nora caught her breath when she saw them. The sight of Indians might always frighten her. But these seemed women like any other and too busy with their own domestic duties to be of any danger.

Arriving at Fort Laramie was the end of a long, stressful several days of travel. Though it was small and roughly thrown together, it offered the first real roof, the first protective walls, that Nora had seen since they left Independence. The wagon company made camp in the afternoon and would stay for the rest of the day, giving each family a chance to recover some of their strength as well as purchase supplies to replace what had been stolen.

"Look for calico, please," Laura said to her husband, as he collected their cash before heading to the store in the fort. "Amy's going to need another new dress already, with the rip and blood in the old one."

"Mother," Amy said with a groan. "No more dresses."

"Oh, you want to run around in your bloomers and petticoat then? Fine. Tell your father."

Charlie just chuckled and kissed his wife's cheek. "I'll see what I can find."

"Whatever other food you can, too," Laura added. "We probably have enough, but any additional would make me feel better. We don't know what we're walking into. And coffee. Always coffee."

Charlie Cole strode off toward the fort, while his wife began heating up water for laundry. Nora had watched this exchange with amusement; she wouldn't mind having a new dress, but she also knew that was an unnecessary extravagance. It was the disadvantage of actually taking care of her things, instead of Amy's way of rushing headlong into anything dirty or complicated.

The afternoon wore on; Charlie returned with about half of what his wife had hoped, but that was better than nothing. And Nora continued to work. After several hours of baking extra biscuits for the days ahead, Nora thought she deserved a break. Everyone else was taking advantage of the afternoon; she would too.

As she washed her hands and made herself presentable, her sister watched her with some suspicion.

"Where are you going?" Amy asked. "I thought you were going to help me compose my letter to the rock scientists back east."

Nora sighed deeply, willing her frustration to dissipate. "Amy, firstly, that doesn't need to be done now. You won't even have a return address to give them. Secondly, you don't need me for that. You are more than capable, and I can't hold your hand at every turn. One of these days you're going to have to do it on your own."

She blinked at Nora, as the words slowly sunk in. "I do lots of stuff on my own."

"You do. Sometimes. When it's convenient for you. But what about when you needed to learn how to cook? Or when you were injured by the Indians?"

"I was shot with an arrow!"

"I know," Nora soothed. "I know, but you also got to watch Dr. Martell remove an arrowhead from Mrs. Alden's leg just a few hours later. You went and did that on your own just fine. It was kind of an exciting day for you."

"But what am I supposed to do by myself? I'm out of books."

"Look," Nora said, pointing. "Here comes Claire. Why don't you two go explore somewhere? There's the river, or the fort, or maybe the doctor will let you follow him around."

"Without you?"

"Without me."

Amy frowned. "Fine. I have been wanting to collect more rock samples to send back east with my letter."

"Perfect," Nora said, though inwardly she had already started thinking about how to talk her out of it.

Amy, likewise, tried to make herself presentable for other people. In her case, however, that just meant she tucked her loose hair behind her ears. She hurried to meet Claire, and though Nora couldn't hear their conversation from where she stayed near the wagon, their animation and excitement was apparent.

But after her sister had disappeared, Nora was left feeling a bit bereft. As much as she knew it would be best for both of them for Amy to exercise a little independence, Nora didn't know much what to do with herself when she was alone.

She took a deep breath, and turned to see her mother watching her surreptitiously.

"Is everything all right?" Laura asked, seemingly casual. "You're not going to go with your sister?"

"You heard all of that. There's no use pretending you didn't," Nora responded with a teasing lilt. "I finished the biscuits. I need a break."

She settled herself on the ground next to her mother and leaned into her, breathing in her scent. Sweat from their travels that day. The comforting aroma of lavender, which Laura had tucked into all of their trunks of linens. And the faint tartness of dried cherries. All of the odors of home and love that had surrounded Nora for as long as she could remember.

"She's fourteen. She's still figuring out who she is and how to be a person in this world," Laura said, as she continued to scrub a petticoat against the washboard. "You should be flattered she looks to you for an example of that."

"I am. But..."

The two women were silent a moment. Nora played with the hem of her apron, wondering what it would be like when Amy finally found her independence, separate from her sister.

"I know," her mother said gently. "What will you do instead today?"

Nora looked around at the campsite. Most of the emigrants had made their trips to the store at the fort already and were settling in for an afternoon of chores or rest. From where she sat by their own wagon, she could see Mrs. Sheldon climbing into their wagon. A bit past her Mr. Larson was sitting on the seat of his wagon, smoking a pipe, and looking out onto the prairie. In the other direction, the Gilroys were both huddled around their campfire, watching whatever they had cooking over it.

"I might go see if there's anything Mrs. Buchanan needs help with. Maybe. If you don't need me, that is. I'd like to just … I don't know what I want."

"No, love, you go on. I appreciate your thoughtfulness and your servant's heart. I'm mostly caught up for the moment on everything that needs doing, so you should enjoy your afternoon."

Nora leaned in again, and kissed her mother's shoulder lightly before climbing to her feet. She brushed the dust off her skirt and shaded her eyes as she looked toward the open prairie just past the walls of Fort Laramie. She was surprised by how safe she felt here, even after enduring the traumatic Indian attack. Any time she looked toward the fort she spotted at least one soldier, and knew there were probably dozens more inside. The Sullivan-Mills company weren't the only group of travelers that had stopped at the fort that day.

She was surrounded by people.

And all of those people could use her help.

Though nearly all the time Nora felt the pull to be of service and offered herself to whoever needed her, in this moment that felt overwhelming. She needed just a few moments to herself. Without going too far outside the campsite, Nora walked out into the open prairie. She turned away from the fort and all the settlement; she tried to shut all the noise from her ears and just appreciate the wide-open expanse of the frontier. In the far distance she thought she spotted a couple wild horses, and smiled to think of all the life that was just beyond her sight.

Every day on the Oregon Trail felt sparse and desperate, but there really was a whole new world all around her. Just because it looked different from what she was used to in Michigan did not make it less real.

"Why, hello, Miss Cole. What brings you here? What do you have planned for your afternoon?"

Nora turned to see that Jasper Stephens had also left the circle of their wagons.

"Hello, Jasper."

He strode toward her across the packed earth, carrying a small barrel in his good arm. He wore a new shirt, in a chocolate brown that perfectly matched his dark hair; the bandage on his injured arm was hidden beneath the sleeve.

Nora felt her face break into the widest smile. She hadn't had reason to visit with him in the several days the company took to travel to the fort. Though she had tried not to think about it too much, Nora couldn't help but wonder what he was doing during that time, wondering if he was thinking about her as much as she thought about him. Hoping that she was not imagining the connection that she had felt the last time they spoke.

"I hadn't decided what I was going to do," she continued. "My mother wants me to take time for myself, and my sister went off with a friend, so I guess I'm on my own. I thought about seeing if Mrs. Buchanan or Mrs. Sullivan needed any help, since they are both one fewer person than when we left Missouri, but I just got distracted here." She gestured at the fort that had so claimed her attention. "I think there might be wild horses out there, past the hill."

"I don't blame you. Feels almost unnatural to see wooden walls now after all these weeks without." He chuckled. "Wonder how long it will take us to get used to it in Oregon."

"I think if I can wake up with just a few less bug bites each morning, I will get used to that real quick."

He chuckled again and Nora blushed at the unspoken approval.

"Well, I don't want to take you away from someone who needs it more," Jasper said, "but if you're looking for someone to help, I need to sort out all these nails this afternoon. It won't be impossible with my injury, but it will go a lot faster with both of us."

"Sort them?"

"When the Indians attacked last week, all of our hardware and tools got overturned and mixed together. There aren't more than a few dozen of these—maybe a couple hundred—but they're in four different sizes and my pa wanted them sorted out now that we have some time. I was thinking I'd go find a spot in the shade, maybe near the water, to sit and get it done. I'd love if you joined me."

"Yes, please, of course," Nora responded without a second thought. "I would love to."

A whole afternoon with Jasper? And being able to help him at the same time? There was nothing Nora would rather be doing that afternoon.

CHAPTER TWENTY-FOUR

That afternoon with Jasper was a memory that Nora lived on for days afterward. Sorting nails of various sizes was easy and mindless enough that most of her attention could be put on him. On the two of them together. Not that their conversation had been particularly intimate or life-changing, but it was the longest stretch of time that she had gotten with him. Doing so had dispelled all her worry that they might not have anything in common or might not know how to be with each other.

But once the wagon company left camp the following morning, there was too much to do and too many miles to cross for her to get to see him anytime soon.

"Nora, Amy," their father called early one morning a couple days after they had left the fort. "I need you to keep an eye on Cinnamon today. She's gonna roam the prairie a bit, but we don't want her to get too far."

"Why aren't you hitching up Cinnamon?" Amy asked.

All the emigrants of the Sullivan-Mills wagon company were finishing up their last packing, final steps, and preparations before beginning the long trek for another day. Before leaving Fort Laramie, they had again collected as much water as they could carry to keep both man and beast alive over the next stretch of trail. But there was so far to go without enough grass or water that the captains were driving the company forward at a punishing pace.

It was taking its toll.

"She's tired," Mr. Cole said. "Did you notice how she was limping a little last night? Captain Mills suggested that those of us that can spare it to let one or another of our animals free for at least a few hours. And then maybe tomorrow, we'll let Cayenne roam a bit. Just a bit of rest without having to haul all two thousand pounds of this wagon will help a lot. We need these guys to last a long way, yet."

"I'm sure having to pull these wagons over the ruts, or even where there's no road, isn't helping," Nora said, gently patting the animal's neck. "You poor thing. You must be more tired than we are."

"We'll make it," her father assured her. "They'll all make it. We just need to be careful now, while we still can be. Before we're asking the animals to haul these prairie schooners up any hills."

Though many of the families took similar precautions over the next couple days, for the Gladwell family it was not enough. One afternoon the entire caravan was held up for an hour or so when one of the Gladwells' oxen collapsed in its harness, splayed across the trail, and refusing to get to its feet again. Slowly, the wagons behind the Gladwells diverted off the trail, around the collapsed animal, until there were enough men free to move the fallen oxen.

Nora looked back over her shoulder after she passed it, her heart broken for the poor creature and for the Gladwells that would now have to keep moving with fewer resources. But at the same time, she said a prayer of gratitude for her own family, her own draft team. They would get over the mountains into Oregon somehow.

The enormous draft animal was not the only thing discarded on the side of the trail. They were beginning to pass litter every few yards or so. Not ten yards beyond the fallen ox, they passed another discarded item. Every family that was attempting the journey to Oregon had to make difficult decisions about what part of their life in the east they would bring with them, and that decision was not always made logically. Rather than put any more strain on the hardy animals that were carrying them west, many emigrants chose to discard their heaviest pieces—occasionally tools or furniture.

Just after the Gladwells' fallen animal, Nora walked past a fine old cherrywood desk, with intricately carved legs and a wide, smooth top. This piece of furniture had been loved enough to be brought this far west; it had maybe even been a family heirloom. But someone had had to make the difficult decision to leave it behind, set out at the mercy of the elements.

It broke Nora's heart for whoever had to let it go.

And it made her wish fervently her family wouldn't need to do anything as drastic.

The trail from Fort Laramie was monotonous and

drudging. Wind blew around the dry dust, through the sagebrush, across the paths the emigrants were striving to traverse each day. The grass for the animals was scarce; the water was sulphuric and bloated their bellies. Worry creased Charlie Cole's brow as he struggled through every day to keep his animals as healthy as possible. The company had to travel fifteen miles each day in order to stay on schedule, and the punishing pace took its toll.

In addition to the discarded furniture or silver platters, at least once every couple of miles the wagon company came upon the rotting carcass of a cow or mule, pulled off the trail. Most of the bodies showed evidence of other animals—wolves and vultures—that had descended once the humans were gone. The carcasses had been moved out of the way of the wagons, but not out of range of the odor. Nora covered her mouth and nose with her apron when she could, but even then it was impossible to avoid the stench.

Through all of it, she found few opportunities to seek out Jasper, or he her. If she wasn't needed by her parents, there were innumerable other ways she could be of service, and nearly all of them far more pressing than anything Jasper might need her for. His wound from the arrowhead was practically healed by now, and there was precious little reason for her to be at his side otherwise.

Nevertheless, Nora found plenty to keep her busy. Though occasionally she had to pretend she had more energy than she did, Nora never said no. The Buchanan children often needed looking after, while their mother attended to the mountain of chores required to survive on the trail every day. Betty and Johnny were old enough to haul water and find fuel for the campfire, but most of the time they were left unattended. Nora regularly found herself helping the Jameson boys, as they had no women in their party, or Eliza Davis, trying to raise three boys on her own. Occasionally, Abby Mills would seek her out for whatever project her mother had set her to, or the doctor asked for an extra hand in dressing a wound.

Nora never said no. There was always a batch of biscuits to make, a pile of laundry to mend, or a stack of dishes to clean. She was getting quite good at all the duties necessary for living life out of a wagon; it seemed as though every family in the company knew she was someone they could call on when they needed aid.

Other than helping Jasper with his wound and bandage that first day after the Indian attack, she hadn't yet found another reason to assist him. He was capable and reliable, and her skills were needed elsewhere.

That just left Nora with more time for daydreams, more space to imagine how her future with Jasper could be.

That same afternoon that the wagon company had to detour around the Gladwells' animal, Amy talked her sister into exploring out on the prairie while the caravan continued on.

"If we go far enough away from the trail, maybe we won't be able to smell all the dead things," she suggested.

"That does sound tempting."

"There's supposed to be these animals called prairie dogs," she said. "I don't know why they're called dogs. They're smaller than that. A foot tall or so."

The two girls strode out a good fifty yards from the trail. They were close enough to be heard if they yelled, but Amy was right that the mess and stench from every-thing that had been left along the trail was far from them. With such space, they walked slowly across the prairie, looking carefully at where she stepped as Nora followed close behind her.

"If they're not dogs, what are they?"

"I don't know. Maybe like rats or rabbits?"

"I'm not sure I care to see a big rat, Amy."

"Look!" Amy whispered, as she pointed to a spot about twenty feet ahead of them. "Hold still."

The sisters froze, watching as a small, sleek tan head poked up out of the ground and looked around.

"It's kind of cute," Nora whispered.

As they watched, a second head and then a third poked up out of the ground from spots about ten feet or so past the first. One of them ducked down again. Another darted out of its hole to collect something on the ground a few feet away and then darted back. The first one, the prairie dog closest to the girls, turned around and let out a kind of chirping bark to the others.

"What are they doing?"

"I don't know," Amy responded excitedly. "That's why we're here! To watch and learn, and maybe I can send a letter describing their behavior to one of the universities back east, and then scientists will know to come out and study them more carefully."

Nora looked at her sister in wonder. This fourteen-year-old was unfailingly confident, despite the oddities that interested her.

But before she could say anything about it, her atten-tion was drawn to a cloud of dust creeping along the trail toward them.

"What do you think that is about?" Nora asked, pointing.

Amy shifted her attention to the new curiosity at once. "Let's go see!"

She hurried on ahead, back to the wagon caravan, toward whatever was heading east along the Oregon Trail. When the girls got about even with the Sullivan wagon, they stopped to watch.

"Captain Sullivan!" Amy called out, bold as brass to the older man. The captain rode his horse alongside the trail, while the oldest Sullivan boy, Junior, drove their lead wagon. "What is that?"

"Turnarounds," he called back. "Folks that have had enough of the struggle and are heading back home."

"Goodness, why on earth would they do that?" Nora asked.

"Imagine if you lost more than one of your draft animals. Or both of your parents. I bet you'd be thinking about turning around too."

"Not me," Amy insisted. "It's just not logical. They're already so far on the way to Oregon."

"Maybe. But some people aren't as strong as you are, Miss Cole. Now, if you'll excuse me, ladies."

The captain tipped his hat at them, and rode off to meet the wagon that was slowly traveling back east.

CHAPTER TWENTY-FIVE

Nora was busy helping Betty and Jack Buchanan practice their addition and subtraction when Independence Rock first came into view. She had been quizzing them as they were walking together near the front of the caravan, parallel to where Billy Whitson was driving the Buchanan wagon.

After learning about turnarounds, that some people so suffered along the Oregon Trail that they couldn't even make it all the way, Nora had thrown herself even more into helping her neighbors than before. They had already lost so much; if Nora could have anything to do with it they would not be losing any more.

She couldn't bear it if one of them decided to turn back if there was anything she could do to ease their burden.

"And if you have three pebbles in one hand and two in the other, how many is that?" she asked the children.

The little ones walked by Nora's side across the plains as the wagons rolled ever westward. The bright sun overhead made Nora grateful for her bonnet, but she could feel the sweat trickle down her back. This dress would need to be washed again as soon as they reached another river. She looked up at the sky as she waited for the little girl's response; there was not a cloud anywhere to be seen. No chance of shade or relief.

"Betty? Do you need help counting?"

"What's that, Miss Nora?"

Nora looked to see where Betty had pointed, to see what had so distracted her. There on the horizon was what she now recognized as another of the enormous granite monuments that had peppered the trail for the last few weeks. Every single one of them had taken her breath away. There was nothing like these monuments in Michigan.

She knew from Amy's repeated lectures that they would be reaching Independence Rock any day. And even with so many of these similar granite milestones on the trail, Independence Rock was different. Independence Rock was one of the most important landmarks along the journey. Amy had told her it was named such because the emigrants would aim to reach it by July fourth, and the Sullivan-Mills company was only a few days off of that pace.

All thought of math forgotten, over the rest of the morning the wagon company closed the distance to the gigantic boulder, excited and eager to have made it this far.

The wagon company made camp in the early afternoon and would be staying the rest of the day at Independence Rock. There they had plenty of room, plenty of water, and if they camped close enough to the rock, they had protection too. As the Cole family settled in to their campsite, Mrs. Cole shooed her daughters away.

"Go on, now. Enjoy an afternoon off. Everything past this point is going to be a lot rougher than we've had to deal with so far, and I don't want you girls thinking you want to turn around like that couple we spotted a few days ago."

Amy didn't need to be told twice. She ran off toward the McKinnon wagon without even a glance back at her sister. Nora supposed she didn't have a right to be hurt by that, given how she had insisted her sister find her own entertainment when they had been at the fort. Still, without her sister to think of, Nora was at a bit of a loss for how to spend her afternoon.

She could do laundry, of course. This dress did need a good scrub.

But still Independence Rock called to her, drew her toward it. She needed to get closer.

Thinking that she might meet a friend on the trail there, Nora set off for the big stone by herself. Solitude was hard to come by these days, with so many people living in such close quarters. She had to go off into the literal wilderness if she wanted to be alone ever.

Even as she had that thought, she was interrupted by someone calling her name from behind her.

"Nora!"

She turned to see Jasper striding up the path quickly. Her face broke into a wide smile.

"Jasper, I haven't seen you in days. Has Mr. Gilroy been keeping you busy?"

"Afternoon off, you know. Would you like to hike up to the rock with me?"

"Up there?" She squinted into the sun. "Goodness, are those people at the top? How on earth did they get up there?"

"There's a path. It's pretty steep, though. Might not be easy to do in your dress."

"Oh, well..." She wanted so badly to give him what he asked for; she wanted so badly to be exactly what he wanted her to be.

But he sensed her hesitation and offered her an alternative.

"Or we can go around it, to the other side by the water?"

"I would love that," Nora responded gratefully.

"Come on."

There was a well-traveled trail that wound around the perimeter of Independence Rock, where years of emigrants had wandered on their journey across the continent. A strong, narrow river crept across the land-scape, around the rock and onward toward the southwest.

Jasper led the way, glancing at Nora repeatedly to make sure she was all right, that she was with him, that she seemed happy. They walked close together; Nora thrilled when the back of his hand accidentally brushed against hers. She kept trying to sneak looks at him, but he seemed to be doing the same. Their eyes met more than once on that short walk, and Nora felt herself thrill all over.

When they reached the river, there were already at least a dozen women and girls there collecting water for whatever chores they had planned that afternoon. Jasper led them farther upstream, away from the crowd, away from listening ears.

When they stopped, around a slight curve in the water and in the shade of Independence Rock, Nora stopped and looked up again at all the silhouettes that peppered the top of it.

"It must be a lovely view from up there," she said.

"You sure you don't want to climb up? I'll make sure you get to the top."

"No. Thank you, though. I think I would rather this quiet view that no one else has. It reminds me of Lake Erie back home. There was so much coastline that I could always find a quiet spot to sit and watch the little waves come in. I would walk for miles just looking for the perfectly smooth rocks that had been worn down to softness."

They were both quietly thoughtful for a moment, before Jasper spoke again.

"Do you miss it?"

"Michigan?"

"Yes. I imagine it was hard to leave your friends ... or your beau," he suggested.

Nora blushed. "There was no beau."

She walked to the edge of the water, thinking about his question. Did she miss it? Life was certainly different now, but she was not at all prepared to say what she had had in her hometown was better, necessarily. And certainly, her dreams about Jimmy Rayburn were long gone.

"I think," she began. "I think what I miss is the idea I had of what my life could be. I spent a lot of time dreaming about creating my own home, and building a family. I had this idea of what my future would be. Every time I sat down to stitch together patchwork my mind wandered over the decades to come. I'm sure I spent more time in the future than in my everyday sometimes."

He listened thoughtfully.

"But none of that was real," she finished. "I miss something that I made up in my mind and was never going to really happen."

They were quiet for a moment. The longer the silence went on, the more embarrassed she became. What must he think of her, a grown woman, imagining things into her life?

"Do you feel like you're still dreaming a lot of the future?" he asked gently.

Nora chuckled. "Not nearly as much as I used to, and yet I'm sure it's still more than a lot of girls. I suppose that's just who I am, always anticipating what comes next."

She moved aside her skirt and sat in the grass that abutted the edge of the river, turning her back on Independence Rock and instead looking out toward the flat land.

"I need to get better at noticing what is actually in front of me," she said without looking at him, "instead of imagining it into what I want it to be."

Jasper sat in the grass next to her, shoulder to shoulder looking over the water. "Don't let go of all your dreams, Nora."

"Maybe just the more flighty ones," she responded with a grin.

"Maybe like those stones you found at Lake Erie...

The Oregon Trail might be wearing you down, but maybe it's just taking off your more impractical edges. By the time we get to Oregon you'll be even more kind and reliable than you had been before."

Nora blinked at him, absorbing his description of her. "I love that," she said finally. "I had been feeling like this journey was changing me, but I think you're right. It could be for the better."

She asked him about his work with Mr. Gilroy. It seemed as though the journey was changing everyone. As though even just choosing to go on such an adventure changed a person.

They talked on and on for hours, until Nora shivered. The sun was low in the sky by that time. She had spent all afternoon with Jasper without realizing how much time had passed. They now sat fully in the shadow of Independence Rock and she didn't have a shawl.

"I should get back. It must be close to supper time." She climbed to her feet.

"You're right." He stood, brushing off his trousers. "Pa will be wondering where I got off to."

"Thank you," Nora said, a little shy now that the prospect of returning to their real life, to their responsibilities, loomed. "This afternoon has been lovely. It almost feels unreal."

"I know exactly what you mean."

They walked back together, along the trail, winding around the monument, back to their wagon company. Shyness stole over Nora now that they were back among people. Jasper seemed different when the two of them were alone, and coming back to the group felt like a spell breaking.

When she got back to her own wagon, her mother informed her that the pastor had been by that afternoon, telling everyone about his plans for a sunset church service.

"We'll have a quick supper," she said, "then go over to the spot at the foot of the rock where he said to gather. Goodness, I'm sure I've missed such gatherings. When Pastor Montgomery said he would be leading worship services, I just about hugged the man."

Accordingly, about forty minutes later, the Cole family made their way to the gathering near the foot of the rock where the pastor had indicated. There were small boulders scattered throughout the space that some women had chosen as chairs. Nora had brought her quilt and spread it over the grass as her own seat.

The Coles got settled as more families joined the gathering.

"Come sit," Amy said, gesturing Claire over.

The two girls settled in next to each other, next to Nora on her quilt.

"Amy said you spent all afternoon with Jasper Stephens," Claire said, her whole face lit up with admiration. "She said you two weren't seen until supper."

Pastor Montgomery moved to the head of the crowd, holding his hands up to quiet everyone down. "Thank you all for coming tonight."

"I'll tell you later," Nora assured the two younger girls with a whisper.

Projecting out over the crowd as he took his place at the front, Pastor Montgomery began the service. "I hope this evening serves as a balm to your souls. But first, let's pray."

CHAPTER TWENTY-SIX

After the worship service that night at Independence Rock, Nora went straight to bed. Though it was still early, only a bit after sunset, she had a lot to think about, a lot of new, sweet memories to pour over and tuck into her heart. She was drained from so much emotion coursing through her, and cherished her quiet night.

Leaving Independence Rock the following morning almost felt like a new chance for Nora. She and Jasper had seemed disconnected for weeks, almost as though they weren't speaking the same language, or on the same schedule. But that small bit of time alone to really talk and share her heart with him had made Nora immensely more optimistic about the future—their future. They had reset. She hoped. But, there was still the fact that he seemed to want to charm everyone he met, and the fact that between his chores and her commitments to the other families, every minute of every day was spoken for.

And it would only get worse from here.

As Nora helped her mother pack up their camp that

next morning, she reminded herself that there was still a long way to go to Oregon, hundreds of miles. She would still need to guard her heart. Katie and Hattie hadn't come up at all in her conversation with Jasper the day before. Was that a deliberate avoidance by him or an oversight by her?

There was too much to consider right now, not when every day they were still fighting for survival.

But maybe it would be okay to hope.

As the wagon company put Independence Rock behind them, Captains Mills and Sullivan set a punishing pace. They were several days behind schedule and each day they spent not yet in Oregon meant food for each person, grass and water for each animal, not to mention the heightened risk of getting stuck in the mountains over the winter. No one wanted to think about what might happen if that happened, while at the same time each person reminded themselves of what had happened to the Donners just a few years earlier. In the meantime, there were still more than one thousand miles to traverse.

The next place the company would stay longer than overnight was Pacific Springs, and the promise of fresh water and sweet grass for the animals kept them all going through the exhaustion.

With the monotony of the Great Plains was behind them, the landscape slowly morphed from flat land with tall granite monuments, to low rolling mounds not quite tall enough to be called hills. Low scrub carpeted every-where Nora looked, the parallel ruts of the trail only faintly cutting through across the landscape. The eleva-tion was climbing, though subtly. Mostly Nora noticed the chill in the air when she woke up. Each morning she would wrap a shawl around her while she went about her chores, and by noon each day the overhead sun had driven her to put the shawl away.

A couple days after the trail began the climb into the hills, Nora was walking with her family alongside the team and wagon when they heard celebratory shouting from up ahead.

"What under the canopy has happened now?" Mrs. Cole exclaimed.

"We must be at the Continental Divide," Amy said, her whole face lit up with excitement. "The guidebook says that it's halfway to Oregon."

"Halfway?" Nora said. "It seems like we should be farther than that."

Cheers and gunshots sounded, drowning out the shouts from the families who were crossing the divide ahead of them.

"I'm going to go see," Amy declared, before darting on ahead.

"Don't let your tiredness keep you from celebrating," her father said to Nora, as he wrapped his free arm around her shoulders. "We've all come a long way. We've gone through a lot to get here. We've made it much farther than most folks, and we should be proud of that. Go on with your sister."

Nora didn't point out that people like Jeb Buchanan or Jeremiah Sullivan hadn't made it this far, despite trying, despite their courage. But her father was right. They were halfway now. There were fewer miles ahead of them than behind them.

But instead of yelling and cheering about it, Nora

walked calmly up the incline to where close to a dozen people of all ages, including Amy, were perched. Like wild children, they waved hats over their heads and cheered on every wagon that crested the low hill to the other side of the divide. She watched the rumpus in grateful wonder.

Halfway. They had made it halfway to Oregon.

If she had known how difficult of a journey it would have been when they left Michigan, she would not have been nearly as eager to leave as she had been. The girl she had been back at home was full of idealized daydreams and romance. Now, she knew the truth of what it meant to set off on what she had once called an adventure. This journey had been far more struggle than the easy fun she had expected.

She lingered at the divide, watching the wagons cross over, until the Stephens family's wagon passed. Nora's heart beat faster at the prospect of seeing Jasper again, even if from that distance.

But that hope was in vain. Mr. and Mrs. Stephens walked with their team, leading the wagon down the trail, but their children were nowhere to be seen.

Where could Jasper be?

She immediately suspected the worst; her mind raced with unfounded suspicions and worries that she couldn't shake. The entire relief of making this milestone was ruined for her. With a heavy heart, Nora made her way down the low hill and hurried ahead back to her own wagon and the rest of the day's travel.

By the end of the day, the wagon company was making camp in Pacific Springs. Amy dragged Nora to the water as soon as she could, eager to see the river flowing west, instead of east, for the first time.

"Do you think it tastes different since it's going west?" she asked. "We should try it. I wonder if we have any water left in one of the canteens to test it against the eastbound water. It will be an experiment."

Nora looked around to the others that had made their way to the river the first thing after making camp.

"You don't see any of the Stephenses, do you? Or Mrs. Tenney?"

Amy looked at her, narrowing her eyes. "Why?"

"No reason, Amy. It's not important. I was just wondering. Let's fill this bucket and then go back to camp and do your experiment. You can tell Miss Atkins all about it when she holds class again."

Amy was thus easily distracted, and Nora tried to follow her example, putting her questions about Jasper from her mind.

Reaching Pacific Springs felt like the end of a race, and yet they still couldn't rest. There was still so far to go. The wagon company remained at that camp long enough to eat, sleep, and again fill every single container they carried with water. It seemed incredible that there could be so many stretches of terrain without fresh water and yet so many men and women had already made the journey, with so many more every year. Why would a person subject themselves to such exhaustion, such testing of their fortitude?

To Nora, such a practice was becoming grating. Why couldn't the earlier explorers have found a trail across the continent with more fresh water? How could this be the best way to get to Oregon?

Through every one of these hurdles, Nora still held an optimistic hope that Oregon would be the fulfillment of all her dreams. She just wished she had more than only a half dozen conversations with Jasper on which to base such dreams. It couldn't be helped that they both had more work than could fit into a single day, but she did wish that he could make her more of a priority.

But her frustration vanished when Mrs. Gladwell showed up at the Coles' camp one night begging for water. One of her children had accidentally knocked over one of the buckets of water the family had been keeping, and there was every reason to think the family would become dangerously dehydrated if their neighbors didn't help them.

They had been on the trail for three months now, since the end of April, and the fatigue could not be ignored. Everyone was being stretched thin. It seemed as though each time they stopped for more than a couple hours someone had a wagon repair to make. Women had to get creative with what meals they could make with an ever-diminishing list of ingredients. More and more spoiled sides of bacon or awkward overstuffed armchairs were being discarded by the side of the trail as priorities were crystallized.

Still, they pressed on, day after day. The company reached another fresh water source, and all the canteens could be refilled. These tiny moments of reprieve seemed just enough to keep each person going, but only just. It was a small mercy.

But before the day came to a close, Daniel Mills came by the Cole family's camp with news of yet another tribulation they would need to get through.

Several members of the wagon company had come down with Mountain Fever. Chills, fever, exhaustion and in some cases delirium had claimed at least eight members of the caravan so far, and threatened to take more. The company would keep pushing west—they couldn't afford to lose any more days—but anyone not sick would need to dig deep to find a heretofore unrealized fortitude.

Nora went to bed that night with thoughts of that quiet, peaceful beach at Lake Erie, that time in her life when the most pressing thing she had to worry about was whether or not Jimmy Rayburn would ask her to dance.

Who knew what new strife the morning would bring.

CHAPTER TWENTY-SEVEN

"Why do you think Mountain Fever hits only in high elevation?" Amy asked. "Is it something in the air here?"

The two sisters were sitting by their campfire at the end of another long day. With so many members of the wagon company taken ill, the labor and capable bodies were stretched even further than they had been. To Nora, it seemed as though everyone was at their breaking point. She had spent that day helping the Sheldon children herd their cows, so their oldest boy could drive the wagon of a different family. Everyone was pitching in; everyone wanted to be done.

"I bet I could ask Dr. Martell," Amy continued. "He must know, don't you think? Do you think anyone will die from this?"

"Goodness, Amy. Hold your tongue for once, please. We shouldn't ever be looking forward to anyone dying, but especially not out here on the trail."

"I'm not looking forward to it," she protested

matter-of-factly. "I'm just wondering. It's interesting to think about is all."

Nora rested her head in her hands and closed her eyes to shut out her sister. She didn't have the energy for this conversation. Keeping track of wandering bovines had been more exhausting than she ever would have guessed. Too late, Nora wished she had thought to learn to drive a team of oxen. She could have been so much more helpful to these people that were so in need.

But Nora was doing her best. Each person in the wagon company was doing their best.

With as swamped as the emigrants had been, Nora had not seen or spoken to Jasper in several days, and the wonder about how he was spending his time wore on her. She hadn't heard that any of the Stephenses had fallen ill, but that was all that could be said.

"Girls?" Mrs. Cole appeared from the back of the wagon, with her hands full. "You're not feeling feverish are you? Extra tired or anything?"

"Of course we're extra tired," Nora said. "Everyone's tired."

Her mother pursed her lips, but didn't comment on Nora's poor attitude. "I'm about to start supper, so you still have some minutes to rest. Just take it easy a bit."

Nora watched her walk away with a pang of guilt, but after her full day of herding she didn't have enough energy to do anything about it. She had felt on the verge of tears since she had woken up; if she was ever granted a moment alone, the tears might come unbidden. After everything the company had been through, now there was this one more thing, another demand on her time.

How much longer could they all do this?

After a quiet moment, Amy said, "I heard John Harper took ill today, too. There's just him and his sister and she's trying to drive the wagon by herself."

"Well, someone has to," Nora said, head buried again in her arms.

Amy, for once, didn't have any response to that.

Later, long after supper, they learned about the death of little Ruth Goldman. She had been only four years old, possibly not even old enough to remember her life back east, but now she would get no farther.

Nora cried herself to sleep that night.

When she woke with the dawn, she sought in vain that bright morning optimism that had carried her so many miles. Away from the home she grew up in, away from the heartache and drudgery. Never before had the first light of day failed to bring with it a clean outlook. But this morning, after so many days of struggle heaped on top of exhaustion and uncertainty, Nora began to feel as though she had simply used up all of her hope. There were no more rose-colored glasses to see this journey through.

Her family was all still asleep for the moment, but Nora needed to get moving. If she stayed curled up under her quilt, the gloom would continue to weigh on her.

Feeling a bit numb, Nora set out to collect the fuel she needed for the morning campfire. There were virtually no trees here on this high desert plateau, and the few that had been here were long ago cut down for firewood by all the wagons that had come before. Instead,

Nora pulled on her boots, tied on a dirty apron, and walked off into the scrub to see if she could find any dry buffalo chips. Even those would be scarce, but without some kind of fuel they would never get a fire.

But before she had gone more than ten feet away from her camp, Lewis Jameson approached, hat in hand.

"Miss Cole, if I could have a moment..." he began. "It's the captain."

"What?" Nora asked breathlessly.

Lewis nodded. "William Sullivan passed in the night."

A sob choked out of her. "Oh, no. Oh, Lewis, no. Captain Sullivan? How much more can we take?"

He shook his head. "Guess we gotta leave that to Providence, Miss Cole. Pastor Montgomery will be holding the funeral service in an hour or so, if you all would like to pay your respects. And then we'll leave right after."

"So soon? Doesn't his family need time to mourn, at least?"

"We can't afford to take any more time, I think. Seems to me Captain Sullivan would want it this way. Now, if you'll excuse me, I have more families to reach."

She nodded, and went to tell her own family the heart-breaking news, before cleaning her face and getting ready for the funeral. The campfire would have to wait.

The captain's death marked one of the lowest points of their journey—more than the Indian attack, more than the deaths of all the children they had lost. This man had been an anchor, a stalwart, to many of the members of the company. Men in the company had gone to William Sullivan to discuss their options for their families, to seek inclusion with the company headed west. Women in the company had gone to William Sullivan to plead for more time or inquire about the doctor or teacher included in their number.

Captain Sullivan had touched the lives of every single member of the wagon company, and saying good-bye to him was one of the hardest things many of them had had to do.

And then they were traveling west again, leaving Captain Sullivan's body in a shallow, hastily dug grave, piled over with stones to discourage the scavengers from disturbing it. But they couldn't stop. They couldn't take any more time. They didn't even have a chance to erect a marker with his name on it.

Captain William Sullivan would be lost to history, recorded only in the hearts of those he had helped get this far on the Oregon Trail.

Onward west, the caravan with its dozen sick members kept pushing.

Nora wished that she could just talk to Jasper, just for a moment. She longed for the security and comfort that she had attributed to his presence. But there was no opportunity. Any free moments she had were few and far between and she couldn't be sure if he had any freedom either. If only their wagons were near each other. If only everyone wasn't so exhausted at the end of the day and there was another dance. If only...

But that's all her days were now... Just a long list of things she wished were different. The burst of enthusiasm that had carried her through the first half of the journey was long gone.

With one of the wagon company captains gone, more decisions had to be made. Captain Mills called a meeting with all the men, one representative from each family, to vote on the next step. The company was at a crossroads, and needed to decide what the biggest priority was. There were two different routes from where they were, each with a drawback but each with a benefit. When Charlie Cole left his camp to join the meeting, Nora took her chance to escape for a bit of alone time.

Telling her mother she was going to look for fuel for the campfire, Nora left the circle of wagons and got some space between herself and others. Just as they had the other night, tears welled up, spilling over onto her cheeks. She was so tired, so worn out. When would she ever get a break?

She had only found a few pieces of buffalo chips when the meeting had evidently broken up and dozens of men spread throughout the camp. Nora had expected to watch from a distance, taking her time to return to her own family, when she realized one of the men was coming straight toward her.

"Jasper!"

"Nora." He quickly closed the distance between them and enveloped her in a hug.

Her breath caught; the juxtaposition of her fatigue and the thrill of seeing him unbalanced her. Though they had touched before, it had never been this close.

"Are you all right?" she asked, muffled into his shoulder.

Jasper pulled away again. "I'm sorry. That was... I'm sorry. I'm just coming from the meeting with all the men and Captain Mills."

She had never seen him so somber.

"What is it?"

"Everyone voted. We're taking the longer route," Jasper said. "It adds about seven days to the journey, but there are enough families running low on food that we couldn't risk bypassing the promise of grass and a fort with a store."

"What if there's not enough at the fort, though? How will we make it with seven more days added?"

"I know, Nora." He took her hand in his and rubbed his thumb lightly over her knuckle. "I had the same thought. But some of these folks are just about desperate. If they don't get some kind of additional sustenance those seven days won't make a difference anyway."

"I can't think about that."

"I know. I know. Me either. So, tomorrow, we'll turn south a bit, to go around by way of Fort Bridger. It will still be a grueling pace, but at least the oxen will have grass and fresh water. There's no telling how many animals we would lose otherwise."

They were quiet for a moment, and Nora longed to feel his arms around her again. Longed to be comforted by his words and his presence.

"Do you think it's the right choice?" she asked quietly.

"I hope so. I just know there's a lot more to worry about now. I thought that seeing you might help me..." He stopped. Cleared his throat. "I need to go. I told Pa

I'd take care of the team before we leave this morning. I'll see you, Nora. Soon, I hope."

She opened her mouth to call after him, but she could see that his mind was on a plethora of other worries. He was no longer thinking about her.

She wondered if he ever did.

CHAPTER TWENTY-EIGHT

To make up time for the additional days they would be on the trail, Captain Mills had ordered that the wagon company would now be leaving at first light every day. With her heaviest shawl clutched around her, Nora went through her morning chores by the faint light of pre-dawn. Many of the families didn't even bother to build campfires, as there was so little time and so little fuel and they had to get moving.

But there was water and there was grass for the animals, and that had to be enough for now.

There were still a number of members of the wagon company laid low by Mountain Fever, but rest and waiting were luxuries none of them could afford. John Harper had emerged from his sick bed in time to drive his wagon, just when Louisa and Josie Hudson had taken to theirs. There was no cure but to keep going. Getting out of the elevation would help or it wouldn't. Their bodies would fight off the sickness or they wouldn't.

They would all make it to Oregon or they would not.

As often as she could find the time, Nora spent at the Valentine family's camp. Both Katie and her youngest sister Alma had been laid low by the sickness. Mrs. Valentine had so many other things on her hands that nursing a couple sick girls was the least Nora could do. It was just one more way she had said yes to helping, despite her own exhaustion.

One afternoon, she sat on the edge of her friend's cot inside the Valentine family's wagon, and placed a cool cloth on her forehead. Over the rumble of the loose crates in the wagon, Nora heard something and realized that in her fevered delirium Katie was saying something.

"Kay... Mbtu..."

Nora leaned forward, straining to hear. Maybe it was important. Maybe she would need to tell the girl's parents. Katie was mumbling, though, barely opening her lips. Whatever sounds she managed to make were not clarifying into words.

"Katie? Are you all right? Can I get you something?" Nora took the other girl's slim, cold hand in her own. "Katie," she whispered. "What is it?"

"Kay...let...Wuv..."

Nora frowned, unable to make any sense of it. Were these secrets? Was she asking for someone? Nora could only hope Katie regained her health, to give her a second chance to communicate whatever she had been trying to.

But by then, Katie had fallen back asleep, turning away from Nora, and burying her face in her pillow.

The next moment, Enid Valentine climbed into the wagon behind her. "I can take over for you, Nora. You deserve a rest, and I know riding inside a wagon can make a person sick."

Nora stood, disappointed to not have heard more. "It does," she said. "But I can manage if you all need me."

"It's my turn. I don't mind, really."

"All right." She looked back at her friend, Katie's face flush from the fever. "I hope she's better soon. I hope we all are."

Nora made her way slowly back to her own wagon. For the first time she fervently hoped that no one else needed her. She was past being done with this journey; every ounce of care had been wrung from her. But that didn't matter out in the wilderness as she was. What choice did she have?

Like Nora, each person in the wagon company just kept putting one foot in front of the other because there was nothing else they could do.

After days and days of helping the families of the sick, Nora was ready to quit. She was ready to just sit in the dirt and let the rest of the caravan pass her by. For the first time since they had left Missouri, Nora understood why someone might get so far and then turn around and go back.

She had collected campfire fuel for the Sullivans, and baked extra biscuits for the Hudsons. She spent a full day at the bedside of Alma Valentine, holding the little girl's hand, and sponging off her forehead slick with sweat. Abby Mills came specially to ask for Nora's help in rearranging her family's wagon and, though she was utterly depleted, she couldn't say no.

And then she stumbled back to her own camp at the end of each day, only to help her mother with the dishes or straightening up the wagon interior or laundry or cooking or listening to Amy or any number of other stresses that were on the Coles.

In spite of everything Nora had done to aid her fellow emigrants it still was not enough. They still lost another of their members.

It was only a couple days into their detour that word was spread around the company that yet another person had passed—the oldest of the Hudson sisters. Louisa Hudson, the strong, spinster, seamstress from Virginia, had worked so hard every day to get her family this far west, and now would be laid to rest before they even got to Oregon.

Nora was tired of all the burials. She was tired of the same cold biscuits every day. She was tired of the smell of burning buffalo chips and of donning the same soiled dress day after day, but still she soldiered on. These people needed her. The widows needed another pair of hands. The orphaned children needed a friendly smile. Nora felt as though she were taking the needs of the entire company on herself, but still she couldn't stop.

Not until they finally arrived in Oregon.

Amy, on the other hand, seemed effortlessly indefatigable. The eager interest she showed for the prairie dogs they spotted, or the birds nest she had brought all the way from Missouri kept her spirts as well as her energy up. It was as though she was unaware of any exhaustion or hardship, as long as she had something interesting to learn about. Nora watched her every day with admiration and a little envy.

All of Nora's hopes were tied up with Jasper Stephens, and she hadn't seen him in days.

After nearly a week on the trail, the walls of Fort Bridger appeared in the valley below them. It wasn't much to look at, just four sturdy log walls topped by a couple of guards. To Nora, however, it held the promise of relief and rest. After so many days of dawn-till-dusk walking, Captain Mills had allowed that they would stop early at the fort and make camp for the rest of the day.

Though the Coles still had just enough food to carry them for another several weeks of travel, Charlie still headed toward the fort once the wagons were settled for the day and the animals taken care of. He was back before long, however, with empty hands. Nora spotted him first.

"Father?"

"I told you I'm not picky, dear," Laura said, as her husband approached. "Anything we could add to our stores would do."

"Wasn't anything," he replied, before sinking to the ground near the low campfire. "Would've got you what I could, but apparently the shipment they were supposed to receive earlier in the summer overturned in the Kansas River. Everything they had before that got picked clean by the companies that came before us."

"Oh, no," Laura said. "Oh, Charlie, what will we do?"

"We'll be all right, at least. We have enough for now, and maybe since we have a few hours this afternoon I'll get a chance to hunt a little. It's the other folks I'm worried about. The McKinnons and the Kirks and others. They had so much stolen and spoiled that they must be really hurting."

Nora's mind raced through what options she had, how she could help these poor families. Though even as she assessed whether or not she could cut her own rations even further, even having to consider such a decision exhausted her.

There was too much. She had already given so much. All of them had. How could the trail wring any more out of them?

After leaving Fort Bridger, the trail turned almost due north. The company would detour only a little to avoid the worst of the mountains and desolate terrain west of the Great Salt Lake. The indirect route would add a couple days to their travels, but would take them through the Bear River Valley, rumored to be a verdant and teeming oasis that would make it all worth it. There was also supposed to be a river full of fish and forest full of game.

Nora would have run all the way there if she could have.

CHAPTER TWENTY-NINE

Captain Mills's lead wagons crested the low hill. Like a line of ants, one after the other the wagons in the caravan rolled over the summit and down the other side into a veritable land of plenty. Just when Nora thought she couldn't take any more of the bleak high desert and the privations of the journey, the trail crossed into the lush Bear River Valley. It was like a breath of fresh air, like plunging into a cold lake on a hot summer day. The difference between the stark landscape they had already crossed and this oasis was like that of an entirely different world.

The trail snaked down into the valley, tall grass and trees on either side. The sound of the river echoed up through the hills, luring the tired emigrants on. The company had several days of travel to get to the other side of the valley, and for what seemed like the first time they had enough water and food to get through it. There was more game and more bright flora than the wagon company had seen in weeks. Everywhere Nora looked was the deep royal purple of lupine, or the fire orange of indian paintbrush, growing straight up out of the tall grass.

Though the company was still many days behind where they had hoped to be at this time of the year, no one could make themselves rush through this valley. Captain Mills almost half-heartedly asked everyone to be ready to leave camp at dawn, but as the days passed that leaving time happened later and later. The trail had curved almost parallel to the Bear River, and no one wanted to miss the singular chance to eat and drink to their heart's content.

Everyone in the wagon company had recovered from their fever, and for the first time in weeks, there was no worry about running out of food or water. Just that small bit of security for a couple days made a world of difference for Nora—for most of the emigrants, really. Eating fresh meat helped lift spirits; seeing the bounty all around them reminded them all why they had chosen to go to Oregon Territory in the first place.

The second and final afternoon they were crossing through the Bear River Valley, Captain Mills called for their halt a good three hours before sunset. That would give those who needed it the time to dry and salt the meat they had harvested, or wash their linens, or even just go to bed a little bit early. With a lazy afternoon to enjoy the last bounty of the valley, Nora felt rested for maybe the first time since they had left Missouri. She decided to use this opportunity to have a little fun.

Jasper found her playing jacks with Betty Buchanan.

The little girl was bright and ebullient as she bossed Nora around, choosing both the game, but where they would play and who would go first. Nora almost couldn't believe that this was the same child that had witnessed her father be killed just a couple months earlier. But she attributed that resilience to Mrs. Buchanan; the widow had from the very beginning been determined to move forward and look toward the future. That sentiment seemed to have rubbed off on her daughter as well.

When Jasper approached them, Nora didn't notice until he was right at her elbow. She had been too focused on the light-hearted entertainment Betty had brought her.

"All right. All seven at once, right?" she said, about to take her turn.

Betty nodded, focused intently on what Nora had to do. The ball was thrown. The jacks were grasped. But then, disaster. Nora dropped one of the jacks in her attempt to catch the ball.

"You fouled that one, Miss Nora," Betty scolded. "It's my turn."

Nora laughed. "You're right. I don't know how you're so much better than me when your hands are so much smaller."

Jasper laughed, startling Nora. He stood over her, and she had to squint to see him with the sun behind him as it was, but that chocolate brown shirt was one she would recognize anywhere.

"Goodness! Jasper. What are you doing here?"

He crouched down next to her, so she no longer had to crane her neck, and offered her an unruly, carefree bouquet of wildflowers that had been hidden behind his back. Red poppies, white daisies, purple lupine and so much more. Nora's eyes went wide, and she laughed in delight.

"What's this?" she asked, beaming at him as she accepted the bouquet. Almost burying her face in the blooms, Nora took a deep whiff. "Oh, Jasper, they're beautiful."

He grinned. "I don't have much time. I was just heading out to see if I could get us a rabbit, maybe a quail or two, but these flowers were just about everywhere. I couldn't take a step but for thinking about you and how you might like a little brightness to your day."

"That's ..." Nora didn't know what to say. She stalled by sniffing again at the daisy closest to her. "I'm flattered, Jasper. Honestly. You didn't have to do this."

"I thought maybe if you can keep them in a little water for a few days, or even press one for later, you might think of me too."

"I—"

"Miss Nora!" Betty said, cutting into their conversation. "It's your turn again."

"I don't want to keep you from your game," Jasper said, as he backed up a couple steps. "I just wanted to see you. Have a good night, Miss Cole."

He tipped his hat, keeping his eyes firmly on hers as he said his good-bye. Somehow the man had managed to imply a caress in the way he said her name. Nora found herself blushing.

"Who's that, Miss Nora?"

Nora looked back at the little girl. "That was a friend of mine. A good friend of mine. Who kindly thought I might like some flowers. They're pretty, don't you think?"

Betty leaned forward, looked behind her, then whispered, "He's handsome."

Nora laughed. "He is that, yes."

As Betty dove back into their game, Nora admired the bouquet again. He had been thinking about her, even when she wasn't there with him. He went through the trouble of both collecting the flowers, arranging them and then coming to find her to give them to her. The gift of flowers was a small gesture, but she couldn't be more pleased than if it had been a pearl necklace.

The following day, the wagon company climbed the trail up out of the Bear River Valley, leaving the promise of game and plenty of water behind them. The trail then wound farther north, for more than five days of vigorous progress, until they reached Fort Hall. The dry desert sagebrush transitioned into uneven volcanic rock, and Nora thought longingly of the green and wildflowers of the valley behind them. The fort was constructed of roughly hewn logs, without windows or any attempt to be appealing to the eye.

But it didn't have to be pretty. It just had to be stocked. Fort Hall, at least, offered substantial relief. Where Fort Bridger had been bare and empty, Fort Hall was at least equipped enough to give them hope. Spread among all the families that needed food, it didn't go far, but it was enough to reassure many of the women that their children would not starve.

Not yet.

The company remained in camp at the fort for half a day, to allow for wheel repairs, laundry and, for the Coles and many other families, repacking the wagons to allow for the new supplies they had been able to purchase.

While Nora and her mother hauled half-emptied sacks of food out of the wagon to take stock and reorganize, Amy sat against the wagon wheel with a small notebook on her knee. She had finally started drafting one of the many letters to the scientists back east that she meant to correspond with. Any inkling that these distinguished professional men might not be interested in the thoughts of a fourteen-year-old girl was far from Amy.

From inside the wagon, Nora heard the murmur of conversation. She stuck her head out from the canvas wagon top to see that they had been visited by Claire McKinnon with her younger brother Ross. The three were huddled together, conferring about something, but seemed to come to a decision quickly.

"Everything all right there?" Laura Cole asked, when she noticed the McKinnons in their camp. "Did your mother need help with something?"

"Mother," Amy began, "Miss Atkins is going to have a science lesson for the older children this afternoon and I'd like to go. With Ross and Claire, please."

"Of course, dear," Laura responded. "Just make sure you change your apron first. The one you've got on is an absolute mess. Maybe wash your face too."

Ross ran on ahead, leaving his sister to wait while Amy changed her clothes and washed her face.

"It's rather impressive how Miss Atkins has managed to lure all of you to give up your afternoon to go to school voluntarily," Nora said, climbing out of the wagon carrying an armful of blankets that needed a good airing. "I'm going to remind you of this next fall when we're in Oregon."

"I've always liked school," Amy said as she hurried to get ready.

Nora set the pile of blankets at her feet and held out her hand for the soiled apron. "I'll take that."

Amy busied herself inside the wagon, looking for a clean apron, while Claire waited.

"You sure you don't want to come with us?" she asked. "I'm sure Miss Atkins won't mind."

"Oh, no. I'm happy to be done with school. And I've got to get started on all this laundry while we have a chance. I have a presentiment we won't get many slow afternoons between here and Oregon."

"What about your beau?" Amy asked as she climbed back out of the wagon. "Will you be seeing him today?"

"First of all, if you mean Jasper, he's not my beau. Second of all, I think he's probably busy. He's meant to be learning from Mr. Gilroy, so I'm sure there will be plenty of work for him to help with today."

"You seem to know an awful lot about how he spends his day for someone who is not your beau," Claire teased.

"Stop," Nora protested half-heartedly. "He's not my beau."

"I keep telling her we should look at the evidence," Amy told Claire. "There's the fact that he spent all day at Independence Rock with her, and then just a few days ago, he picked a bouquet of wildflowers for her."

"Yes, but there's also the fact that he danced with Hattie Larson, didn't he?" Claire asked, fully invested in the hypotheticals. "And you have to admit, she doesn't see him quite often enough to really consider this a serious courting."

"Both of you. Enough," Nora said. "None of this is necessary or helpful. Don't you have somewhere to be?"

"Yep. We do." Amy dried her face on her fresh apron, rubbing vigorously. "Ready, Claire?"

"We're just teasing," Claire whispered with a shy smile, before she followed after Amy.

But Nora was flustered the rest of the day, thinking over what the girls had pointed out, as well as objections to every bit.

The following morning, the wagon company left the fort behind. With a collective, anticipatory breath, they hit the trail early, heading westward into the foothills and the mountains beyond. The next stretch of trail would be demanding for new and different reasons than they had dealt with yet. Nora wasn't sure how much more she had to give.

CHAPTER THIRTY

As she used sand to clean off the burnt bit of biscuit at the bottom of her pan, Nora glanced over her shoulder to where Jasper was chatting with Caleb Kelly and Sean Gilroy at the latter's camp. Katie Valentine was there too, standing just outside the men's circle, but still listening. Nora wondered what she was doing there; Mrs. Gilroy didn't appear to be anywhere in sight.

Jasper removed his hat and wiped the sweat from his brow with a ragged navy-blue handkerchief he had fished out of his front pocket. She looked away again before he noticed her watching.

The wagon company had stopped for the day, making camp in the hour or so before sunset. This late in the summer they had enough daylight to fully wear out the draft animals and cover at least a dozen miles each day. It was grueling, but at least they did not have to make camp in the dark.

And, so, Nora still had daylight left after supper to get all their dishes clean. She heard a burst of laughter and glanced again, noticing that Jasper seemed to be saying his good-byes to the Gilroys.

Jasper was spending more and more time with Sean Gilroy and Nora felt so proud she could burst. Not that she could tell anyone, or draw attention to the fact that she knew he was there or why. Whatever connection she and Jasper had, it was still new. It was still sacred and private. And, if Nora was being honest with herself, she was a little afraid of getting her hopes up. She didn't want to repeat the same mistake she had made with Jimmy.

"Why, Miss Nora Cole. Fancy meeting you here."

Nora turned to him, with a broad welcoming smile. That leather and campfire smell that accompanied him made her heart beat just a little bit faster.

"Good evening. You coming from the Gilroys'?"

"There's always something for me to do there, though Mr. Gilroy wants me to start small. Says I can start with just keeping his tools cleaned and organized before we get to Oregon, then I'll be in good shape to start my official apprenticeship before the end of the year. Says with all the new folks settling in the territory this fall we should have our hands full. He can go on and on about how everything has a place, and that's how he can get so much done." He chuckled. "So I guess keeping it that way is my job now."

"That's wonderful! Oh, Jasper, I'm so happy for you. Are you excited?"

"I think so. There's something about blacksmithing that feels more..." He looked off to his right, as though trying to find the best word. "It feels more final to me. At the end of the day, I can see what I've accomplished and be able to measure it. Farming always felt like just endless chores. I think I'll really like this."

"And I'm sure Mr. Gilroy is right that there will be a big demand for your work. Especially as more folks pour into the territory every year."

"Probably."

He pulled the dirty handkerchief from his pocket again, and Nora could see that it was more just a scrap of fabric than a hemmed or starched handkerchief.

"That looks familiar."

"This?" He held up the wad of blue fabric. "Just a rag. It used to be the shirt I was wearing the day the Indians attacked, but the arrowhead ripped too big of a hole in the sleeve to be able to repair it. I got Ma to help me rip out the seams and I've just been using it as a handkerchief sometimes."

"That's smart. We can't waste anything out here. You should have heard Mother giving Amy grief about the bloodstains on her dress."

"It reminds me of you, you know?"

Nora looked at him in surprise. "It does?"

"Of course." His smile softened and he seemed to move almost imperceptibly closer to her.

"I... Well..." she stammered. "That's... very sweet. I don't know what to say."

"Well, it was a rather memorable day all told, wasn't it?"

She laughed.

"I had no reason to expect anyone but my mother and sister would bother with my injury," he continued, "but then there you were. You didn't have to help me— you didn't have to help anyone, but you did. You went out of your way. That was the first day I really got to have a long conversation with you and I will always be grateful for it. Maybe I should throw away these rags, or find something more practical to do with them, but seeing this shirt reminds me of that day."

"That was a special day," she said softly.

He grinned at her. "Independence Rock was a special day too, wasn't it?"

She grinned back. Nora couldn't help it. This man standing before her had a way of making her feel special and worthy of attention. She always felt more relaxed and grateful, no matter the circumstances, after she had talked to him a bit.

Jasper had a gift.

And she wanted some way to remember him too.

In a flash, an idea popped into her head.

"Do you have more pieces of that shirt?"

"This shirt?" He held up the crumpled fabric ball again. "Yeah, a couple. Why?"

"I wonder if I might have that scrap. I think I'll start a new patchwork quilt before winter really sets in."

"I bet there's not a lot of scrap fabric just sitting around your wagon, huh?"

"There's not. But, you're right. That shirt, even just a patch or two, will remind me of that afternoon after the Indian attack. If you can spare—"

"Of course. Yes. Absolutely. Do you want me to see if my sister will wash this first or...?"

"I'd love to take it now." Nora held out her hand. "If that's okay."

Jasper closed the distance between them and offered the piece of his shirt. Nora placed her own hand over the fabric, her fingertips brushing against his palm. All of a sudden, she became acutely aware of the fact that they were talking right next to her family's camp. Hopefully Amy was focused on writing her letters and was not trying to eavesdrop.

"Thank you."

"You'll have to show me that quilt once it's done. I'll look out for more fabric scraps for you too, if you like."

"I would love that. Thank you. I'll be honest. I haven't done any sewing since we left Michigan. It'll be good to get back to it."

"I bet you've been too busy helping everyone else, huh? Math with the little kids or bandaging someone else's sprained ankle?"

Nora laughed. "Who told you I was doing math lessons?"

He grinned again. "People talk. You're more popular than you realize."

"Really? I... I guess I don't know what to say."

"You don't have to say anything. I'm just passing along the praise." He winked at her. "Now, if you'll excuse me, Miss Cole, I need to be getting my chores done for Pa so I can get up early and do more chores for Mr. Gilroy. I'll see you soon, I hope."

"Bye," she answered softly, as he walked away.

She looked down at the navy-blue fabric that she held crumpled in her hand. Holding it to her face, she took a deep whiff of it. Sweat and leather and campfire. And it was as soft as a feather. This would be the perfect piece for her to begin her next patchwork quilt.

Nora had another idea.

"Mother, what happened to Amy's dress? The one with the tear in the arm?"

Both of the older Coles had been sitting on the wagon seat, watching the sunset over the hills in the west. When Nora called to her, Laura turned but did not get up.

"Oh, I tucked it away. Thought it would be useful to keep the medicine bottles from rattling too much."

"Can I have it?"

"Whatever for?"

"I want to start a new quilt. With some of the pieces that have been along the trail with us. I thought it would be a nice little memory and reminder of these last few months if I could incorporate her dress into the patches."

Laura Cole gazed at her oldest daughter with admiration. "I love that, Nora. That's a lovely thought. Go ahead. In the medicine chest, as I said."

Nora darted off to the wagon, climbing in and letting her eyes adjust to the dimmer light. As she stood there, between the narrow cots and sorting through the chaos for the medicine chest, Nora looked down at the faded yellow dress she was wearing. It had been stained beyond cleaning in a couple spots, and the bottom hem was ragged from all the time she had spent outside and in the dirt. This was the dress she had been wearing when they had left Independence, and more than anything else she owned it reminded her most of her time on the Oregon Trail.

And also more than anything else she owned, this yellow dress probably needed to be relegated to the rag bag.

But a new dress was a luxury her family could not afford. Not now. Not when they were so close to making it to Oregon. Every spare cent they had would be spent on food to get them there or to build a home once they arrived.

She could put up with this dress for a few months longer, if that's what it took to get to the other end of their journey unscathed.

And in the meantime, she could start her new patchwork quilt with the cast-offs from others. It was exactly the project she had been looking for to help keep her mind on the possibilities of the future instead of the hardships of the present. This quilt would be her fresh start, the first step toward her building a new life in Oregon.

CHAPTER THIRTY-ONE

For the third time that day, Nora crept to the edge of the cliff and looked down. From where the trail was cut into the rock high above the Snake River, she could easily hear the rushing rapids but not see them. The rushing water echoed off the tall rock walls, offering the constant reminder of their environment, even when it was not in sight.

To remind herself that she wasn't imagining so much water nearby, Nora found herself repeatedly checking to be sure that the river was still down there. It was maddening to be so close to so much fresh water and not have an easy way to access it, but she wasn't about to climb down over a hundred feet of sheer rock face just to fill a canteen.

The Sullivan-Mills wagon company had passed American Falls only a few days prior, and the promise of so much water had lifted everyone's spirits. Now, though, as they had to pass along the narrow cut of trail high above the river, it seemed far enough away as to be infuriatingly tantalizing. They would follow the river for at least a week, but only be in easy reach of the water for a small part of that.

The trail was too narrow, right up against the ravine, for Nora to wander very far. She and Amy walked close to the wagons, a far cry from their exploring of the great plains that they had been able to do just a few weeks earlier.

"Mr. Gilroy told me if I want to be a blacksmith, I have to start with cleaning his tools and things." Amy grimaced.

"Yes, that's what Jasper told me he'd be doing too. What did you think, Amy? That you'd get to start right away with pounding on metal?"

"Maybe. I could, you know. I could be just as strong as some of these boys."

"That's not the question," Nora said. "The point is that being a blacksmith is a proper career. There are no short cuts. Especially for a girl."

"Why is everything different just because I'm a girl?"

Nora sighed. "I don't know. That's just the way life is, I guess."

She moved to the edge of the ravine to look down again, longingly, at the river far below them.

The wagon company was traveling toward Shoshone Falls. They had crossed into Shoshone Indian territory just a few days prior, and Nora felt like she had been holding her breath the whole time. Ever since the wagon company had been attacked by the tribe near Fort Laramie, she had half expected another attack any time.

So far, they had been lucky, but the danger was

always there. For all she knew the local tribe was watching them follow the trail right that moment.

Nora looked around. They could be anywhere.

"What's your beau doing today?" Amy asked, appearing at Nora's side by the edge of the ravine. "Cleaning tools too?"

"Come on, let's get away from the cliff." Nora led her sister back closer to the wagons, back to where it felt a bit safer. "You are far too comfortable looking out over steep precipices."

"You're avoiding my question."

"Amy," Nora said, trying to be patient. "I assume you mean Jasper, and I am going to reiterate that he is not my beau. And as far as what he is doing today, I imagine he is doing the same thing everyone is doing right now—leading a covered wagon or walking alongside one."

Before Amy could respond, Caleb Kelly pushed past them, at a run, heading up toward the front of the caravan. He didn't even acknowledge the Cole girls, in his haste to get wherever he was going.

"What do you think that was about?" Amy asked.

"I hope it's nothing bad."

The girls continued to walk with the wagons, though now both remained in thoughtful silence. Nora glanced back at the Gilroy wagon following behind the Coles. She had almost talked herself into going back to check on that family when movement ahead of them stole her focus.

As they followed the caravan, the Sheldon family moved their wagon off of the trail. They followed the rest of the company, toward where everyone was making camp not far from the edge of the canyon.

"It shouldn't be time to make camp yet," Charlie said with a frown. "There's still plenty of light in the day. Strange. Something must have happened."

"But..." Nora protested. "We don't have time for a detour. What is the captain thinking? We only have so many days left before it snows in the mountains."

"I don't know, dear," he said. "Why don't you go on ahead and see if you can be of service. As I said, there must be a reason, and we have to trust Captain Mills to know what is best to do."

"If you're sure you don't need me?"

"Amy can help if there's anything. You go on ahead. I know you'll feel better once you know."

Resolutely, Nora walked to the head of the train, looking carefully at each family she passed for a hint of what might be different, what might be wrong.

She got as far as the rear Sullivan wagon before anyone had any answers. Junior Sullivan had been leading their team, and the worry on his face told Nora that he at least had some idea of what had happened.

"Junior," Nora called, breathless from her hurrying. "Do you know why we're making camp?"

He looked grim. "It's Mrs. Van Anda's time. Caleb ran up to the front to tell Captain Mills her pains had started and now, I guess, we're here for the rest of the day. The captain didn't want to have to stop here, but ... I don't know anything about babies. I was always sent away when it was Ma's time with the little ones. Do you think it'll take very long?"

"I don't know. Oh, but I hope everything goes smoothly. Thank you, Junior. Make sure you tell your ma I'm happy to help if anyone needs anything."

"I know, Miss Cole. I'll tell her."

She headed back to her own wagon, to help her parents make camp for the rest of the day. The Van Andas' wagon was just a few behind the Coles, but when Nora went by about an hour later there seemed to be more than enough help on hand, including the doctor and his wife. The new mother's low groans could be heard through the dirty white canvas of her wagon.

Nora didn't like feeling helpless, but there was not much else to be done.

"Just enjoy your afternoon, dear," the doctor's wife said kindly as she directed her away. "All we can do now is wait."

Wandering away from the Van Andas' wagon, Nora wondered what they would tell the child about his birth when he got older. Maybe he would grow up wild and unpredictable just like the landscape he had been born into.

Well, thought Nora, if the doctor didn't need extra help, she could be sure that her sister would be happy to have her attention. She was just about to go back to return to her own wagon again when she almost ran straight into Jasper.

"Nora, thank goodness. I was just going to come find you."

"You were?"

"There was another accident. A death. It must have happened right about the time Mrs. Van Anda went into labor, but no one knew right away. I wanted to make sure you were all right."

Nora gasped and put a hand over her mouth. "Oh, no. What happened?"

"John Harper. Trying to climb down to the water and must've slipped. A few of the men are going to try to recover his body."

"Goodness, that's terrible."

"It is," he agreed. "Tomorrow morning we'll have another funeral. Seems like those never end, doesn't it? And that leaves his sister on her own to continue on. That poor woman. Helpless as a child from her days as a New York City heiress, and now she's got to manage the wagon and her whole future on her own."

Nora felt a wave of hurt and panic wash over her, but she managed to keep her voice steady. "Sister?"

"Caroline. You've met her, haven't you? Sweet girl. She's really come a long way since the first days on the trail, from what I hear. The whole Sullivan family really admires her."

"Oh." Nora swallowed hard, her thoughts racing. "Who... Um..."

Every rule of propriety and polite society she had been raised with told her she should keep quiet, that she shouldn't be so quick to show her hurt, but it had all become so hard. Nora was exhausted. She had been exhausted for months, and between the hunger and her sister and having to constantly look the other direction when Jasper flirted with every female under the age of eighty, Nora had had enough.

"Nora?" he asked, as she trailed off. "Are you all right?"

"Fine." She beamed at him, though it took all her willpower to hold the insincere smile. "I'm just fine. I think I'll go check on the Van Andas. They can certainly use some help tonight, don't you think?"

"Right, yes." He nodded, though continued to watch her carefully. "I heard they named the baby after John Harper, by the way."

Nora gasped. She couldn't say why that bit of news affected her so much, but tears welled up in her eyes, hearing that the new little boy was named after the man who had died the same day. Nora had put a hand to her chest, and bowed her head to compose herself.

"Nora," Jasper said softly. "Are you all right? Did I say something?"

She blinked back the tears before she looked up again. "Fine," she repeated. "I'm just fine. That sweet baby will have quite the story when he gets older, won't he? Do you know what Miss Harper will do now?"

"I haven't heard, beyond the fact that the pastor will help bury him in the morning and then we'll leave camp again."

"All of these deaths. When will it all end?"

CHAPTER THIRTY-TWO

One more grave. One more family broken up. One more delay on the journey west.

One more poor woman left alone, thought Nora, as she stood at the back of the crowd that had come to pay their respects to their fallen neighbor. She had no idea what she would do if she were in that girl's shoes.

She had no idea what she would do if yet another member of the company didn't make it to Oregon.

Later that morning, the wagon company left another grave behind and continued down the trail that ran parallel to the Snake River. Having to cram their grief into such small pockets of time before traveling again was taking its toll. It felt as though they were so close to their destination, and yet there was still so far to go, and everyone was being worn down to nothing. Nora noticed Mrs. Sheldon weeping into a handkerchief even as she helped her husband hitch the animals to their wagon.

To make up for the shortfall of miles the previous afternoon when they had to stop for little John to be born, Captain Mills now set a punishing pace. None minded, however, as the faint roar of Shoshone Falls drew them closer with every rotation of wagon wheel. It would take all day, but at least there would be a reward at the end.

They arrived in camp near the falls after dark. The roar of the enormous waterfall lent a current of energy to their work as each person made camp and ate supper in faint light of the campfires. Everyone seemed to be in a hurry to go to bed. There was the promise of fresh, swiftly running water and the several hours to take advantage of it waiting for them in the morning.

They had some time the next morning before leaving camp, and many of the members of the wagon company stole away to see the falls. Some even bathed or played in the pool at the bottom. Nora didn't plan on staying long enough to do that, but she did want to see Shoshone Falls before they left this site. In all her guide-book talk, Amy had said this was supposed to be the largest waterfall west of the Mississippi River. It must be something to see, and something that she would not get the chance to see again.

Before Amy or anyone could stop her, Nora ducked out just after breakfast. She made her way toward the narrow trail that wound down to the pool beneath the falls. Before she got there, from the other side of camp she noticed the tall form of Jasper walking down the trail ahead of her. Nora's heart soared. It was fate. She would have another quiet moment alone with Jasper that morning, another memory to live on over the final weeks of traveling and chaos before they got to Oregon.

"Nora, wait for me!"

She glanced back to see her sister frantically trying to pull on her boots. Amy was too impatient to sit and do it properly, but in rushing she ended up losing her balance and falling to the dirt without even having fit the boot over her heel.

Nora turned back toward the trail and pretended she hadn't heard Amy. She wanted those moments with Jasper if she could. Amy had gotten plenty of her time, every single day of her life.

"Nora!"

She hurried her steps, eager to get out of Amy's line of sight. There would never be a chance for alone time with Jasper as long as her sister kept hanging around.

Jasper with his long strides managed to get far ahead of her. The trail from the campsite cut through low scrub, from the plateau winding down to the edge of the water and down the hill. It was steep in places, and Nora had to slow her steps to keep from running headlong down the incline.

The roar of the falls covered most other sounds—birds, voices, even Nora's own footsteps. As Nora drew closer, she forgot about Jasper, she forgot about Amy, she forgot about all the sacrifices she had made on the Oregon Trail to get to this point. All she thought about was the power and beauty of Shoshone Falls, thousands of gallons of water pouring over every second. She paused to watch for a couple moments before remembering her original goal.

Farther down the trail was the bottom of the waterfall and the pool of water that curved around before continuing on as the Snake River. There was a group of about half a dozen different young people watching the water and standing at the edge. From this distance, Nora could identify most of them. The oldest Carter boy. One of the Waters men. Several women.

She slowed her steps.

There was Jasper. She would recognize him anywhere, his long arms, his broad shoulders and that chocolate brown shirt that she was beginning to love.

But who was he talking to? Hattie Larson she spotted, recognized by her forest green calico. The other of the girls had her back to Nora; her dress and bonnet weren't any Nora could place immediately.

Jasper had been holding a single wildflower in one hand, held low at his side, and as Nora watched, he raised it to his nose, sniffed it, and handed it over to the woman. She accepted it immediately and, judging by the smile on Jasper's face, accepted it gratefully.

Let it be someone's mother, Nora thought, as she continued a few more steps down the trail. Let it be Mrs. Sullivan or Mrs. Mills or even his sister.

Even just having to wonder exhausted Nora all at once.

She was so tired of constantly doubting Jasper's attention. She was tired of having to wonder what he was doing or what his intentions were. After how she had been fooled and then hurt by Jimmy Rayburn, Nora didn't have it in her to go through the whole thing again.

The roar of the falls masked her steps.

She was still several yards away, and stopped to watch before anyone else realized she was there.

The girl who had been gifted the flower turned to talk to Hattie and Jefferson and when she turned in profile, Nora finally recognized her.

Her vision went spotty in her fury and pain.

It was Katie Valentine.

Pretty, charming, fancy-free Katie Valentine.

Katie Valentine who always seemed to be hanging around the Gilroys' camp when Jasper was there.

Katie Valentine who Nora had considered a friend.

Nora had seen it with her own eyes. Jasper Stephens had given Katie Valentine a flower, not more than a couple weeks after he had done the same for her.

Who was this man that seemed to have so little regard for her feelings?

She whirled around and hurried back up the trail. No longer would she stand for being toyed with by Jasper Stephens.

"Nora!"

She heaved a deep sigh and slowed her steps but she didn't turn around. What could she say to him that she hadn't already? Though she really did know better than to pick a fight with Jasper, there were things she needed to say. He had hurt her, and she was tired of pretending otherwise.

"Nora, wait."

She schooled her face, and turned back to him.

"Nora, thank goodness. I've been looking for you."

"Me? Whatever for? I'm sure there are plenty of other girls who would be glad for your attention. Hattie. Miss Harper. Katie Valentine. Goodness, I bet even Claire McKinnon or Abby or Hannah or any number of other girls. I'm sure the list goes on and on."

"What are you talking about?"

"I *saw* you. I saw you with Katie just now. I saw you with Hattie at the dance. And of course you're sympathetic to poor Miss Harper, left all alone. Did you already offer to drive her wagon? It seems like every time I turn around I hear about some girl or another who is being charmed by you. Do you really not have enough responsibility to your family or Mr. Gilroy to fill your time? You have to go flirting with every pretty girl who looks your way?"

"What has gotten into you?" He looked stunned, but Nora noticed he was not denying it. "I thought we had put this behind us."

"So did I. Imagine my surprise, then, when I see you just now. Giving flowers to Katie Valentine. That seems to be your favorite gesture, doesn't it? Like with me in the Bear River Valley. Who else have you picked bouquets for?"

He frowned. "I wasn't giving her flowers."

"Oh, really?" Nora couldn't help the sarcastic bite in her voice. "I cannot believe you are such a cad as to deny it. I saw you, Jasper. A beautiful single wildflower handed over gently to Katie Valentine. What was that? A daisy? A black-eyed susan? How sweet. Maybe she will dry and press it to think of you."

"Nora, please—"

But Nora didn't want to hear it. She was so tired of giving and giving and being understanding and patient.

"Stop," she said, taking a step back and putting a hand up between them. "I wish you the best, Jasper. I really do. But I need someone who is not going to take me for granted. Someone who is going to give me the security I need and not keep me wondering all the time where I stand or if he's going to show up for me."

"When have I not shown up for you, Nora?"

He sounded frustrated, almost angry, which made Nora even more upset.

"I don't know what you do when you're not standing right in front of me. Oh, wait. I do. You do chores for Sean Gilroy while Katie watches and fawns over you. I had been wondering why she spent so much time at their camp and now I know."

"It's not like that at all." He sounded angrier now, but she was not about to listen.

"Nora!"

Jasper and Nora's fight was interrupted by a third voice. They both turned toward the new sound, the clear distress of Amy calling for her sister, only barely heard over the roar of the nearby water.

"Is that your sister?" he said with a concerned frown.

"Yes." Nora sighed. Of all the times for Amy to demand her attention. "I'm sure she's fine. She did this before. Remember, at the Kansas?"

"Are you sure?"

"Nora Cole!"

She sighed. "Everyone always wants attention from Nora."

"NORA! Please!"

"Yes, I'm sure she's fine," she said, answering his earlier question. "I'm tired of always having to come running to her. She needs to learn how to be on her own eventually."

"Oh. Well..."

"I can't deal with this, though," Nora said, defeated. "I'm going. I can't ... I can't keep wondering if..."

She stopped herself from saying more, but the tears came anyway, spilling over her cheeks. As the wave of heartbreak crashed over her, Nora took several steps back, wresting her hands from his grasp.

"I can't."

She turned and ran, before he could protest, before he could try to charm her and change her mind. Nora ran up the trail, through the scrub brush, with no destination in mind. All she wanted was peace. She wanted to put this all behind her. She wanted to forget that such a person as Jasper Stephens ever existed.

CHAPTER THIRTY-THREE

"Amy, stop it with this. Where are you?" Nora called into the wilderness.

She had left Jasper standing on his own on the trail near Shoshone Falls, after finally being honest with him. She couldn't take it anymore. Maybe it was all innocent like he claimed, but his inconstancy had hurt her, and the constant doubting exhausted her. He had been so sweet and attentive at times, but at others seemed to ignore her completely. Seeing him gift flowers to another girl—especially after he had just done the same for her—was the last straw. Nora was tired of having her feelings played with like that, but it still was a difficult conversation to have.

After everything she had wanted, everything she had dreamed about when she left Michigan, now it felt as though that future was further away than ever.

She was even a little bit grateful to her sister for calling to her, giving Nora the perfect reason to leave Jasper behind.

But only a little. Amy's constantly expecting things of her needed to be curtailed.

"Amy! Come on, don't pout. I'm here now. What do you need?"

The sun was high overhead, stretching toward noon. As Nora walked through the brush toward where she thought Amy would be, she tried to push down the annoyance. She had thought that Amy's friendship with Claire had gone a long way to the younger Cole developing more of an independence than she had before. But now where was that independence? It was one thing for Amy to interrupt Nora's more important conversations, demanding her attention, but to do so and then disappear was more than what she had thought her sister capable of.

"Amy?"

Nora stopped in her tracks. Though she hadn't precisely been looking for it, now she found clue that seemed too important to ignore. To the side of the trail—the side closest to the water—there was a clear break in the brush, where something had pushed through between the plants. Nora was not a tracker and never would be, but it was clear that something big had been here.

Someone had left the trail.

"Nora..."

"Amy?"

That was Amy's voice, there was no mistaking it, but she sounded so weak. Though Nora seemed to be getting closer to her, maybe she was too late. She felt as though her heart had stopped in panic. Where was Amy? The fear she heard in her sister's voice had never been there before. The blatant begging for Nora to help her was far more than Amy had ever asked of her. This was different. Her sister needed her.

"Amy!" she called again, louder, desperate. "Amy, where are you?"

"Nora, help me!"

"Amy?"

Nora diverted from the trail through the gap she had found and cut through the low brush toward the edge of the water. With every step she prayed that Amy had not been so reckless as leave the trail. But if anyone would forget about the risk of being on her own, in the wilderness, in the interest of science, it was this girl. For all Nora knew, her sister had followed a bird or something right off the cliff.

"Amy!"

She ran faster. The thin, pointed branches caught her dress, pulling at her with every step. She heard a rip; her faded yellow dress caught on a sharp branch as she ran. But Nora didn't stop. She couldn't stop when her sister could be in danger.

"Nora! Hurry!"

Her voice sounded weaker now, as though all of her strength was being poured into keeping herself alive. Faintly, only barely noticeable over the sound of the waterfall, Nora thought she heard her sister's rapid breaths and grunting. Whatever she was doing was quickly using up all her energy.

Nora pushed through the bushes, hurrying toward the sounds.

But still she had not seen her sister.

"Amy, where are you?"

"Nora? I'm here. Over here!"

Nora looked toward the voice, toward where her sister must be.

It was coming from the edge of the plateau, from the drop to the pool and river below.

At second glance, Nora spotted two pale hands, covered in scratches and valiantly grasping the narrow roots of the red dogwood bush that grew out of the top of the cliff.

"AMY!"

Nora dashed to the edge, careful as she got closer, and dropped to her knees to look over the edge. The plateau here was high above the river, with some boulders directly below where Amy hung.

Everywhere were signs of struggle. Amy had tried to keep from falling, had clearly tried to climb back up. But she was just too far and couldn't get enough leverage.

"Amy, hold on!"

Her hands had been scratched. A long strip of dried blood on the branch that strained over the edge told the story of Amy's grip slipping. Carefully, Nora crept closer. The last thing they needed was for her to tumble after her sister.

"I'm okay," Amy said, though her voice cracked. "There's a little ledge just under my toes. It's holding some of my weight, but I can't— I tried, but it's so..."

"Don't worry," Nora assured her, though she had no idea how she would be able to get Amy back up.

She backed up a foot, trying to assess what she had to work with.

"I don't know... I don't know..."

She looked around desperately, as though some solution would magically present itself. There were no ropes, no sturdy branches. There was nothing Nora could use to pull her sister up but her own body.

"You have to help, Amy. Listen to me." The authority in her tone demanded that her sister give her full attention. "I'm going to help pull you up, but I can't do it by myself. You have to help. You have to do your part. I cannot—can *not*—take care of you this time, do you hear me?"

"Yes," she murmured. "Just hurry. My hands are really starting to hurt."

"All right." Nora tried to sound confident. "We can do this, right?"

She inched forward again on her stomach, completely destroying her dress in the dirt. Creeping forward little by little, Nora tried to anchor herself on the plants nearby. She wrapped one ankle around the base of the nearby dogwood bush, and hung over the edge of the cliff from her chest up.

"We can do this, Amy Cole."

Amy nodded, eyes wide.

Nora took a deep steeling breath and leaned far over the ridge. Her arms were not strong, but they could hold on. Being careful not to jostle Amy's already precarious grip, Nora tucked her arms under her sister's armpits and tried to grasp her own hands again behind her small body. Even at this impossible angle, Nora held her as close as she could.

"Ready?" she whispered.

With her arms wrapped tightly around her sister, Nora heaved. She pulled. leaning as far back as she could, Nora struggled to haul her sister's scrawny body up over the edge of the cliff.

"Don't let go," Amy pleaded breathlessly.

Amy's feet slipped, but she quickly gained purchase again, and was able to do some of the work to pull herself up.

"Come on, Amy," Nora said, barely able to get it out.

"I can't."

"Yes, you can. Don't let go."

Nora's arms burned with the effort, but she didn't stop. She couldn't stop. She would not lose her sister. The sound of Amy's feet scrambling for purchase drove her on through the pain.

"Once more," she managed to get out. "Here we go."

With one big tug, Nora had pulled Amy the rest of the way over the ledge until her sister was half sprawled on top of her.

The two girls lay in the dirt breathing hard, getting their bearings. Nora could feel sweat trickle down her scalp, and soak into the fabric of her bonnet.

After a moment, Nora groaned. "Okay, you need to get off of me."

Amy laughed weakly and rolled off, backed away from the cliff, leaving Nora still laying in the dirt and panting.

Once she had finally caught her breath again, Nora sat up and scooted farther away from the edge of the plateau that fell down into the river.

"Amy," she began, trying to stay calm, "what... What happened?"

"I don't know," she mumbled. Nora couldn't remember the last time she had seen her sister unsure of herself. Two days earlier she would have joked that Amy didn't know the phrase 'I don't know.'

"Tell me."

"I just... I was watching and I guess not paying attention, and then all of a sudden, the dirt under my feet fell away and I was hanging off the cliff."

"Don't make me ask again, Amy. What were you watching?"

"A snake," she responded, almost in a whisper. "And a hawk."

"Why would you do that?" Nora demanded, almost shaking her sister. "How could you do something so reckless? What were you thinking?"

"I don't know. It was such a big snake, Nora. Kind of yellow with dark stripes. As long as my leg—"

"Amy," Nora interrupted, forestalling what was sure to be a long, detailed description, "tell me precisely what happened."

"I was going to follow you, but then a little field mouse ran across the trail, and it was all by itself. It darted into the shrubs and I wanted to see if it was going back to a burrow or something, so I followed the mouse. And then I spotted the snake, coming at it from a different direction. I thought it would be interesting, and if I stayed back far enough it wouldn't notice me. I've never seen a snake hunt before and what if I didn't get a chance again? I had to investigate, Nora. I couldn't help it."

"Amy..."

"And then a hawk swooped down," she continued excitedly, "and tried to get the mouse from the snake and it was the most exciting—"

Nora groaned. "I thought I was going to lose you. Do you understand? I thought you were gone forever. You can't do that. You can't do that to me."

"I'm sorry, Nora," Amy blubbered. "I'm so sorry. I'm so stupid. That was so stupid."

Nora held her sister close, trying to curb her tongue. The poor girl had been scared enough; she didn't need any more scolding.

"Promise me you will not do anything like that again. In fact, promise me you won't go out into the wilderness by yourself ever again. Take Claire or someone. Anyone. Even if you had still gone after the snake, and still fallen over the edge, at least there would have been someone to go for help. Promise me, Amy."

"But what if—"

"Amy Cole!"

"All right, I promise."

Nora wrapped her arms around her sister and hugged her close. Amy slumped over, cuddled in her sister's arms in the dirt while they sat quietly together letting their hearts calm.

"It was a beautiful snake," Amy finally said softly. "You should have seen it. All muscle and stealth, pouncing on the field mouse."

Myriad emotions roiled in Nora, but finally she realized there was nothing she could do but laugh. "Oh, Amy," she said, hugging her sister tight. "This might be the most Amy thing you've ever done. And please don't ever do it again. Come on."

She nudged her sister and got to her feet, brushing the dirt off her skirt as best she could, even while knowing it was a lost cause. "We need to get back and get those scrapes looked at. We'll probably be leaving camp soon, too, and I want to make sure you eat something before we do."

As the sisters made their way back to the trail to return to camp, Amy slipped her arm through Nora's.

"Did I tell you about the owl I saw last night?" she asked.

CHAPTER THIRTY-FOUR

The Cole sisters walked back to camp together, from the edge of the trail near Shoshone Falls. Nora's arm was wound around her sister's waist half in hug and half in supporting her in case she was weaker than she let on. Truthfully, though, even if Amy had been perfectly fine and without a scratch, Nora still wasn't sure she would want to let the girl go. That had been far too close of a call.

"I almost lost you," she murmured for the fourth or fifth time.

"But you didn't," Amy said, all cheers and optimism now that she was safely back on solid ground. "And I got to see a snake pounce on a mouse and fight off a hawk. It was amazing, Nora! You should have seen it."

Nora was saved having to respond when their mother met them as they approached their campsite.

"Girls, goodness. There you are. Amy, what happened to you? Nora, you look filthy! Never mind. We don't have time for that this moment. I need your help."

"What's wrong?" Nora asked.

"The Shoshone tribe is requiring a toll for our wagon company to cross through their land."

Nora's stomach dropped.

"A toll?" Amy perked right up at the chance to learn something new. "What would they do with greenbacks?"

"Captain Mills convinced them that we are cash-poor travelers and they would never get the money that they're asking out of all the families. So instead, we are to give them belongings. Clothes, tools, food. Whatever we have to spare."

"But we don't have anything to spare," Nora protested.

"I know that. And yet we have to find something. Come help me look."

Mrs. Cole climbed into the wagon ahead of her daughter.

"You have to understand it from their point of view," she was saying. "As long as we are on their land, their usual paths for hunting or fishing are all taken up. Animals scared away. They don't have to let us pass at all, you know. What if we were forced to go around the long way? And it does seem fair that they get some kind of compensation for the loss of their regular life."

Nora climbed in after her, overwhelmed at this new demand. Her brain didn't seem to be working well; it was as though she had completely blanked on all options. "But none of that matters if we don't have anything to give."

Laura turned to face her daughter in the cramped space under the wagon cover.

"We must have something. We weren't cleaned out

like some of the other families. You've been away helping others for at least a couple meals, so maybe there's a little bit of extra food. We *must* have something we can part with, to help the company pass through peacefully. What would you give them?"

A wave of emotion she couldn't identify crashed over her. Nora broke down in tears.

Her mother looked at her in shock. "Goodness, child, there's nothing to cry about. I'm not going to make you give away anything important. Whatever is the matter?"

"I'm sorry." She wiped her tears away. "I'm sorry, I'm just... I'm sorry."

"Oh, Nora." Her mother reached for her, wrapping her arms around her oldest daughter and pulling her close. "I'm sorry. I've been relying on you for so much on this journey and there was bound to come a time when it was too much. You poor thing. Do you want to tell me about it?"

Nora shook her head. "Just... I'm tired. It's so much, all the time. And then Amy almost falling over that cliff this morning."

"What!?" Laura interjected with alarm.

"And then coming back here," she continued, "and having to decide what *else* we are going to have to do without for the remaining month. It's just so much all at once."

Nora had buried her face in her mother's shoulder, but could tell that she was wavering over what part of her surprising speech to address.

"I know," she soothed. "I know. I'm sorry. Tell you what, you go outside again and take some deep breaths.

Enjoy the last bit of time we have, and rest and I can decide this on my own."

"Are you sure? I feel so bad... If you need me, I want to be able to help."

"The best way you can help me right now is to rest. So you're all rested up for the next time I really need you."

Nora nodded. The strength of her relief surprised her, and she was happy to do what her mother asked.

"And when I'm done here," her mother added as Nora left the wagon, "you and Amy are going to explain to me exactly what you meant by her falling over a cliff."

In the end, the Coles managed to cobble together a little bit of food, a dented pan and a couple other small things to hand over to the native tribe as gratitude for being able to cross their land unmolested. Between all the families of the wagon company, they managed to collect enough.

Nora felt guilty that she couldn't be of more help to her mother, but she was so worn down. Between the stress of the trail, the drama with Jasper, and then Amy's terrifying ordeal, Nora was beat. For the short time she had in camp before they left again, she spent it sitting on her wagon's seat, just watching the families all around her.

Just after noon, the wagon company pulled up their stakes and left camp. The trail wound away from the water, down the less steep incline, before curving back again. Nora stuck close to her sister. She was determined that they would not have a repeat of that morning.

Where the trail curved back toward the water, it ran straight into the dead end of a rocky ravine before climbing up again. The bottom of the ravine created a bit of a bottleneck. The trail was so steep that most of the wagons had to be doubled up—twice as many draft animals yoked together to haul two wagons up at a time. The chaos and organization required to make that happen delayed everyone. So many of the oxen and mules were malnourished and exhausted that it wasn't certain how easily any of them could drag the wagons up. Just as they had seen at many places along the Oregon Trail, at the bottom of this ravine, even more belongings were discarded.

Nora spotted a moldy side of bacon, a crate of books and a broken rocking chair. And that was just at first glance. The crate of books, for example, was sitting on top of some abandoned piece of furniture Nora couldn't identify from where she was.

"Maybe the Shoshone will come collect it all," Amy suggested, from where she stood already leaning over the books. "It's too bad folks couldn't have included all this in the toll we just paid, huh? Think I can take some of these books?"

"One," Nora said. She didn't have the heart to refuse her sister. "And you have to carry it up."

"Obviously," Amy responded, already elbow-deep in sorting through the books.

Nora looked up the path, out of the ravine, and realized there was a small gap in the wagons.

"Come on, Amy, make your choice so we can go. We'll walk on up ahead," Nora told her parents. "And wait for you at the top and see if anyone there needs help."

"Wonderful idea, girls. Don't go far."

"Amy," Nora called again.

She looked up, looked back down at the books and finally made her choice. She closed the distance to Nora with a book in either hand.

"What?" Amy said, with fake innocence. "You said what I could carry."

"That's not what I said." But Nora didn't stop her. Two new books would keep her sister busy for at least, oh three days or so.

"Amy! Wait!"

Nora and Amy turned to see Claire McKinnon hurrying toward them, weaving her way through the crowd. At one point, Nora held her breath, certain Claire was going to get hit by one of the big animals that were being herded to the narrow trail, but she soon was by their side albeit panting a little from her exertion.

"Are you two walking up?"

"Come with us," Amy said eagerly. "Wait till you hear what happened to me this morning."

"Amy," Nora said in half a groan, half a laugh. "This was not some big, exciting adventure that you're going to repeat ever."

"I know. But it makes a good story, doesn't it?"

Nora laughed. "Fine. As long as you are treating this as evidence—to use your own word—and not suggestions for what you want to do this afternoon."

Claire laughed at that, and Amy plunged into her story, as the three girls began their climb up the trail out of the ravine. Nora listened to Amy's version of the morning's stress with some trepidation. Despite the rest and quiet her mother had allowed her, Nora still felt tightly wound, as though anything might set her off in tears again.

But maybe that's how she would feel every day, until they got to Oregon. Until she got settled in her new life and had some security.

When they reached the top of the gorge, Nora looked around. Only a fraction of the wagons had come up thus far. They still had some time to wait before the whole of the caravan was ready to keep moving. Amy and Claire had continued chattering away, and walked off toward the shade of one of the lone trees that overlooked the canyon.

Nora stayed closer to the top of the trail, always with a weather eye out for someone who might need an extra hand.

There were still several hours of daylight, and the wagon company would not be stopping here for camp. They were still on Shoshone land and the agreement had been that they would cross it as quickly as they could.

With a resigned sigh, Nora started walking west. She couldn't stop now.

CHAPTER THIRTY-FIVE

When the wagon company had left Shoshone Falls and climbed back out of the ravine, the trail then wound away from the water, across the broad plateau of high desert, before curving back to following the length of the Snake River. For three full days the wagons traveled parallel to the water. This time, however, they had fresh water in reach instead of hundreds of feet below them. The trail gently curved down and down and down to the bottom of the valley, until the only place to go was across the river and continue northwest.

Late summer was the only time of year that the Snake River was low enough that it could be safely forded; there was no ferry or bridge to get them over. The emigrants would have to take this small window when they had it, or risk losing everything.

Even beyond the one chance to cross the river, the Sullivan-Mills wagon company was running out of time to get to Oregon. It was already nearing the end of August. Every wagon company that had left St. Joseph or

Independence, Missouri, in April wanted to be over the mountains into the Willamette Valley by the first of September, or as soon as possible after that.

At this rate, Nora thought, they would be lucky if they made it to Oregon before October. She might be spending her nineteenth birthday in the wilderness of the Oregon Trail.

But first, the wagon company had to get across the Snake River. The trail took them through the water at Three Islands Crossing, before heading farther north and west toward Oregon. Even with everything lined up and efficient as it could be, only half of the wagon company could cross in a day. Each man had to lead his team slowly through the water, across the sand, being careful not to go so slow they got stuck, but also not go so quickly they overturned. It was a delicate balance, and emotions ran high, as the company prepared for the crossing.

The Coles made camp with the rear half of the caravan while they waited for their turn to cross the river the following day. Though Amy tried to talk Nora into watching chipmunks with her, she had to take care of the more important things first. Immediately after breakfast, she visited Mrs. Van Anda and the newest tiny member of their wagon company.

"Hello?" she called in a loud whisper as she knocked gently on the side of the wagon. "Mrs. Van Anda, how are you feeling? Is there anything you need?"

"Come in, Nora."

Accordingly, Nora climbed into the wagon. The dim interior was cozy and warm, compared to the early fall air outside. Mrs. Van Anda sat up in her cot that ran the length of one side of the wagon, with her new baby swaddled and nestled against her chest.

"How is he?" Nora asked, continuing to whisper.

"He is really enjoying the wagon sitting in one place, I can tell you that. The jostling over ruts in that last stretch was not this little boy's cup of tea."

"Can I hold him?" She reached for the newborn hesitatingly as she sat on the edge of the bed.

As the new mother carefully put the child in Nora's arms, she sighed. "If all this help from neighbors continues when we actually get to Oregon, I won't have to lift a finger for this fellow."

"I'll do my best."

Nora chuckled softly, not wanting to wake him. She pulled the blankets away from his face, and gazed down at him. Though only days old, his cheeks were full and pink, and he had the same light brown wisps of hair that Jory Rayburn had had at the same age.

Nora's breath caught at that memory; the last time she'd held a baby, she had been dreaming of her own. She had been so focused on imagining what her life could look like—babies and a husband and a home—that she didn't see the reality right in front of her.

"You excited to have one of your own someday?" Mrs. Van Anda asked, her eyes still watching her child.

Nora knew the answer—she had always wanted to be a mother. But after everything she had been through, and all her disappointment over the last year, she was hesitant to say any of it out loud.

"How is he eating?" she asked. "Can I bring you something? Maybe the Sheldons' cows have milk to spare."

"If they do, I would be very grateful. So far, it's been fine, but I worry about my body being able to maintain this over the next few weeks before Oregon. Any charity anyone can spare would be most welcome."

Nora nodded and handed the child back to his mother. "I'll do what I can. And just send someone to come find me if you need anything. Really. He's simply darling, and I want to help."

"You're a sweet girl, Nora Cole. And a generous woman. You're far too kind to me."

"It's nothing," Nora said lightly as she left the wagon. "I'm happy to do it."

But if she was more than available to Mrs. Van Anda, and the other women of the company, Nora was more than reticent when it came to Jasper Stephens. She had put up the wall around her heart when it came to that man, and she couldn't imagine ever taking it down again.

The Stephenses stayed on the south side of the river for the same day that the Coles did, and Nora did her best to not run into him. It had been days since she had seen Jasper. Though Nora was sure he had spent many mornings and evenings at the Gilroys' camp just next to the Coles, she avoided even looking that direction. Instead, she invented reasons she needed to be in her family's wagon, and stayed there far longer than her made-up chores should take her.

When, partway through the second day, it was finally the Coles' chance to cross the river, Nora grabbed her sister and made her way purposefully to the banks.

"Let's go now," she said. "The sooner we get to the other side, the sooner we can start drying off. There's already a little chill in the air."

Nora hesitated at the water's edge. There were three sand bars that stretched the width of the river—the three islands of the crossing's name—but the water between here and the first small break seemed faster and deeper than Nora had been ready for. This was not the ankle-deep muddy fording of the Platte River. Their choices were to ride in the wagon, adding to the weight the animals had to haul, or get soaked through walking on their own.

She needed to just start.

"Ready?" Amy asked from next to her. "The current looks fast."

"Where are Mother and Father?"

Looking over her shoulder to see how close her parents were with the wagon, Nora noticed Jasper Stephens. Less than fifty feet away. He was headed straight toward her, and seemed as though he would not be distracted from his aim. Lifting his hat, he caught her eye and greeted her from afar.

"Not now," Nora murmured to herself. Then, turning to her sister said, "Let's just go. If we wait for the wagon, we'll just be in someone's way. Let's cross now."

"Just wade across?" Amy's face lit up.

"You're right, though; it looks like it's a bit of a strong current, so we'll have to stick together."

But Nora was already two steps into the river. She could feel Jasper watching her, feel him getting closer, but she refused to acknowledge him. Let him feel what it was like to be so disregarded. Let him wonder what she was thinking for once.

Nora's heart hurt, and she felt like she was on the

verge of tears, but Amy's eagerness helped her forget all about that.

"Here I come!" she declared, wading into the water after Nora.

"Careful!"

With her hands wrapped in her heavy skirts and petticoat, Nora had a hard time keeping her balance as she waded through the water. Though it wasn't too deep, the current was strong and the riverbed uneven. She kept her eyes looking ahead to the first island sandbar and then the next, as she and her sister made their way across the water.

She tried to push Jasper from her mind, concentrating instead on where she would put her next step.

Stumbling up onto the low sand island, Nora waited for her sister. They only took enough time to catch their breaths before plunging in again and again, until they finally reached the other side of the river safely.

"Golly," Amy said, excitedly. "I'm soaked!"

Nora looked back to see where her family's wagon was. "We can get dry as soon as Mother and Father get across with the clothes and towels and things."

Scanning the opposite bank, she didn't see Jasper at all. He must have given up on her rather quickly.

Nora's teeth chattered from the cold and the wet.

Between the physical discomfort and the emotional turmoil the trail had brought her, Nora wanted nothing more than for this journey to be over.

When Charlie led his team of mules up the north bank, Nora and Amy made a beeline for their wagon, and the trunk of dry blankets within.

The moment everyone was across the river, the wagon company continued. The Oregon Trail followed along the stretch of the Snake River for another day and a half, before it curved northward. They had one last fort to visit between here and the end of their journey, one last chance to purchase whatever supplies they could before the final push over the mountains into Willamette Valley. The land here was as flat as the prairie had been back in Missouri, only now the sight of the tall, snow-capped mountains in the distance urged them on.

They were in the last stretch of the Oregon Trail, so close Nora could almost imagine what Oregon would be like. She filled her days as much as she could, finding that when she was worrying about Mrs. Buchanan or Mrs. Van Anda, she had far less time to wonder how Jasper was filling his time.

But despite all her best efforts, after several days of avoiding him, Jasper finally managed to track her down. One night after supper, when she was walking back to her own wagon from the Buchanans, Jasper sought her out, following her and almost sneaking up on her before she noticed.

"Nora."

With a small gasp of surprise, she looked down at her feet, away from his eyes, and moved to the side. He stepped in front of her again, blocking her path.

"Please," he said, "just give me a minute. Please."

"Jasper..."

"Nora, why are you avoiding me?"

"I'm not."

"I watched you plunge into the Snake River instead

of having to talk to me." He chuckled self-consciously. "That seems like avoiding to me."

"I never give you a thought," she responded airily.

"Nora..."

"No." She took a step back, putting more space between them. "Honestly, Jasper, I just ... I don't have the time or energy to worry about you right now. There are too many other people who actually need my help, and are not just flattering me into changing their bandage."

"Nora, that's not what I did—"

"I almost lost my sister," she said, choking back a sob. "I was so caught up in you, and what you could be—what *we* could be—that I stopped paying attention when one of the most important people in the world needed me. If I had stayed even a moment longer to argue with you at Shoshone Falls, Amy could have been really hurt. She could have died, Jasper. Because of *me*."

"I'm sorry," he spluttered. "I'm so sorry, I didn't know."

"No, you didn't know. Because you are only ever paying attention to yourself. To what is best for Jasper Stephens at any moment."

"Don't say that..."

Tears spilled down her cheeks at this, but Nora brushed them angrily away.

"I don't have time for this," she repeated deliberately. "I am... I need security, Jasper. I need someone who won't make me doubt myself, and who won't keep me from the other important things in my life. I've been hurt, before. In my past. Back in Michigan. I told you about them, and you still didn't take my feelings into consideration."

"I'm sorry, I—"

"Stop saying you're sorry, and... *do* something, Jasper," Nora concluded in a whisper. "I'm exhausted. I have my sister to look after. I have so many other friends and loved ones in this caravan who count on me for compassion and labor. I don't have the time to also teach you how to be considerate of other people."

She tried not to think of the hurt expression on his face as she walked away.

CHAPTER THIRTY-SIX

Jasper's meager attempt to rekindle any kind of friendship with Nora infuriated her for the rest of the day. But by the time she had crawled into her narrow bed inside the wagon that night, she had worn herself out with her anger. He was not worth so much of her time, she told herself, and certainly not so much of her energy.

Nora finally fell asleep that night listing to herself all the other members of the wagon company who needed her help, who cared about her feelings, who she should be spending her time on instead. By the time she woke the following morning, she had thoroughly relegated thoughts of Jasper to the furthest corner of her mind.

Nora Cole had a full day, and Jasper Stephens didn't need to be any part of it.

As the trail wound away from the Snake River, northwest toward Fort Boise, the land again grew flat. It was a different kind of flat than they had traveled through to this point. Nora had walked west, alongside the wagon train, through the flat of the prairies, then the flat of the high desert, the flat of a plateau above a river. Amy walked with her, talking about some new kind of an animal called a marmot, that was "like a prairie dog, but not really," that she hoped to see before they reached Oregon.

"And then when we get to the new territory," she continued excitedly, "there will be a whole bunch of new things to learn about."

Nora listened patiently as they continued west. Gone were the days of trying to get rid of her sister as quickly as she could. The experience of almost losing her had shown Nora what her sister meant to her with crystal-clear clarity. It was the apparent loss of Jasper Stephens in her life that she would have to get used to now.

This stretch of country was slightly greener than previous expanses of desert, and the tall mountain range was ever in sight. In this stretch of country, the wagon company could travel for miles without seeing a single tree. No wonder the fort had been built here, Nora thought. How else could anyone survive in such a stark environment than if they brought in the supplies?

"We're almost there, Nora," Amy said with a happy sigh, as the two sisters walked along the hard dirt. "It didn't seem real when we left Michigan, even though logically I knew it must be. But now we're actually almost to Oregon."

"I know just what you mean. So much about this whole adventure has felt unreal. It seems strange to be traveling through this country and know we will never see these things again, doesn't it? I wish I could sketch. So I don't forget any of this."

"I've been trying to write down as many details as possible for the letters that I am going to send to the universities back east. I'm sure those scientists will be grateful for all I can tell them."

Nora hid a smile. "You know they probably all have copies of the journals of Captain Lewis and Lieutenant Clark, right? That's why the president had them published in the first place."

"Well, yes, but that was *years* ago," Amy protested.

Nora laughed, which quickly turned into a surprised, gasping cough when Katie Valentine suddenly appeared directly in front of the Cole girls. She seemed to have come down the length of the caravan on the other side of the trail, hidden from their view by the wagons, before darting between the wagons to surprise them. Katie had all but cornered her, not unlike the way Jasper had just a couple days earlier.

"Nora, can I talk to you?"

She felt a pang, immediately assuming the worst, but helpless to avoid it. But Nora could be polite, in spite of everything. "Of course. Yes. What can I help you with?"

"Can we, um...?" Katie gestured for Nora to follow her away from listening ears. Nora looked at her sister, nodded, and then walked out away from the trail with Katie.

"Watch out for snakes," Amy called after them.

"She says she saw a big one back near the falls, and now it's all I can think about," Nora added as they got some distance from her sister.

"Oh, heavens," Katie murmured, looking more intently at where she stepped. "Well, then, I'll make this quick so we can get back to the caravan."

"Is everything all right, Katie? Are you feeling sick again?"

She shook her head, and peered at Nora intently. After taking a deep breath, she said, "You know there's nothing between me and Jasper, don't you?"

Nora blinked, confused, wrong-footed somehow. Whatever she had been expecting Katie to say to her, this wasn't it.

"I— But—" she stammered. "What do you mean?"

"I don't want to... It's really none of my business, but I saw you running away from us that day at the falls, and then Jasper mentioned later how you had said that he had given me flowers. And I... I don't want there to be any confusion. I'm not going to pretend to speak for Jasper, but for myself, I can assure you there is nothing more between us than simply good comradeship."

"He told you what I said?" she asked in a small voice.

"Only a little. Only because I asked. I could tell he was upset. He doesn't just go around telling your secrets, of course. But I thought maybe since he knows you and I are friends— We are friends, aren't we?"

Nora paused before responding. She took a deep breath.

"Katie. We could be as close as sisters, but I know what I saw. He handed you a wildflower, didn't he?"

"It was from Caleb," she said softly.

"What?"

"Caleb Kelly. The Gilroys' nephew. Jasper spends a lot of time with both Mr. Gilroy and Caleb, and that morning he's the only one who had a chance to get away so he brought me that flower and message. From my beau."

"Your *beau*?" Nora could not be more surprised than if Katie had said that little Jack Buchanan was her beau.

"We've been keeping it quiet, since my father doesn't like the fact that Caleb is an orphan from 'across the ocean,' but yes. He's been courting me almost since Independence. We'll be announcing our engagement as soon as we can talk Pa around, but please keep this quiet."

"Your beau," Nora said again. "This explains so much."

"What do you mean?"

Nora laughed self-consciously. "Oh goodness. I'm such a fool. Did I ever tell you that you talked in your sleep when you were delirious with fever?"

"Enid told me I was awfully noisy for someone who couldn't work." She smiled. "But she didn't say anything else."

"You mumbled, so I can't be sure what you were saying, but now that I think about it ... You were probably asking for Caleb. You said Kay... something. That must have been what you meant, don't you think? Caleb?"

Nora's heart melted at the romance of the scene in her memory. There Katie was, too sick to even know what she was saying but she was asking for her beloved. And here Nora had been blaming the other girl for coming between her and Jasper.

"I'm sorry," she said. "Katie, forgive me. I didn't realize about you and Caleb. I only saw the way Jasper makes himself available to everyone, including you, and that flower, and ..."

"He has a generous heart like that," she agreed. "Not unlike yours, you know."

"I ... He..." Nora trailed off.

Was Katie right?

Before she had to come up with a response, the girls were interrupted by Mrs. Buchanan appearing at Nora's side.

"Oh, good, Nora, there you are." She took a deep breath and offered her an apologetic smile. "I'm so sorry to interrupt. But I wonder if I might prevail on you to help me this afternoon? Both of the boys are needed elsewhere today, and I have to drive my team, and with the little ones underfoot I am far too distracted, and I just know I'll spend the whole afternoon worrying about something happening."

"Of course," Nora responded. "Katie and I are done here." She glanced at the other girl, who nodded curtly. "Katie, will you tell my sister where I've gone?"

"Thank you. I can't tell you how much I appreciate you." Mrs. Buchanan chattered on as she led Nora back to her own wagon. "I know I might be worrying for nothing, but of course with what happened with their father—"

"Really, Mrs. Buchanan. You don't have to explain yourself. I'm happy to help."

As Nora collected the Buchanan children and led them out a bit away from the trail to walk for the afternoon, her mind went to what Katie had said.

Jasper had never been flirting with her. Katie had been spoken for, and what's more, Jasper had known it.

Nora was so embarrassed. If she wasn't so happy about learning this piece of information, she might be hesitant to even show her face. She had been such a goose, imagining that every girl in this wagon company wanted Jasper Stephens.

She should apologize to him, but she had no idea how to even start. Even the thought of talking to Jasper just now made her want to cry, overwhelmed with a torrent of emotions. She had been so hurt, and needed time to forget, to recognize her errors.

"Miss Nora," Jack asked, interrupting her thoughts, "what's the name of that thing again?"

He pointed to a little tan head sticking up from the otherwise flat, dry earth.

"I think that might be a marmot," she answered. "But you know who would know better? Miss Amy."

CHAPTER THIRTY-SEVEN

"Amy Cole! Be careful!" Nora scolded with exasperation.

"Sorry!"

But it was too late. She had already spilled dirty, greasy dish water all over Nora. It soaked straight through her apron to the ruined skirt of her faded yellow dress.

Nora looked down at herself, exhausted. "I didn't think this dress could get any worse," she murmured.

"Oh, dear," her mother said, sympathetic. "Here's what we'll do. If we can't get those stains out of the apron, at least, you can just wear one of mine until we can afford to get you something new."

"Thank you, Mother. But ... Oh well. There's nothing else to be done, I guess."

The wagon company had finally reached the last fort on the trail before they reached Oregon. They arrived shortly after midday, and had the rest of the afternoon to rest and make camp before leaving in the morning.

Fort Boise sat nestled in a curve in the Boise River.

Whitewashed and clean, this final fort before they reached Oregon was also the most welcoming. It was as though the trail knew the emigrants needed one last boost to get them over the final stretch of terrain. Three small buildings behind a log stockade wall were the whole of the structure, but it was enough.

After they made camp, Mrs. Cole made her family a small meal with some of their sparse rations. Mr. Cole went for more supplies, while Nora began washing dishes. That is, until Amy accidentally lost her balance, fell into Nora, and spilled the whole tub across their campsite.

Nora was wringing her skirt out into the dirt when her father made his way back.

"The fort is mostly out of supplies, but I heard the salmon are biting," Mr. Cole said as he returned. "Would you all like some fresh fish for supper?"

"Can I come?" Amy asked.

"I think I might check on Mrs. Van Anda again," Nora said. "If that's all right? Mrs. Sheldon was going to save some milk from the one cow still producing for her, and I said I'd take it."

"That's sweet, dear," her mother responded. "Just be back for supper. If your father and sister bring back fish, I'll need help salting any extra."

Nora left her campsite and walked into the center of the company. The Van Andas' wagon wasn't far from her own, but she wanted time for her skirt to dry a little more before she presented herself. As they were settling right next to a fort, the wagons were not pulled into a tight circle but rather a chaotic hodgepodge, the usually rigid caravan turning this way and that as each family found the most advantageous spot to stay for the afternoon.

Nora wandered through the middle of the mess, passing cows, horses, dogs, children. Waving to women she knew and pretending she didn't see men's uncouth spitting into the dirt. After so many months on the trail with these people, Nora felt as though she had found her place. There, standing in the middle of their campsite, she took a deep, contented breath and checked again to see how damp her skirt still was.

A tall man with dark hair that matched his chocolate brown shirt approached Nora though the throng of animals.

"Nora? I'm sorry. Do you have a minute, please?"

"Jasper." She sighed, and took a step back away from him. She was not ready for this. Even with the news from Katie, Nora was an emotional mess and didn't know what to say.

"I know you don't want to talk to me, and I understand, but this is just ... it's a little thing."

She had spent so much time trying to forget about him, and trying to forget the way she felt when she was with him. And then after talking to Katie, she had spent the intervening couple days trying to put everything back in her mind, trying to remember how special it had been spending time with him, trying to forget how he had hurt her.

Nora felt like a mess when it came to her feelings about Jasper Stephens.

And now he was standing in front of her asking for a little bit of her time.

"I was on my way somewhere."

He didn't need to know that she was stalling, or that she had specifically come out to the middle of the camp to avoid people.

"I'm sure you are." He smiled gently, and took a few steps closer. Nora noticed he held a brown package under one arm. "You're always on your way to help someone."

Nora smiled tightly. Her heart hammered. "Was there something you needed from me?"

"No," he answered quickly. "No, I don't need anything but just a couple minutes. I, um... I got you something. I wanted to give it to you away from other people, so you didn't feel, I don't know, obligated in any way? But, well you know. There are always people around."

"You got me something?"

He nodded, taking another shy step toward her. "I remembered what you said about your sister's new dress. And a couple people said some things here and there that gave me an idea." He held out the package with both hands. "Open it."

"This?" She looked up at him. "This is for me?"

He offered it a little closer. With hesitant hand, Nora pulled at the string-tied bow that held the package together. The top fold of paper came up and she gently pushed open the other fold, revealing what Jasper had got for her.

Nora gasped.

Jasper held a folded sky-blue dress, covered in small white flowers that matched the wide white lace collar. The fabric was a bright blue, clean and crisp.

"It might be a little big, but it's a finished dress, not

just the fabric. But also, I thought if you have to take it in or hem it, maybe there can be some extra you can use for your quilt?"

Nora picked up the dress by the shoulder seams, and let it unfold, falling almost to the ground as she held it up to admire. In the bright afternoon sun, the blue seemed to match the sky almost perfectly.

"Jasper," she said. "It's beautiful. Thank you. How did you know?"

He shrugged. "I pay attention. Heard something from Mrs. Gilroy, and from Abby Mills. A little bit here and there, and I put it together. No offense meant, but that dress of yours has seen better days."

Nora groaned. "You don't know the half of it."

"And you deserve to feel your best," he concluded softly. "I've been saving the little bit of wages Gilroy has paid me for my help of the last few months. I had thought I might use it to outfit my home or something when we get to Oregon, but this feels like a better use for it."

"You didn't have to do that, Jasper. You shouldn't have done that for me."

"I wanted to. I can always make more money. There's nothing more important to me than making sure the people I care about are taken care of. That's why— Well, Katie told me that she talked to you and she explained... I'm so sorry. I should have realized how that gesture might appear to anyone else, but at the time I was just trying to do something nice for my friend. Caleb was caught up with helping Gilroy, and couldn't get away and ... Well, you saw what happened. I wasn't thinking."

"Yes, she told me." Nora felt a wave of shame come

over her, remembering how hurt she had been, how embarrassed she had felt chasing after a boy who didn't seem to care for her.

Jasper started talking faster now that he was sure he had Nora's attention.

"And, I mean, my sister tried to tell me too, I think, in her own way, that I needed to be careful about how my actions were perceived by other people. But I never really cared what anyone thought about me until... Until I met you."

"Me? Why?"

"You just have this... There's something about you that makes me want to be a better person. You're always so generous and so thoughtful. It makes a fellow feel self-conscious." He ran his fingers through his hair. "I wanted to live up to your standard, Nora. A man you care about would be just as generous as you are, I guess."

"Oh" she let out in a soft gasp.

"So, anyway." He cleared his throat. "So, the dress. You deserve it, and I thought maybe you could use some of the scraps from this yellow dress for the patchwork quilt you're starting. Some of this. Some of your sister's dress. My shirt. Maybe I'll see if I can snag one of little John Van Anda's blankets that is stained beyond help too. We'll see what else we can find you and you'll have a new finished blanket in no time."

"A blanket that represents all of the steps of this impossible journey," she concluded, allowing herself to sink into this feeling of being appreciated. Of being looked after properly. "That's... that's amazing, Jasper. Thank you. Thank you so much. I can't even tell you what this means to me."

"You really like it?"

"I really do. Oh, Jasper, this is one of the kindest things anyone has done for me in such a long time. I am so used to taking care of everyone around me, I don't know if I ever realized what it felt like to be taken care of in turn."

He sighed in relief. "I'm so glad. I just want to help."

"You are. You do. I mean… well, just the fact that you noticed I had a need and didn't wait to be asked that just … It speaks very well of your character. You're just as generous as you seem to think I am. I didn't see it before, but that says more about me than it does about you."

"Oh, I wouldn't say that."

"Really," she insisted. "I'm sorry. I don't… um. I think I need time, you know, to think about all this new information and put everything into place in my mind, but I know for certain that I owe you an apology. So. I'm sorry. Truly. I … I made a mistake and I'm very sorry."

"Well. Good, then. Great." He grinned, pleased with himself. "I know you have things to do; I don't want to keep you."

"Thank you," she said again, softly, as he backed up several steps before turning toward his own wagon, looking at her over his shoulder all along the way.

CHAPTER THIRTY-EIGHT

Charlie Cole caught just enough salmon at the Boise River to feed the family. Laura cooked some rice to go with it, and Amy had brought back to camp some wild onions for tiny bit of flavoring. The Cole family ate richly that night, and Nora could not remember when she had last had such a full stomach.

"Were you going to tell us about that new dress, daughter?" her mother said, as the four Coles sat around the campfire after supper. "Did you suddenly come into some inheritance your father and I didn't know anything about?"

"It was a gift." Nora looked down at the dirt in front of her, where she had been using a small twig to doodle little flowers. The folded dress sat in her lap where she had continued to admire it even after supper. She wanted to wait until the fresh beginning of the next morning before donning the clean new dress.

"Really?"

There was a brief quiet moment and Nora looked up

to see her parents exchanging looks, having a whole conversation without saying anything out loud.

Amy, as usual, had her nose buried in one of the books she had rescued from the crate at the bottom of the ravine, and Nora couldn't be certain that she was listening at all.

"Do you care to tell us who gave you that gift?" Charlie asked.

"Um. Well. Okay, before you say anything, just know that, um, the intention was good," Nora began. "And I don't think there were any ulterior motives nor any debt implied by my accepting the gift."

"You are not making me feel much better about this," Laura said with eyebrows raised.

"It was Jasper Stephens," she finally said. "Jasper saw that my yellow dress was practically a rag already and he used some of his wages from Mr. Gilroy and bought me a new dress."

Her parents were silent, again exchanging expressions without enlightening Nora as to their thoughts. Finally, after a long quiet moment, Mrs. Cole nodded and turned to Nora.

"It's a beautiful dress. You're very lucky."

"Um. Yes. Thank you. I think so too."

After a pause, her mother added. "Is there anything else you want to tell us about this, Nora? Or about the boy?"

"No." She blushed. "There's nothing. That is... Um. There might be something. Someday. In the future. Right now it's just a dress, I think."

Mrs. Cole nodded. "All right, then. You just promise me you'll talk to us if anything changes, won't you?"

"I will."

She leaned forward, took Nora's hand and squeezed it. "I have never been more proud of you than over these six months, dear. And whatever else happened, I think you should be proud of you too. It seems like this young man probably is."

"Thank you," Nora replied in a whisper. She looked down at the dress still folded in her lap and fingered the crisp white collar.

After a moment, her mother turned to Amy with a question, and Nora was left alone with her thoughts.

———

When the Sullivan-Mills wagon company left Fort Boise the next morning, Nora felt full and rested and hopeful for the first time in many weeks. They were so close to the end of the trail, she had on a fresh, clean dress—albeit a little big—and she was again on speaking terms with Jasper. True, of course there were risks about the remaining journey, but on the whole Nora felt like she could see the end. If she kept putting one foot in front of the other for a few more weeks, they would be in Oregon in no time.

But those days of inching their way westward would be tireless. Captain Mills insisted that the wagon company push as hard as they could, and they traveled several days in a row without stopping for a midday break. More than once, Nora had to make extra biscuits after dark when they stopped for the night, just so her family would have some form of food to eat the following day as they walked.

There was only a small window of time left to get over the Blue Mountains before the snow, and Captain Mills was determined that his company would make it.

Several days into this punishing pace, Amy and Nora were walking with the Valentine girls again, along with Claire McKinnon and Abby Mills. All six of the young women were exhausted; it had taken so much for each of them to get to this point on the trail. In spite of this, they had plenty to keep them excited and hopeful for the remaining few weeks of the journey.

"There's not much longer now, girls," Abby Mills said. "Once we get higher up into the mountains, Pa is going to send Daniel on ahead to scout. We could be just a couple weeks from a real town."

"All right, then," Amy said. She was walking backwards along the trail, so she could face the line of girls that walked just behind. "That means I am running out of time to do my thorough research. Raise your hand if you need me to describe again what a marmot looks like. I still haven't seen one, but maybe with all of us looking—"

"Amy," Nora said. "What if we just point out to you any animal we see today and you can determine what it is?"

Amy deflated only a little, before saying, "You promise? You'll tell me if you see *any*thing?"

"I promise," Enid volunteered.

"Me too," added Claire.

"See?" Nora said. "Six pairs of eyes. You couldn't ask for better."

"Only five pairs," Enid corrected her. "The future Mrs. Kelly is too busy looking for her beau."

Katie shoved her sister playfully. "Stop."

"Is it official, then?" Nora asked. "Your father relented?"

"Caleb and Katie Kelly," Enid said, with a snorting laugh. "That sounds made up."

"Ma talked him around," Katie said with a modest smile, ignoring her sister. "Papa insists that Caleb has to have a home for us before he will consent to the wedding, but he's a hustler. I'm hoping that we'll have a spring wedding, maybe even in our own parlor."

"There's no parlors in Oregon," her sister said slyly.

"Fine," Katie responded. "Our room, then. Our single, one room cabin with a tiny bed crammed in one corner and a wood stove in the other. But it doesn't matter because it will be ours and we'll be together. And if you're not nice about it, Enid Valentine, I won't invite you to the wedding."

"I'm your sister!" she protested as the other girls laughed.

"Which is even more of a reason you need to behave. Don't you want a second home to visit when Alma or Bea get on your nerves?"

Enid thought a brief moment before cuddling up to her older sister, with big innocent eyes. "Forgive me, dearest sister of mine. Don't leave me out in the cold with those hellions."

"Can I come too?" Claire asked with a laugh. "Lizzie has about worn me out with all her shenanigans now without Alexander around to entertain."

Nora wondered how the rest of the McKinnon family was doing; she had barely had a chance to talk to Claire since her brother had died. Her mother had kept her too close to home for too long. It seemed an unexpected treat to have Claire with them today.

But before she could mention anything about it, Nora felt a light tapping on the top of her bonnet. She looked up into the gray sky, only to get pelted in the face with several large raindrops as the sky opened up.

Enid and Amy shrieked with laughter, as all the girls scattered, darting back to their own wagons to take cover from the torrential storm. The rain fell so hard and so fast that by the time the Coles reached their own wagon, the wheels had slowed almost to a stop. The churning mud would keep the caravan from crossing as many miles as they'd hoped today.

"Get in, get in!" Nora prodded.

Careful, so as not to get her already-heavy-with-wet skirt caught, Nora leapt into the wagon, with Amy right behind her.

"Girls! There you are," their mother exclaimed from inside the wagon. "I had hoped you weren't too far."

Amy unbraided her hair and shook it out to dry it, before sticking her head back out from under the canvas cover to peer at the sky. "I think this is the biggest storm yet."

"Might be. Your poor father."

"He probably should have had more children then," Amy said, matter-of-factly. "Maybe one of them would've been a boy and then Father could be in here with us."

Nora and her mother burst into laughter. "Oh, Amy."

CHAPTER THIRTY-NINE

"Nora, could you start the coffee for us, please?"

The fire had been started, with the meager twigs and dried pine needles she and Amy could gather on that stark mountainside. The needles burned quick and hot, and they smelled horrific, but the emigrants didn't have many options at this point in their journey. They only had so much fuel. Nora didn't have much time before the fire died out, so she went right to work.

The bucket of water had frozen over in the night. Amy had gone with a few of the other girls to collect it the day before, from a spring well off the trail. It was to be used for their coffee, but first they needed to break the ice covering the surface. Nora's hands were so cold that she almost couldn't feel her fingers. She had been putting off wearing her gloves, saving that moment for when she *really* needed the warmth. That moment had arrived.

With a pointed stick almost as thick as her finger, Nora poked at the layer of ice, breaking it from the circumference of the bucket and then breaking the layer into smaller pieces.

The wagon company had spent a monotonous week climbing into the mountains just to the east of Oregon. They were so close. Just over this ridge would be their destination, their own promised land. But somehow that ridge never seemed to get closer. Nora knew it must be, knew that the perception of distance was askew. But now almost six months since they had left Missouri, the seemingly unending trail was all that she knew. It felt as though there was nothing before this, nothing after this moment.

But there was nothing here. No grass for the animals, water only in dribbles when they were fortunate enough to stumble across a spring. It was colder than many of the emigrants had prepared for, having planned to already be settled in Oregon by this time. Nora didn't know how long they could keep going under such circumstances.

She filled the pot with ice water and positioned it over the fire to heat up. Rubbing her hands together to warm them, Nora reminded herself again to find her gloves before they started on the trail for the day.

Her mother approached where Nora stood near the fire, shifting her weight from one foot to the other to stay warm.

"Here, open your hand."

Nora obeyed, curious.

Her mother dropped five small, dried cherries into her open palm. "That's the last of them. At least for a while."

Nora popped just one in her mouth, determined to

savor them. "Maybe we'll get lucky and Father can purchase an orchard."

"Wouldn't that be wonderful?"

Both women were studiously ignoring the fact that it was almost impossible there would be a settled orchard in the wild territory.

"Where's Amy?"

Her mother pointed. "She said she wanted to see if the cold was affecting the wildlife, so she went off into the trees before we left for the day. Will you go collect her, please?"

With a small seed of worry, Nora strode off to the edge of the camp, toward where some of the other wagons were crammed as close to the line of pine trees as they could get. The trail in this part of the mountains was haphazard, with few wide-open areas like the emigrants had been used to on the plains.

Nora tried to put from her mind the last time Amy had gone off into the wilderness alone. Surely the girl had learned her lesson and would at least look out for cliffs before she tumbled over one.

As she approached the forest that spread out across the mountainside, Nora finally spotted her sister. Then she stopped, amazed at what she saw. Amy wasn't alone.

That was Jasper, sitting close to Amy and peering at whatever she held in her hand. Nora easily recognized those broad shoulders, that dark hair. Amy was leaning close to her hand, with the other one cupped over it, intensely studying what she had found.

And that was Jasper. Just as intent as she was.

Nora almost didn't know what to think, but the idea

of this man embracing her sister's more curious and queer traits made her want to cry with relief.

"Amy," she called out. "You need to get ready to go, please."

There was no response. Nora wasn't sure if Amy just hadn't heard or if she was too focused on what was in her hand to listen. As she drew closer, she saw that Amy had a giant beetle, almost as long as her thumb.

"Amy," she said again, when she was standing right behind the two. "Amy Cole."

Finally, her sister looked up at her, blinking into the morning light as though she had just emerged from a cave or tunnel.

"Is it time to go?"

"It's time to go," Nora confirmed, as Amy climbed to her feet. "And Mother has a little treat for you."

"Does she?"

"The last of the dried cherries."

"All right."

"Maybe leave the beetle behind though."

"Oh." Amy looked down at the creature that was still crawling slowly over the back of her hand. She turned to Jasper. "Do you want it?"

"No, thank you."

She shrugged, and bent down to let the bug crawl onto the dirt. "I bet we can find more of this fellow when we get to Oregon anyway."

With that, Amy turned and strode toward their camp, not looking back or waiting for her sister at all.

Jasper chuckled, but Nora just shook her head.

"One of these days, we might be able to teach her to

get out of her own head and notice the other people around her."

"Oh, I don't know. I kind of like the way you never have to wonder with Amy. She's always exactly who she is, take it or leave it."

Nora smiled. "That's... insightful. That is precisely what to expect from her. What were you doing looking at that big beetle, by the way? Amy's interest I can at least kind of understand."

"Just curious, really. I was walking back to my own camp from the Gilroys, and she waylaid me."

"I did make her promise she wouldn't go off alone. At least I know now she listened."

Jasper chuckled. "Your sister is quite convincing. She talked fast and practically dragged me with her. I wanted to make sure she was all right. But when I saw what she was looking for I got just as interested as she is. Did you know that a lot of bugs hibernate?"

"Did you know she has a bird's nest tucked in the gap between her cot and the wagon and she's kept it since Missouri at least? "

"Of course she does. And now she's off to eat the last of the cherries."

"I have two left," she said, offering her open hand to him. "I'll share them. If you want."

"Really?" Jasper's whole face had lit up. "Are you sure?"

Nora grinned. "I already had more than this just on my walk over here. Go on. It's nice to share with someone so appreciative."

He grinned back and accepted the last two cherries,

moaning appreciatively at the taste. "Perfect. Will your parents try growing cherries again in Oregon?"

"I think so. Cherry trees are supposed to grow well in the valley, but of course it takes more than a few months to grow a whole tree."

He nodded. "There are a lot of decisions to make now. For everyone."

"Do you know what your family will do when we get there?"

"I don't think my pa has big ambitions. Really as long as they have a farm, and me and Rebecca are settled, I think they'll be happy. I'll need to help them build their home. And as soon as Sean Gilroy can claim a piece of land I'll be helping him set up his forge and all that. I foresee myself being very busy for a while once we finally get off the trail."

"I wish I had such set plans. Other than helping my parents get settled, I don't know what I'm going to do with myself. I just hope we'll be able to stay near all these folks. I want to watch Betty and Jack grow up, and go to Katie and Caleb's wedding."

"If I know you, Nora Cole, you will find plenty of ways to fill your time helping your neighbors. Someone's going to need to keep an eye on you to make sure you don't overdo it."

He winked at her, and Nora blushed. No one had ever teased her the way that Jasper did, and there was something about it that made her feel as though he knew her better than anyone else did. As though he recognized her tendency to take herself too seriously and wanted to help her. He certainly was the only person aside from Nora herself, who noticed she had run herself as ragged as that yellow dress.

"Yes, sir," she replied coyly. "I'll see what I can do."

CHAPTER FORTY

Nora yawned, then shivered.

More days had passed as the company climbed the mountain, days in which each family's food supplies dwindled to almost nothing.

It was the brightest part of the day, but the cold and the hunger were making her tired. Her body wanted to hibernate, and she thought longingly of the previous year around this time when she could just sit in front of the Coles' little wood stove and stitch her patchwork together. But now, on the side of a mountain, a desolate trail in their final push westward into Oregon, there was no relaxing. There was no putting her feet up after a long day. She was lucky that she had enough warm clothing for this current environment. Not all of the members of the wagon company did.

The wagon company had stopped for a break at midday. Many of the families didn't have enough food to eat three full meals each day, but that was all the more reason why going slowly and resting in the middle of the day was necessary. It felt as though their progress was going as slow as molasses in January, and that this stretch of trail was interminable.

Nora just kept putting one foot in front of the other, and keeping herself busy by checking on her friends. Everyone was struggling. Everyone needed her help.

As her father unhitched the team for the short rest, and her mother went looking in the wagon for more winter clothes, Nora decided she needed a change of scenery. Something to wake her up a bit.

"I'm going to check on the Buchanans," Nora said.

"You're sweet." Her mother kissed her cheek. "Don't go using up all your energy on other people, though. We're going to have to start moving again soon."

"I know. But sitting here won't help me either."

Her mother nodded and turned back to the wagon while Nora headed off to the far side of the campsite. Since there wasn't really enough space on this stretch of mountainside, the company had not bothered to pull the wagons into a secure circle. Instead, the fifty wagons were a chaotic hodgepodge, stretched out across the trail. The Buchanans' wagon was near the front of the company, and so Nora headed up the small incline toward where they would be.

Each family she passed seemed worn down. Some were eating, heating up their last handful of beans, or gnawing on a cold johnnycake. But many of the emigrants were simply leaning or sitting against their wagons, arms wrapped around themselves, conserving their energy. Nora spotted the Buchanans, and when she approached, the two children were huddled together, each clutching a cold biscuit to them.

"Nora," Mrs. Buchanan greeted her. "How are you holding up?"

"How are *you* holding up?" she returned. "These two look like icicles."

"I know, the poor dears. I think our food will hold out," she said. "I suppose there is one good thing to come out of losing my husband—our supplies stretched longer. But this cold..." She held out a palm and looked up, as though expecting flurries any moment. "I grossly underestimated what we would need. We don't have weather like this in Alabama. I don't know what we're going to do this winter. It's only going to get worse."

"You're right. I wouldn't be surprised if we get the first dusting of snow in a few weeks. Maybe sooner."

The other woman shook her head. "Maybe we can buy coats or blankets or something when we get to the other side. Otherwise, this is going to be a terrible winter for us."

Nora thought about the trunks of winter clothing her family had brought from Michigan. They had enough. If only there was something she could do for this poor family.

The solution popped into her head, and Nora perked up.

"I have just the thing. It's not a lot, but it will help," she assured her. "Just stay right here. I'll be right back."

She hurried back to her own camp, intent on her goal before she could give it too much thought. Without even greeting her family, Nora climbed into her wagon and went straight to her cot. She had made her bed that morning, folding up the quilt that she had been sleeping with since they left Michigan. It was mostly clean, though well-loved, but Nora didn't think Mrs. Buchanan would mind.

She climbed back out of the wagon and made her way again to the Buchanans.

As she walked, Nora clutched the folded quilt to her chest, breathing in the fresh lavender scent that all their linens bore as she crossed the campsite. This was the quilt that she had put together over the days and weeks that she daydreamed about her life with Jimmy Rayburn. This was the project she had poured all her hopes and dreams into before those had been ripped away by the truth. Though it had taken her two thousand miles of obstacles and trials, Nora felt that she was finally ready to let go of the girl she had been back then.

It was time. They would be in Oregon any day and she was ready to start her new life. Even if it didn't precisely match the dreams she had had, she would be very happy here.

"Mrs. Buchanan," she called as she returned. "Please, take this quilt. It's not much, but any extra layer will help in this weather."

"Oh, my goodness," Mrs. Buchanan said. She reached out and gently fingered the hemmed edge of soft patch-work. "Honey, this is just gorgeous. Did you make it? I couldn't possibly take this."

"Yes, you can. Please." Nora held it out to her again, her eyes picking out the deep red patches she had made from Jimmy's discarded shirt. "I've gotten plenty of use out of this. I'm not going to pretend it's a new gift, made just for you. It's time for me to let it go."

Mrs. Buchanan chuckled, as she took the folded quilt.

"But I would feel better knowing you and the children all had this extra layer," Nora finished. "Who knows how much longer we'll have to be living out of these wagons. You can't do anything if you're not warm."

Before Mrs. Buchanan could protest again, they were interrupted by a chorus of male voices coming up the trail toward them. Both women turned to watch, confused, as no fewer than a dozen men, each loaded down with heavy bags, or leading a packhorse that was itself carrying multiple bags, approached the camp.

"What is this?" the older woman whispered.

Nora could only watch, so surprised was she at the sight of not only so many strangers but so much food.

"Excuse me?" Mrs. Buchanan called to one of the visitors as they passed through the camp. "What is all this?"

A scrawny young man who couldn't be older than Amy approached the Buchanans' camp.

"Rescue mission, ma'am. One of your men came down a couple days ago and told us you all were close. After what happened with those folks in California over the winter a few years ago, we're not taking any chances if we can help it. Better to take a few days to get you safely over the mountains than risk the worst happening."

"Rescue mission?" she repeated.

The young man reached into the bag he had slung over his shoulder. "Those your little ones?" he asked, nodding to the children who were watching with wide eyes. "Would they like some jerky?"

CHAPTER FORTY-ONE

The rescue team that had come up the mountain from the Willamette Valley was more welcome than they could have guessed. Some of the families in the Sullivan-Mills wagon company were down to their final grains of rice; some were trying to make tea or broth out of the handfuls of weeds that could be sourced on the mountainside. Each person was exhausted, hungry and desperate.

And then kind strangers came up from the valley to help get them to their new home. They were like angels, sent down from on high, to some of the travelers.

When Nora heard the young man explain to Mrs. Buchanan who they were and what they were doing there, she all but flew as she ran back to her own camp to share the news.

The men from Oregon dispersed throughout the camp, distributing food to every family, providing aid and making sure that each person had everything they need to make it down the other side of the mountain.

Winter weather was upon them, but the emigrants had successfully journeyed to the Oregon Territory.

Nora's family were in better shape than many of the others, even with Nora constantly going off to help the Buchanans, or the Van Andas and others. Even so it was only with the rescue teams help that they ate a full meal for the first time since Fort Boise.

With the boon of enough food, the Sullivan-Mills wagon company finally had the energy they needed to make the final push up over the mountain into Oregon. They pushed hard that afternoon, getting as far as they could with the added power.

The next morning, the excitement in the camp was almost palpable. The wagon company so close to their goal. By the end of the day, they could be putting down stakes, and that promise had most of the men and women up with the sun. But beyond being so close to their destination, every person had a full belly for the first time in weeks. Some maybe for the first time since leaving Independence.

The sun was rising later and later, so not long after sunup, Captain Mills called to his team, and set his own lead wagon heading up over the last ridge of the mountain and then down the trail on the other side. The western side of the mountain was steeper, but the wagons would be going downhill and would have a hot meal at the bottom.

The trail down from the mountain cut into the rock and terrain in places, wound away from the edge in others. The wagons had to take it slowly, turning at the hairpins and keeping the animals from rushing headlong down the straightaways. It would take them all day, most likely, but every single member of the company was happy to stay on the trail as long as it took to finally camp in the Willamette Valley that night.

As the wagons curved around one of the switchbacks, Nora spotted Jasper out a dozen feet or so at the very edge looking over the side of the mountain. From this distance, it wasn't clear what he would have a view of but it must be entrancing. He was just standing there hardly moving as he gazed out.

"There's your beau," Amy said with a grin. She nudged Nora with an elbow.

"Is he?"

"Isn't he?"

Nora looked at her sister. "I honestly don't know."

"Well," Amy began, thoughtful and thorough as ever. "Let's look at the evidence."

"Amy, not everything can be explained by evidence."

"Most things can. Go see what he's looking at."

"I don't want to interrupt him," she demurred.

Amy sighed. "Fine, then I'll go see. I want to know." She made to walk toward Jasper before her sister stopped her.

"No, no. I'll go."

"And then report back. I want to add it to my list of evidence."

Nora stepped off the trail and made her way to where he stood at the overlook. She approached Jasper quietly, but he must have sensed her. After glancing over his shoulder at her, he gestured her to come stand by his side. She stepped up to the edge, next to him but not touching. Her head barely reached his shoulder, and even without looking she could sense his peace, relaxing into this final culmination of so many months of work.

"What are you looking at?"

"Where do you think might be the best place for a farm?" he said, casually.

Nora's heart began to beat faster. "Oh, well ... um..." She faltered, before pausing to take in the view and really consider his question. Where would she like to live if she had the choice. "It's all gorgeous, isn't it? With the leaves beginning to change, you can just picture how our next harvest season would be. But, I think I'd love to live kind of in the middle of everything. Maybe around there." She pointed. "Not too far off the main road, but close to the river?"

"Accessible to all kinds of folks visiting? Probably also a good spot for a blacksmith to be headquartered." He nodded. "I believe you're right. That seems like the perfect place for a home. And a family. A lovely little wife who is beloved by our neighbors and adored by our children."

Nora's breath caught. Her heart pounded so hard she felt lightheaded. "Our?" she said faintly.

He turned toward her and took her hand in his. "I'm probably getting ahead of myself." He grinned down at her and winked. "I apologize. But let me be clear. I want to court you, Nora Cole."

She gasped.

"I know we've had our misunderstandings and I haven't always made you feel sure of my affections, so let me tell you now. As we are taking these final steps into Oregon. I greatly admire you. Your dedication to others, your kind heart, your generosity. Hearing your name on the lips of everyone in this wagon company, extolling all that you have done for them, just made my heart sweet every day."

"Jasper, I... I don't know what to say."

"Say..." He laughed. "Say whatever you want. Tell me what you need from me, how I can at least ensure that I get to stay in your life now that we'll no longer be so desperate for survival on a minute-by-minute basis."

Nora looked back out over the valley, the welcoming view of what would be her future home. She had come so far since Michigan, so much more than the two thousand miles would imply. She had grown in ways that she never would have if she had stayed at home, even if she had married Jimmy Rayburn.

"I thought I was in love in Michigan," she began slowly. "But now that I look back on it, I was just ... letting my daydreams bleed into my reality. I've never actually been courted." Nora took a deep breath and turned to him. He took her second hand in his as well. "I would be honored to be so by you. I would love that."

"Me too." He leaned in and whispered as though sharing a secret. "We're going to have so much fun."

Nora laughed, sinking into the safety and peace that she felt just being in Jasper's presence. It was such a far cry from the tiny sliver of notice she'd sought so desperately when in Michigan. She turned to look out over the view, but this time stepped closer to Jasper, leaning into his tall body and allowing him to put his arm around her.

"We are going to have so much fun," she agreed.

She would have to tell her sister about this new evidence.

Thank you so much for joining another family of the Sullivan-Mills wagon company. Of all the books in this series, *Fierce Dreams* is probably the closest to a proper romance (but even then, the relationship between the sisters is probably just as big of a character arc as her relationship with Jasper). The sweet, hopeful romanticism of a teenage girl in the 19th century who had limited options is always interesting to me.

I gave Nora some of my interest in homemaking skills. When I was a child I adored *Anne of Green Gables* by L.M. Montgomery and went through several phases where I tried to learn to garden and sew and bake and all of that. While I'm still only very amateur at all of it (I haven't even attempted to can anything), those are the kinds of skills that a girl like Nora would pride herself on. Whenever I reread this book I want to try again.

Jasper was loosely inspired by my brother. He is younger than me, and it's just the two of us, but he was always the handsome, charming one that everyone adored (he probably still is).

One more thing about this book that is important to me: Amy Cole is one of my absolutely favorite characters in this series. There's just a thing about the 'weird girl' in fiction—the gothic teenager, the one not easily bending to the feminine traditions expected of her—that tugs at my heart. I'm sure part of that came from my own growing up—I was always the girl that was "too much"—and part from my childhood love of Anne Shirley.

As of the time of this writing, Amy and Nora appear in *Snowbound Promises*, book three of the Oregon At Last series. Amy will be one of the main characters in a future Oregon At Last book. And I'm even considering introducing her in a totally different series that takes place 30 years later.

I love her.

I hope you do too.

But in the meantime, there are still several books of this series to read! I hope you love *Seeking Home*...

A.T. Butler

April 2025

FREE PRINTABLE OREGON TRAIL MAP

Sign-up to download a FREE custom printable map of the Sullivan-Mills wagon company's journey on the Oregon Trail.

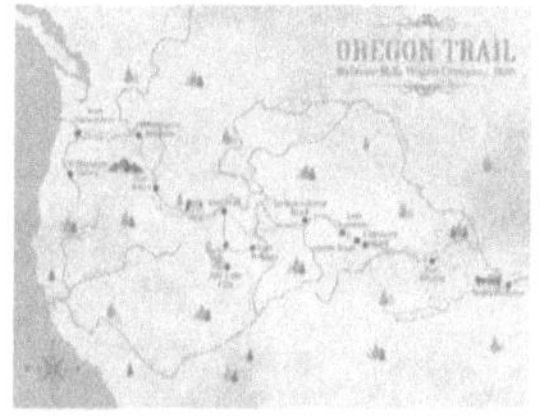

You'll also get news of future releases, updates for promotions and discounts, as well as occasional other exclusive goodies, created just for my subscribers.

https://atbutler.com/ot-free

The next book in COURAGE ON THE OREGON TRAIL series is available now.

**Grab SEEKING HOME here!
(on Kindle and Kindle Unlimited)**

Nothing will keep her from settling in the Oregon Territory.

When Hope Waters gets the chance to move west to Oregon, she doesn't hesitate. Her husband and all six of her grown children (plus their spouses) dive headfirst into the adventure, all eager to start a new life on the West Coast. It finally feels like the  final pieces of a happy life are coming together for her family. She has worked so long for this moment and nothing will get in her way.

But Hope has a secret.

That secret is eating away at her. That secret could ruin her family, and break their hearts. That secret could change everything, including her chance for a new life in Oregon.

Her sons are hard-working and her daughters are brave. And all Hope wants is to find the home that has eluded her for so long.

Can she make it all the way to the Oregon Territory and the final home she is looking for without hurting everyone around her?

She thought the hardest part was behind her.

The Oregon Territory, October 1850: After nearly a year of living out of a covered wagon, day after day of grueling work and heart-breaking tragedy, Caroline Harper has finally reached the Oregon Territory where her new life will begin.

She thought she had given all she had to give; she thought she had become the strong woman the frontier requires. But every day brings a new challenge for the settlers.

When unexpected obstacles appear that keep her from getting married, from finally finding her security, Caroline learns that becoming the woman she needs to be will be far more difficult than she had realized.

Can Caroline find her new path or will this journey be the end of everything she thought she had achieved?

For all the stories of how these brave pioneers got to Oregon, look for the book series Courage on the Oregon Trail by A.T. Butler.

Oregon At Last Series:
Journey's End (Caroline's story)
Christmas in Oregon (Annie's story)
Snowbound Promises (Nora's story)
The Pastor's Baby (Olivia's story)
Frontier Fortune (Rebecca's story)
Reluctant Spring (Sadie's story)
Summer of Promise (Margaret's story)
Eden Valley Sunrise (Leah's story)

ALSO BY A.T. BUTLER

Courage On The Oregon Trail Series:

Westward Courage

Faithful Trail

Frontier Sisters

Unyielding Heart

Wild Promise

Fierce Dreams

Seeking Home

Trouble and Grace

Oregon At Last Series:

Journey's End

Christmas in Oregon

Snowbound Promises

Pastor's Baby

Frontier Fortune

Reluctant Spring

Summer of Promise

Juniper Falls Series:

The Juniper Hotel

Building the Dream

Snowflakes and Sugar Cookies

Marrying a Sweet Sister Series:

The Sweetest Bond

The Sweetest Spark

Jacob Payne, Bounty Hunter Series:

Trouble By Any Name

Danger in the Canyon

Justice for Jasper

Blood on the Mountain

Outlaw Country

Death By Grit

Desert Rage

Arizona Legend

Fool's Demise

Silent Night

Bountiful Justice Series:

Loyalty's Price

Riding for Justice

Trail of Redemption

Other Western Novels by A.T. Butler:

Hawke's Revenge

Stories from Juniper Falls

ABOUT THE AUTHOR

I grew up in the southwest—California Missions, snakes and constant threat of drought weaving the backdrop of my childhood.

But it wasn't until I moved to Texas a few years ago that the magic and mythology of the American West began to seep into my soul.

I'd love to write about western adventures, strong women and noble men for a long time.

If you enjoyed this book, a review on your favorite retailer would be greatly appreciated.

- A

Fierce Dreams is a work of fiction. Names, characters, places and incidents either are the product of the author's imagination or are used fictitiously. Any resemblance to actual persons living or dead, events or locales is entirely coincidental.

Copyright 2022 by A.T. Butler

Cover by Striking Book Covers

All rights reserved.

No part of this publication may be reproduced, distributed, or transmitted in any form or by any means, including photocopying, recording or other electronic or mechanical methods, without the prior written permission of the publisher, except in the case of brief quotations embodied in critical reviews and certain other noncommercial uses permitted by copyright law.

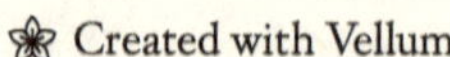 Created with Vellum

www.ingramcontent.com/pod-product-compliance
Lightning Source LLC
Chambersburg PA
CBHW021245190726
48289CB00005B/1504